MW01139312

Copyright © 2019 by Roberta Kagan

ISBN-13 (paperback) : 978-1653364787

ISBN-13 (hardcover) : 978-1-957207-15-5

DISCLAIMER

MILLIONS OF PEBBLES

ROBERTA KAGAN

PROLOGUE

Spring 1941

Benjamin Rabinowitz's heart sank as he heard the door of his apartment slam shut. The Lodz ghetto was bursting with life as he ran to the window and looked out and down onto the street. It would be getting dark soon, but children played and women huddled in groups. His palms were wet with sweat as his eyes were glued on his wife and child, who were walking across the street and turning the corner out of his life forever.

Everything in his small world was changing. Ben felt a chill run down his spine as he watched Lila through the dirty glass window. She was carrying their son in her long, slender arms. She was leaving him. This could very well be the last time he would ever see her. And even though she'd always been a difficult woman, he knew he would miss her. Their arranged marriage had not been easy. So when she'd decided that she was going to find a way to escape so she could get their son out of the ghetto, Benjamin knew that he might as well just agree with her. It was dangerous, but if she succeeded it would probably be the best thing that could happen to his son, Moishe.

Moishe was a small, skinny child, with pale skin that was so transparent that it was easy to trace the markings of his blue veins, a sickly and weak boy who looked half his age of four. It broke Ben's heart to see that Moishe was not growing properly. And at four years old, Moishe still had trouble getting around without falling down on his skinny, bowed legs. Ben knew that Moishe's chances of survival in this filthy and disease-ridden place were slim. And he also knew that Lila was determined that her son would not die. This determination was both Lila's greatest asset and her most devastating weakness. When she wanted something she could be relentless. And this was not the first time that Ben had seen Lila's indestructible will at work. She had stood up to their entire Jewish community when Moishe was born, refusing to have Moishe circumcised. The rabbi had come to their home to try and convince her. But she was immovable. Everyone suggested that Ben take the child to the mohel and have it done without the mother's consent. But he didn't. He was afraid of the power of her wrath. And he knew that she would have been furious. Her strong will was something he would not miss.

She got what she wanted. All during their marriage she'd had a way of making him feel powerless, and he hated it. So he had secretly rebelled by being unfaithful: not with one woman but with many. However, none of them had ever captured his heart even though they made him feel like a man—something Lila failed to do.

Now as he watched Lila carry his only son out of his view, he wondered if he would ever see the boy again. Tears filled the corners of his eyes as the figures of his wife and son grew smaller.

"God be with you, Moishe," he whispered. Then he added softly, "And you too, Lila."

He'd only returned from his ten-hour shift at his job at the ghetto tailor shop on Lagiewnicka Street a few minutes ago, where he spent all day making coats for the German army. This was work he hated. He had been going to university to become a teacher when the Nazis invaded his country and forced him out of school. But his hatred for this job was not because he thought it beneath him or because he was lazy, but it was unbearable for him to think that his hard work was helping the Nazis in their war effort. He would never have chosen this particular job. And before he started, Ben had never even operated a sewing machine but been assigned to it. And since so many others had no work, and without work starvation was lurking right around every corner, he was grateful for the small amount of money his job provided and the noonday meal every worker was entitled to. But more importantly, he was happy to have any job because it helped him to provide for his wife and son. So when Rumkowski, the head of the Judenrat, had assigned him to the tailor factory he accepted without complaining. And silently thought that at least his family would eat for another day.

For a long time Ben sat at the window gazing out at the misery of the Lodz ghetto. He watched as a group of children, who had been strapped to a cart like horses, made their final deliveries for the day. They were just children, boys of perhaps ten or twelve, he assumed, but their bodies slumped with defeat, and their heads rolled forward like those of old men. He watched them working like animals and thought, *I hate to admit it, but Lila was right to get Moishe out of here. The Nazis work the Jewish children to death. And if the hard work doesn't kill them, the lack of food, the filth, or the rampant spread of disease will. My boy, my only son, my only child, for that matter, is gone. Tomorrow morning, for the first time since he was born, I will not wake up to his smiling face. I will not be able to hold him in my arms and be in the presence of his childlike innocence, even if only for a short time, and forget that we are prisoners here in Lodz and put the horrors of what we are facing out of my mind.*

CHAPTER 1

BEN WAS STILL GAZING OUT THE WINDOW WHEN HE CAUGHT SIGHT OF a familiar figure: the bastard who was known as the Jewish king or the eldest of Jews. His name was Mordechai Chaim Rumkowski.

Rumkowski moved through the ghetto with the confidence of a king expecting the obedience of his subjects. Ben hated him, perhaps even more than he hated the Nazis. That was because Rumkowski was born a Jew, but he collaborated with the Nazis against his own people. He was a mean, heartless man, who worked the Jews in the Lodz ghetto as hard as any Nazi would have. Age did not give a person exemption from painstaking, physical work. The old and the young must earn their keep: this was Rumkowski's motto.

It was a beautiful spring afternoon just before the sunset of evening. Rumkowski wore a light jacket and black-rimmed glasses. His white hair erupted out the back and sides of his black fedora as he surveyed the ghetto with a serious frown. Ben spit on the floor three times as he watched Rumkowski enter an apartment building across the street.

I'll bet Lila let that old, ugly bastard have his way her so that he would look the other way when she took Moishe out of the ghetto. Lila would do that. She would do whatever she had to do for her son. And how can I blame her. I couldn't help her or Moishe. I am worthless. I can't count the number of times I would see my wife standing on the streets and flirting with Werner, that SS guard. He might have been the one who helped her. I don't know. But I doubt she would have been able to leave this place without Rumkowski looking the other way; he is far too powerful. What kind of man am I that I can sit here and think about my wife spreading her legs for other men? I hate myself. I hate that I am too weak and helpless to protect my family. My wife had to behave like a common whore to save her child. And all I could do was sit back and feel sorry for myself. This was not the life I had planned when I married Lila. I never saw all this coming—this ghetto, this starvation, this suffering. I have always hated the fact that Lila is stronger than I am. I wanted to be the man in our marriage. I wanted to protect her and our children. I wanted to provide for them. But even before the Nazis came, everyone said Lila was a tremendous force. Her will was always stronger than mine. She was always relentless, and she always won. I am not sure whether I ever loved her. Sometimes I think I did, other times I think not. But I know for certain that I love that boy of ours, and I will miss him. There is nothing I can do to change this. Lila and Moishe are gone. And even if I could change it and keep them here with me, I wouldn't. The boy is better off with his strong mother than his weak and worthless father. All I can do is pray for him.

The following day several guards came to question Ben about the whereabouts of his wife and son.

"My wife left me," Benjamin said, trembling. He was so terrified not only that he would be beaten but that the guards would find Lila and Moishe. "She took my son."

"Where did she go?"

"I am sorry; I don't know. Perhaps to live with another man in the ghetto," he said, deliberately lying in hopes of buying Lila and Moishe more time to get away.

The guard shook his head. "She didn't show up for work today."

Lila worked at the knitwear shop on Brezinka Street just a few streets from the apartment.

"Perhaps she is ill and stayed at home today? I don't know. She left without telling me where she was going," he said.

"Why did she leave you, Rabinowitz?"

"She said she'd met another man, and she was going to move in with him."

The guard nodded looking disinterested. "Who is it?"

"I don't know. She wouldn't tell me his name."

The guard took a whip that had been attached to his belt and hit Ben across the face. Ben felt the leather cut into his skin like a razor blade. Then the guard shook his head. "You are a poor excuse for a man. I can see why she left you," he said and walked out of the apartment.

CHAPTER 2

NOT EVEN A FULL WEEK AFTER LILA LEFT, THE LIPMAN FAMILY moved in to the already crowded rooms where Ben and the other couples lived. There were four Lipmans. Asher, a strong and coarse man who spoke very little; Zelda, his young and pretty wife, and their two children: Sarah a quiet girl of five, and Solomon, a precocious and funny nine-year-old boy. Ben liked the boy. Having Solomon in the apartment made Ben think of Moishe. He watched Solomon's curiosity at the world and wondered what Moishe might have been like as he grew up.

Asher Lipman worked at the metal works factory on Krotka Street. He was a rough but handsome man with hard features and perpetual dark stubble on his cheeks and chin, who often came home dirty, covered in sweat, and in a foul mood. Wiry muscles stood out like snakes in his otherwise slender arms. He never spoke to Ben only huffed at him in passing. And although Ben had no justification for his feelings other than his own insecurities, he felt that Asher thought of him as a soft and useless man.

Even though she had the two young children, Zelda worked as a carpet weaver. Her fingers were always red, covered in small cuts and callouses. The children worked too. Instead of going to school as Ben thought they should have, Sara and Solomon spent their days sewing Nazi insignias on uniforms. Partially, this was Asher's decision, but Rumkowski, like Asher, saw no need for the children to attend school. However, each night, regardless of how exhausted they all were, Zelda sat down at the table with her two children and forced them to practice reading with the precious books she'd hidden inside her skirt when she was arrested and forced into the ghetto. Asher scoffed at her and went to bed. He thought it was more important to get his rest than to worry about whether his children could read or write. Ben overheard him say to Zelda that they were all doomed, so what was the point in learning. Sometimes after a bad day at work Asher would lash out and hit Zelda. The other men living in the apartment tried to look the other way. They didn't want to come between a husband and wife. But even though Ben had always been a coward, he longed to stand up to Asher. It broke his heart to see the way Zelda's husband left her hurt and humiliated.

Asher had another bad habit. He liked to drink, and drink in excess. Many times he drank away all his earnings leaving his family struggling to pay their rent and still have enough money to buy food. But poor Zelda was a quiet girl, not a complainer. Ben knew by the way Zelda obeyed her husband that she was afraid of him. So rather than argue with Asher about his wasting money they needed for food, Zelda just didn't eat. Ben didn't interfere, but it broke his heart. Each week, everyone who had enough money in the ghetto was able to buy one loaf of bread. This loaf had to last for an entire seven days. Asher bought his own loaf first, then if he had enough money he bought the loaves for the rest of the family. Once he finished his, which only took him a couple of days, he ate what he wanted of his wife's and children's.

Solomon was growing fast and always hungry. He gobbled his food quickly. He was a courageous child who forged friendships with street-savvy children. They formed gangs and stole from the vendors. Zelda was worried about Solomon. Sometimes he would go out at night and not return until morning, and she'd heard from other people that he snuck out of the ghetto in the middle of the night. She didn't know for certain that he was leaving the ghetto and engaging in illegal trade, but what she did know for sure was that he was often outside of the apartment after curfew. And if he were caught, he would face Rumkowski, who was not at all kind or understanding toward children. It was rumored that Rumkowski had once run an orphanage, and he'd treated the unfortunate orphans very badly. However, as hard as Zelda tried to reason with Solomon, there was no talking to him. He would not listen. One night Asher returned late from work. It was getting dark, and Solomon was preparing to leave for the night. Asher walked into the apartment stumbling as if he had been drinking. He turned and grabbed the sleeve of Solomon's shirt. "Where the hell do you think you're going?"

"Out."

"Oh yeah? I am sick and tired of you running around here like you're some kind of an animal. You are just a child, and you're going to act like one."

Solomon pulled his arm free of his father's grasp. "Leave me alone," he said.

"I'll leave you alone. When your ass is black and blue. That's when I'll leave you alone. You disrespectful, ungrateful piece of shit."

"Grateful? What the hell am I supposed to be grateful to you for? You are nobody. You can't stop the Nazis, and you are scared to death of Rumkowski and his Jewish thugs. I have no respect for you."

Asher pulled the belt out of his pants, then he doubled it up and began whipping Solomon. For all his bravado, Solomon was still only a child. He fell to the floor. Asher continued to rain blows on him. His lips were bleeding, and he raised his hands to cover his face. Ben was terrified of Asher, but he couldn't stand by and watch this. He had to do something. His palms were sweaty as he gripped the corner of the wall with a white-knuckle grip.

Zelda was crying. "Please, Asher," she begged, throwing herself on top of Solomon. "He's just a little boy. Talk to him; reason with him, but don't hit him. You're hurting him."

"Shut up, you stupid bitch. You should learn to keep your mouth shut when a man is disciplining his son." Asher turned around and slapped the leather belt in Zelda's direction. She let out a yelp and moved out of the way, then Asher turned his attention back to Solomon. "You are the most disgusting little ingrate I've ever seen. A man works hard all day to feed his family, and this is the thanks he gets. A wife and son who conspire against him." Asher cracked the belt across Solomon's shoulder. Solomon let out a cry and tried to stand up. Asher took his foot and knocked Solomon back down to the floor.

Ben's heart was racing. "Asher, please stop," he managed to say.

"Mind your own business, Rabinowitz. Your family walked out on you because you are half a man. You let them walk all over you. My wife is going to learn today that she and my son had better treat me with the respect I deserve or . . ." Asher raised the belt again. From the corner, where she cowered, Zelda let out a cry of fear.

"Asher," Ben blurted out, then he quickly added, "Come with me, and I'll buy you a drink. I've heard that Shlomi Kaufman has set up a makeshift tavern in his apartment. He's got some black-market alcohol. Like I said, I'm buying. But we'd better hurry. I don't know how many bottles he has or how long it will last."

"It's almost curfew," Asher said, but the thought of a drink distracted him from his violent rage.

"We can make it quick. Come on. Let's take a walk. What do you say? A vodka or a beer? Sounds good, no?"

"Yes, yes it does. And it sounds even better if you're paying," Asher said.

"Of course I am paying. Come on, let's go."

Asher slid his belt back through the belt loops in his pants. Ben thought he could hear a sigh of relief come from Zelda. Solomon was bleeding and still in tears, but from what Ben could see, all the wounds appeared to be superficial.

Ben opened the door for Asher, then he followed him out. As Ben turned around to close the door, he saw Zelda. She was kneeling at Solomon's side. She glanced up at Ben quickly, and he saw the gratitude in her eyes. He smiled and closed the door, leaving the apartment in peace.

It cost Ben plenty that night. It would leave him short of money for food that week. But at least he had stopped Asher from beating the boy for a little while.

CHAPTER 3

THE FOLLOWING DAY WHEN BEN WAS RETURNING FROM WORK, ZELDA was waiting for him outside the apartment building where they lived.

"I don't know how to thank you," she said. "My husband has a hot temper, and my son provokes him."

"I know. It's all right," Ben said, smiling.

"I waited out here because I didn't want the others to see me talking to you. I was afraid they might say something to Asher. And I just never know what will set him off."

"I know. I see how difficult things are for you."

"My little Sarah is my only joy in life. She gives me no tsuris, no aggravation. Solomon is a lot like his father. He is independent and refuses to take advice—ever."

"Yes, I can see the independent streak in him, but it's not necessarily a bad thing. He is only nine years old. Perhaps he will grow out of it."

"Yes, he is only nine, and I don't think he realizes the consequences of his actions. I don't think he is old enough to grasp what can happen to him if he is caught out after curfew," she said, wringing her hands.

"I know. I understand how hard it must be for you," Ben offered.

"Asher is stubborn; Solomon is stubborn. What am I to do?"

"I don't know what to tell you. I wish I had some answers. I have made more mistakes than anyone, so I am not the person to ask for advice."

"What happened?" she asked then quickly added, "I don't mean to pry. I'm sorry. I don't know what came over me. It's none of my business."

"No, please, it's all right, really. I was a weak husband to a very domineering wife. My wife set the rules and I followed. She refused to have our son circumcised. I was so ashamed. All the men in town told me to take the boy and bring him to the mohel without her permission. But I didn't. I let her do what she wanted. She always did whatever she wanted. Before you and your family moved in, she left me and escaped the ghetto with our son. I know it is probably best that she found a way to escape the ghetto with our son, Moishe, but I knew she was having sex with other men to get them to help her, and I couldn't confront her. I just didn't have the courage." He shrugged not knowing why he'd told her so much about himself.

"Oh," she said in a soft voice as she looked at the ground.

"I'm sorry. I don't know why I am telling you all of this except perhaps it's because of what happened yesterday. You see, you might find this strange, but I feel good about myself for the first time in my life."

"What do you mean?"

"Well, yesterday when I stood up to Asher, I was afraid, and yet I did it anyway. That's the first time in my life that I found the courage to stand up to my fear."

"You were very brave," she said and then added, "and I have never said this to a man before, but you are very handsome."

He blushed and looked down at his shoes.

Ben had always been considered handsome with his cocoa-brown eyes and boyish smile. And since he came of age, he realized there were two types of women who were attracted to him. One, like his wife, Lila, who was a strong woman who wanted to dominate him, and the other was a gentle girl, like Zelda, with a strong need to mother him.

"I'm sorry, did I embarrass you?" Zelda asked.

He shrugged. "Yes, maybe a little."

"I didn't mean to. It was bold of me to say that."

"I know you didn't mean to embarrass me. And, well, thank you. It was, after all, a nice compliment."

She hesitated and then turned to go inside. "I'll see you later?" she asked.

"Yes, that would be nice." He smiled.

After Zelda went into the apartment, Ben walked for a while. It wasn't dark yet, and he wanted to think. He'd had quick one-night stands while he was married but never with married women. He'd justified cheating on Lila because her strong will always left him feeling castrated. Zelda, he knew, had a violent and hateful man for a husband, who was even worse when he drank to excess. Ben had seen the fear in the eyes of Asher's wife and children, and he completely understood why Zelda was flirting with him. And since Lila and Moishe left, Ben felt terribly alone in the ghetto. He had no real friends to speak of, not even at his job. Most of his free time was spent by himself. Zelda was pretty, not nearly as pretty as Lila but pretty enough. She had wavy, dark hair and a slim figure. Her features were even except for her nose, which was slightly big for her face. Zelda's dark eyes were kind and filled with compassion. Ben knew she liked him, and he could easily have become her lover, but he was terrified of Asher. *The next time she flirts with me I'll tell her that I can't become involved with her. I hate to admit that I am afraid, but I'll tell her the truth, that her husband is not the kind of man I want to provoke.*

CHAPTER 4

THE FOLLOWING AFTERNOON, ZELDA FOUND BEN AT THE MARKET where he went to purchase food. They stood in line together talking softly about the terribly small rations the Jews were given. Then they walked home together. He was carrying her purchases, looking for the right time to tell her that he could not allow himself to become involved with her.

Two days later, when Ben walked out of the tailor shop after work, he found Zelda waiting to walk home with him. She explained that she had just gotten off work too and had only waited a few minutes. They walked slower than usual sharing tidbits about their day and laughing about annoying coworkers. The more Ben got to know Zelda, the more he wanted to spend time with her. He was still afraid of Asher, but he'd begun to really enjoy her company, so he found he was willing to take the risk.

When Asher's back was turned, Zelda shot Ben smiles as she prepared dinner for her children in the cramped apartment. Ben found himself eager to see her. She became the light in his dark and lonely life. They had not committed adultery with their bodies, but they had begun to do so with their hearts. He brought her small gifts that he was able to steal from the tailor shop. Just a few pieces of ribbon for her hair or a few buttons, but it was the gesture that touched her heart.

"I wish I could give you more. I know that these things are so miniscule. But they are all I have to give," Ben said.

She smiled. "I cherish them because they come from you," she said as they rounded the corner toward the apartment building.

He didn't know what possessed him, but he grabbed her hand and pulled her into an alleyway between two buildings. She didn't resist. He pushed her against the wall and kissed her passionately. Zelda sighed. He pulled her farther into the alleyway. She followed him. It was as if he was overcome with need, and he couldn't think straight. Before either of them had a moment to come to their senses, Zelda's dress was above her waist, and Ben was fumbling with his pants. His hands trembled with desire. Her breath was hot on his neck. She sighed when he entered her. A tear fell down her cheek and onto his shoulder. She grasped him tighter. He kissed her and kissed her again. And then it was over.

"I'm sorry," he whispered as he came to his senses, turning away from her to zip his pants.

Zelda pulled her dress down and steadied herself. She didn't speak. But when he turned back to look into her eyes, he saw that she was crying.

"Are you all right?" he asked, wiping her tears away with his thumb then gently caressing her face.

"Yes, I'm feeling so many conflicting emotions. I'm happy, so very happy. But I feel selfish and guilty too. I never thought I would commit adultery. Never."

"Are you sorry for what we did?" he asked in a small voice.

"That's the thing that's bothering me. I'm not sorry, and I feel like I should be. But, Benjamin Rabinowitz, you make me feel like I matter. You make me feel loved. I've never felt this way before in my entire life."

"You do matter, Zelda. You matter to me. And your happiness is so important to me." He looked into her eyes. "And I hope for the rest of our lives I will have the privilege of making you feel loved, because you deserve to be loved."

"Oh, Ben, thank you. Thank you for caring."

"I do. I care more than you'll ever know. I've never felt this way about anyone else either."

"We should get home. Asher will be home soon. I don't want him to wonder where we are."

"You're right. Let's go."

Gently, he took her hand and led her out of the alleyway and back toward home. They could not openly hold hands on the street because Zelda was married, but they walked together side by side, their hearts alive with the fire of love.

"You're so beautiful," he whispered.

She looked up at him and smiled.

But . . . unbeknownst to Ben and Zelda, someone lurked in the shadows. Someone had seen them. Someone was watching.

CHAPTER 5

Lodz Ghetto
Caleb Ornstein

WHEN HE WAS GROWING UP, CALEB ORNSTEIN WAS ALWAYS IN trouble, womanizing, stealing, and fighting. He was handsome to a fault, conniving, and dangerously sexy. Not only that, but to match his charm and looks, he was wildly good in bed. After his initiation, at thirteen, into the pleasures of sex by the thirty-five-year-old woman who lived next door, Caleb quickly learned what women wanted and how to give it to them. The Ornsteins were poor but respectable people. Both Caleb's father and his mother worked all day at the textile factory trying to make ends meet.

Caleb's earliest memory occurred when he was only six. He had awakened from a nightmare one night to overhear his parents whispering in bed. They thought he was asleep. His father said that he wished they'd never had children because even with both of their salaries they were finding it very difficult to afford to raise Caleb. He'd never forgotten those words.

Then when Caleb was nine, his mother had an accident at the factory leaving her permanently disabled and unable to keep working. He was forced to wear ragged, hand-me-down clothes given to him by Jewish charities. His shoes were old, used, ill fitting, and broken. At school the other children made fun of him, especially the boys.

At fourteen, Caleb's parents were called into the principal's office at school. Caleb had been caught stealing a wallet from his teacher's jacket pocket, which the teacher had left draped across the top of his chair during the lunch break. His father was filled with shame. He slapped Caleb's face with the back of his hand in front of the school principal, who shook his head gravely at Caleb. His face red with shame, Caleb gave his father a look of pure hatred, but then Caleb caught a glimpse of his file folder which sent him into a fit of uncontrollable laughter. On the front, handwritten carefully, it said, "Caleb Ornstein: Absolutely Incorrigible." He laughed wildly in spite of the glares from the principal and both of his parents.

"I'm sorry," the principal said, trying to control the anger in his voice, "but he has no remorse, so my only option is to expel him from school."

Caleb was expelled. He was not distraught at all. In fact, he was glad because he was now free to wander the streets all day. About a year later on a Sunday afternoon, he met a girl in an ice cream parlor. She was dressed in a cashmere sweater and a wool skirt. Her clothing told him she came from money, and that made her all the more attractive to him. Her wavy, brown hair was accented with a pink ribbon tied into a perfect bow. The color was a perfect match to the flowers in the pattern of her white dress. She was with three other girls, but none of the others caught Caleb's eye the way this one did. He glanced at her as she talked to her friends in soft whispers. She said something to one of the other girls, and they all broke out in a fit of giggles. Caleb saw her glance at him and he smiled. Then he walked over to her and introduced himself.

"Pardon me for staring at you. I couldn't help but notice you," he said. "Has anyone ever told you that you should be a model? You are really beautiful."

She giggled again clearly taken aback by his words. Close up, he could see that she couldn't have been more than fourteen.

"I'm Caleb Ornstein," he said.

"Bina Bloomberg," she said, casting her eyes down in a flirtatious manner.

He smiled. "May I join you ladies?"

The girls at the table blushed.

"All right," Bina said, nodding.

That day Bina Bloomberg fell hard for Caleb, and they began dating. When the chill of winter came they were still together taking walks on cold winter afternoons, holding hands. They stopped every so often so Caleb could hold her tightly and kiss her as the snow fell, dusting her hair. He brought her chocolates, which she loved. She never knew that he got them by blackmailing the chocolate maker, who he knew was having an affair.

One very chilly afternoon, Caleb knew his parents would be out, so he brought Bina to his family's apartment and there he slowly seduced her. From that day forward they made love as often as they could. A month later Bina brought him home to meet her parents. He was in awe of the big brick house with the large picture windows, where she lived. The house was also beautifully furnished. To Caleb, such finery only existed in museums. Bina's family had a maid to clean the house and a French cook that her father had hired and brought back with him from France, to prepare their meals. Caleb could see himself living in this fine house, eating expensive food and wearing nice clothes. He considered marrying Bina, but the Bloombergs did not welcome Caleb with open arms; they treated him coldly. Caleb was hurt. They made him feel inferior, but he knew he had an advantage: Bina was mad about him. And every time she lay naked beneath him, it gave him a deep sense of inner satisfaction to know that he, the poor boy from the poverty-stricken family, an outcast, was having sex with their rich, precious daughter.

When spring began, Caleb found himself growing bored of Bina. Women rarely held his interest for very long. And besides, he'd met another woman, an older woman with a wealthy husband and plenty of free time on her hands. She bought him expensive gifts, like diamond cufflinks and tailor-made suits. She even had a tuxedo made for him, which she paid for with her husband's money. Then she took him to the theater and to the opera in his new clothes. She was attractive and elegant, if not young and beautiful. But he found that he enjoyed his time with her far more than the quick sexual encounters he shared with Bina. One night, Caleb and the older woman sat at a table in a fine restaurant enjoying a glass of expensive port wine after dinner. Caleb took a sip and rolled it around in his mouth. *Nothing like a good wine*, he thought.

"Have you ever wondered why I am not afraid that someone might tell my husband that I have been seen with you in public?" she said. She toyed with him sometimes, but Caleb didn't mind. The money and material things she gave him made up for it.

Caleb shrugged. "I never gave it much thought," he said without emotion.

"Well, I wanted to let you know that you needn't worry. My husband and I have an understanding. So there will never be a problem."

So, he thought, *she wasn't playing with him this time. This was actually good news.*

Caleb gave her his brightest smile. It was nice to know that an angry husband would not come looking for him on some night when he was least expecting it. But whether she knew it or not, Caleb had never been planning to have anything serious with this woman. From her attitude, it seemed that she, too, was looking for a good time, and that suited him very well.

By now, he'd had enough of Bina and had to find a way to get rid of her. Caleb took Bina out for dinner one evening. He rarely spent any money when they were together, but he had been planning to break things off with her gently, and he thought she was far less likely to make a scene if he broke up with her in a public place like a restaurant. The waitress gave Caleb a flirtatious smile as she placed the food on the table. He had no interest in her, but out of habit he flashed a smile back at her. Her attraction to him was obvious, and for a moment it made him feel good. But Caleb was hungry, and the food was far more interesting than a waitress or the conversation he was about to have with Bina that he knew was going to be upsetting. So he decided to take a few minutes to enjoy his dinner before he delivered the bad news to Bina. But as he took his first bite, he looked up to see that Bina was staring directly at him. Her face was flushed, and she appeared excited but also afraid. She was wringing the side of the white tablecloth in her fingers, then she looked down at the floor and then back up at him. She cleared her throat and said, "I'm pregnant."

Caleb almost choked on the piece of chicken he was chewing. He could not speak, but he stared at her in disbelief. His entire body began to shake. His face was red with anger. Caleb had been so worried about Bina making a scene, but instead, it was Caleb who was making a scene. He stood up and leaned forward across the table, his face close to hers, his breath hot on her cheeks, then he growled, "Why didn't you do something to prevent this? I don't want a child."

She put her hands over her face and began to cry. Caleb pounded his fist on the table shaking it until a full glass of red wine slid into Bina's lap staining her pink dress.

She looked down at the dress, but she could not look at Caleb. Instead, she shook her head not knowing what to say. This Caleb was not the man she knew. This was not the Caleb who was her lover. That man was a calm, devil-may-care sort of fellow. But this man who sat in front of her now was a scarlet-faced, raging tyrant. And he was blaming her for everything that had gone wrong.

"What do you expect me to do about this? You had better not be thinking I am going to marry you. I don't want to marry you or anybody else." He groaned. Everyone in the restaurant had turned around to look at them, but that didn't stop Caleb's anger. He hollered at her, "Besides, Bina, how the hell can I be sure it's mine? I don't know how many other men you lay down and opened your legs for."

· · ·

23

The ugliness of his words sent her running out of the restaurant with her hands covering her face. She ran as fast as she could through the dark streets until she arrived at her home.

Bina's mother was still awake. She was in the living room knitting quietly in the dark. When Bina came flying through the door, her mother looked up. Bina was whimpering as she fell down at her mother's feet.

"What is it? What's happened?" her mother asked.

"I'm pregnant. It's Caleb's."

"Oh, no," her mother said in a deep and pained voice. "Oy, Bina, the shanda, the embarrassment. You're going to have a child out of wedlock. What will the neighbors think of you? How will you ever outlive this shame? No decent boy will have you now. Dear God, no, this is the most terrible thing that could happen to our family," her mother muttered, biting her lip. "And what's even worse . . . how am I going to tell your father? He will be livid."

Bina nodded. "I know, Mommy. I know. I'm so sorry." Bina was sobbing.

Bina's mother told her father. Both of her parents were angry and devastated. The only choice left to Bina was to marry Caleb, and he was not the kind of man they'd hoped for as a son-in-law. Not only was Caleb poor, but they all lived in a small Jewish area, where a man's character was well known by his neighbors. And Caleb was well known to be a less-than-savory character. So not only was it a terrible embarrassment to be pregnant out of wedlock, but the child's father had a terrible reputation. The Bloombergs went to see Caleb's family and told them the news. The Ornsteins, unlike the Bloombergs, were hopeful. Perhaps, Caleb's parents thought, this might be a good thing for their son. Perhaps if Caleb settled down with a wife and child, he might straighten out his life. The Bloombergs had no choice but to plan a quick wedding. They knew it was inevitable that people would learn the truth that the baby was conceived before the vows were taken. After all, people weren't stupid, and they could easily count nine months from the wedding day. Still, the Bloombergs tried to keep the secret of Bina's pregnancy at least until the couple were married. Bina's mother began to arrange the wedding as quickly as possible.

Meanwhile, Caleb felt trapped. He couldn't see himself stuck with a wife and child for the rest of his days. The very idea of being buried under the mundane day-to-day life of a working father gave him anxiety, so he outright refused to marry Bina. He told her parents that he didn't want to be her husband and would not treat her well if he were forced into this marriage. Her father, in turn, threatened to kill Caleb. And Caleb's father, furious with his son for not seeing the blessing in the opportunity to marry into a rich Jewish family, threatened to help kill Caleb himself. But Caleb's mind would not be changed. He refused to see Bina. She was heartbroken. She was also ashamed as her belly grew, so she stopped attending school. In her young eyes, this breakup with Caleb was the end of her life. So one autumn afternoon when her parents were not home, and she could see no other means of escape, she ran a hot bath and sat in the tub crying until the water grew cold. Then she slit her wrists. Blood turned the water red just as it did when Moses went to speak to Pharaoh begging him to let the Jews leave Egypt. And Pharaoh had denied his request.

CHAPTER 6

Caleb felt bad about what he'd caused. He blamed himself, but he did not go to speak to Bina's family to apologize. Instead, he moved out of his parents' home and into the home of a middle-aged Jewish widow whom he'd met only a few days prior when he'd gone to buy clothes. He saw the admiration in her eyes and asked her who owned the store.

"I do," she said.

They talked for a while, and then she closed early. Caleb ended up spending the night in her bed. She liked him; he could see it in her eyes. They all did. In the morning as she prepared his breakfast, she said, "Why don't you move in with me?"

"I'll be your lover," he told her, "but I am never going to marry you or anyone else. And if you ever start to think that you own me, I'll be gone before you can count to ten."

Caleb was an experienced lover. He was handsome and charming if occasionally cruel. The woman was lonely. She'd been a widow for five years, with a desperate need to feel cared for. Caleb's offer was not romantic or ideal, but she accepted it anyway. He stayed for a few months until he felt her becoming possessive, and then he found another woman. The women he met and lived with on and off paid all his bills and gave him gifts of clothing and cash. This was his way of life until he was arrested and sent to the ghetto.

Caleb knew the Germans had taken over Poland because the women he lived with were frightened by the constant bombing. He was worried and afraid that the homes where he stayed might take a direct hit. But he didn't know much about the Nazis or what they stood for. He thought they were just another political group taking over Poland and that once they were in power the bombing would stop, and their government would have little to do with him.

Caleb was more interested in women and what they would do for him. He searched for the wealthiest, loneliest women he could find, and even as Germany descended upon the people of Poland, Caleb Ornstein had more women than he knew what to do with. Both Jewish and Gentile girls fell prey to his charms. He flirted with the poor ones but spent his time with the rich. He came to appreciate and expect their gifts, and he developed a taste for fine dining. They didn't need to be pretty, although some of them were, and as long as they were willing to pay for a good time, he kept them around. Once in a while, he indulged in a one-night stand with a young girl who had nothing to offer but good looks and a firm body. However, by morning he was gone. Sometimes a father or older brother would come looking for him. And more than once he'd been challenged and had to fight his way out, but he took it all in stride. He knew what he was doing was wrong, but it was easier than working.

On a few occasions, Caleb saw his mother at the market. She begged him to stop living the life he was living. "Come home, Caleb. Start over. You've made mistakes, but you're young. You can get a job . . ."

Caleb listened, and then he just touched her cheek and smiled, shaking his head. This was his way of life, and he had no intentions of changing. Then got to know the Nazis firsthand. Caleb, like all the Jews in Lodz, was arrested.

Even before Caleb's arrest, he'd been no stranger to the Balut section in Lodz. This was where the ghetto was built. The Balut was a seedy part of town filled with criminals of all kinds. It was here that, for a year before the Nazi invasion, Caleb had established a small business as a procurer of women. He knew which taverns to frequent in order to find prostitutes whose sexual favors he sold to men in the better sections of town. The prostitutes were easy prey for him. They were girls with low self-esteem who were swept away by his charisma. So when he told them they were very special to him and asked them turn tricks for him, they did as he asked and gave him most of the money they earned.

Caleb was appalled at the living conditions in the Lodz ghetto. Never could he have imagined a more repugnant place. There was no running water and no toilets, only outhouses that were filthy, stinking holes in the ground. He had no privacy. Instead, he was forced to live with two young married couples. He might have found the living arrangements entertaining had either of the women been rich or attractive. However, they were neither. One was skinny, with a face covered in warts. He could hardly bear to look at her. But at least she was childless. The other, however, had four young, loud, and obnoxious children whom Caleb despised. To make matters worse, the husband of the childless woman was a sickly, balding man who had contracted a terrible case of dysentery. He found it hard to make it all the way down four flights of stairs to the outhouse. He often had accidents that left the small, two-room flat smelling like a zoo for hours. Caleb searched the ghetto in desperation for a wealthy woman with influence who might be able to help him better his situation. But he found no one. Instead, he only found more poor and desperate people just like himself. He couldn't bear to go on living the way he was. He had to find a way out of that apartment.

Before his arrest, Caleb had been having an affair with an older Gentile woman. She was generous with cash and gifts. But when he'd been arrested, and he'd asked her for help, she had turned her back on him. Caleb never expected anything more from her. Her husband was a government official, and Caleb was a Jew. When the Gestapo questioned her, she quickly denied ever knowing Caleb. However, when they were lovers, she'd given

Caleb some cash, and he still had a little left over. First, he took a few of the reichsmarks and exchanged them for rumkies, which was the money used by the prisoners in the Lodz ghetto. One reichsmark was worth ten rumkies. And then he watched and waited for an opportunity, keeping his eyes and ears open. In order to save himself, he needed to know as much as possible about the operations of the ghetto. He learned that a man named Mordechai Chaim Rumkowski was the head of the Judenrat. Rumkowski was powerful; he was right under the Nazis, and he was a cruel and demanding man who was hated and feared by his fellow Jews. Caleb studied him. He asked everyone he met what they knew about him. What he discovered was abhorrent. There were rumors that before Rumkowski came to the ghetto he had been in charge of orphanages where he was accused of sexually abusing children. Caleb knew that Rumkowski could be manipulated. He was an evil man, a self-serving bastard. He was perfect, and he was Caleb's mark. Caleb continued to study Rumkowski. The more he knew, the more ammunition he had. Rumkowski was from Russia. He'd gone to Jewish schools, known as cheders. *He is a cruel, selfish, and conniving man, perfect for my plan*, Caleb thought.

The blacksmith, Heimy Klein, was known to everyone as a slow-thinking man. People in town had nicknamed him the dimwit. A dimwit was another easy mark, Caleb decided, so he kept an eye on Heimy. When Caleb had a little free time, he went to visit with Heimy pretending to befriend the blacksmith. And as Caleb suspected, Heimy's lack of intelligence made him easy to control.

"You want to earn a little extra cash?" Caleb asked as he pulled out a few rumkies.

"How?"

"Well . . ." Caleb hesitated and looked into Heimy's eyes. "Can I trust you?"

"Of course. You know you can trust me. Tell me what you want me to do."

"Okay . . . so here is the plan." Caleb convinced Heimy to attack Rumkowski when Rumkowski was making his rounds. "When he goes into the empty store across the street to count his money, you slip in behind him. Then you start beating the shit out of him."

"He'll have me killed, Caleb. Everyone knows he's really powerful here in the ghetto."

"Yes, of course, he is. But would I let him hurt you? I am your friend. Come on, Heimy. Don't I come to talk to you all the time? No one else does, do they?"

"No . . ." Heimy studied his shoe.

"Exactly right. I am going to protect you. You have to trust me. While you're beating him up and robbing him, I'll come and save him, then I'll tell him that you and me are friends. And since he'll have seen how strong you are on account of how you beat him up, I'll tell him that you would make a great bodyguard for him."

"You think he would believe you?"

"Yeah, of course he would," Caleb said, patting Heimy's back. "And I'll bet he could use a strong fella like you."

"Yeah, you're right," Heimy said, nodding. "And if he hired me as one of his bodyguards, I'd get special treatment, like extra food and maybe a nicer place to live."

"You sure would."

"Yeah, you're right. This is a real good idea, Caleb. I'm glad we're friends." Heimy nodded his head.

"And once he sees how strong you are, I'll bet he'll want you as not just one of his sonder, but his chief bodyguard."

"Who are the sonder?" Heimy asked.

"You know who they are. They're the special forces here in the ghetto."

"Oh, you mean the special police, not just the regular police, right?"

"Yeah, Heimy, right." Caleb was trying hard not to lose patience with Heimy's stupidity. He had to remind himself that if Heimy was smarter, he would never attack Rumkowski. He would not even entertain the idea.

"What if I kill him by accident?"

"You won't 'cause I'm gonna show up and save him. Make sure I can see the whole thing from the street; that way he won't suspect anything."

"Like, what would he suspect?"

"Like, that I knew about this in advance, you amoretz."

"You called me an idiot." Heimy clenched his fists.

"Sorry." Caleb smiled at him and tipped his hat. "It was just a term of affection. Anyway, in good faith and all . . . let me give you an advance toward this job you're doing for me. I'll give you half the money now, then I'll give you the rest the day after you do the deed. You attack him on Monday at five o'clock in the afternoon, and then I'll meet you here at the shop on Tuesday morning at four to pay you the rest."

"What about me? Won't Rumkowski come after me with the law?"

"I already told you not to worry about that now, didn't I?"

"Yes."

"I said I'll protect you, and I will. But right now here is some money to buy you some extra food."

"That's true. You did promise to protect me." Heimy nodded. "And I could sure use some extra food. I'm hungry all the time."

"Right, and if all goes well, I'll get us both jobs working directly for Rumkowski. That will mean better food and more food. Right?"

"Sure, Caleb. You're so smart. You always know what to do."

"So don't forget to take care of this thing on Monday, all right?"

"Yes, Caleb. I won't forget."

Caleb patted Heimy on the back again. "Good. Now remember, I'm trusting you," Caleb said.

"I know, and I'll do what you ask."

Dimwit, Caleb thought as he left and went back to the filthy, overcrowded apartment.

He would not have worked at all, but if he didn't work he would be forced to forgo the afternoon bowl of watery soup that only those who were employed were entitled to. So when he first arrived he'd found a job at the hatter's shop, making hats. He hated it, so he charmed the foreman's wife with a few clandestine afternoons in her bed, after which she eagerly covered for him, making up excuses, so he was able to come and go as he pleased. Today he'd left after lunch to go and see Heimy. On Monday he would claim he wasn't feeling well and leave early.

Caleb was nervous on Monday. *I can't believe I have to depend on this idiot to put this plan into action.* He thought about taking the day off, but it would give him too much time to sit and dwell on the plan. So he went into work acting as if he were very ill. After lunch, he went to the boss's wife, who also worked in the store. "I've been up all night," he told her. "I've been vomiting."

One of the other workers overheard him. "Who isn't sick in this ghetto?" she asked, groaning.

"I can't answer that," Caleb retorted. Then he turned back to the boss's wife. "I'm afraid I might be contagious. Look at this rash," he said, pulling up his shirt. There, he revealed an ugly, red rash which he'd created by using a lipstick he'd stolen from the handbag of one of the women who lived in the apartment with him. He'd made tiny red dots then covered them with her facial powder so they wouldn't smear.

"That does look bad, Caleb," the foreman's wife said.

"Can you cover for me? This morning when I left, the rash didn't look nearly as bad as it does now, and I am afraid that if it's something serious it could close this whole place down."

"Of course. Go home and rest. I'll stay late, so I can put in your share of the work today. That way you'll still make your quota," she said.

"Thank you. You know how much I appreciate everything you do for me, honey," he said, looking around before he gently caressed her cheek.

"Of course. Go home now, Caleb."

Caleb quietly walked out the door. If everything went as planned his life would change forever today. He would never have to return to that horrible job again. Walking slowly, he kept out of sight by ducking in alleyways until he saw Rumkowski come marching down the other side of the street. His heart beat fast. *Come on, you idiot, do your job*, he thought, and then Heimy came strolling out of his blacksmith shop and followed Rumkowski into the nearby building. He grabbed Rumkowski and pushed him against the wall. Caleb waited a few minutes but not too long, then he walked in to find Heimy pounding his fists into Rumkowski's stomach.

"What's going on here?" Caleb said, his voice strong and filled with shock.

"Help me!" Rumkowski yelled.

Caleb drew the gun he carried and shot Heimy point-blank in the head. Blood flew onto the walls as Heimy fell on top of Rumkowski. Together, Caleb and Rumkowski pushed him off. Caleb helped Rumkowski to his feet. "Are you all right?" he asked.

"I think so. He was trying to rob me." Rumkowski was standing now, bent over at the waist and breathing hard.

"Yes, I'm sure he was. Are you sure you're all right?"

Rumkowski nodded. "Thank you," he said.

"Don't mention it," Caleb answered and turned to leave.

"Here, wait. Take this," Rumkowski said as he took a couple of bills out of his pocket.

"No, that's all right," Caleb said. "I didn't do it for a reward."

"I owe you. You saved my life. What can I do to help you out? Better housing, better work detail?"

"I sure would like to work for you, Mr. Rumkowski. I'd like to be one of your policemen. I think I could serve you quite well."

Rumkowski studied Caleb and smiled. "I think you're right," he said. "I believe you're right."

And that was how Caleb came to work as one of Rumkowski's henchmen in the sonder, the special forces police in the Lodz ghetto.

CHAPTER 7

THE FIRST TIME CALEB SAW ZELDA LIPMAN, SHE WAS STANDING IN line at the butcher shop with her two children by her side. Initially, he was not attracted to her. In fact, he thought she looked small and helpless like a baby bird. Her long, crooked nose reminded him of a beak. He noticed she had bruises on her face and collarbone, which she'd made a futile attempt to cover with some old makeup that didn't match her skin. Caleb knew who Zelda was married to because he listened to the rumors that spread through the ghetto, and word had it that Asher Lipman was known to be a brute.

But one afternoon he'd happened to see Zelda in the alleyway between two buildings embracing a man, with her skirt hiked up over her waist. This would not have mattered much to Caleb; he saw this sort of thing happen before, but the man was Benjamin Rabinowitz. From the first time Caleb saw Benjamin, he hated him. Benjamin was the husband of Lila Rabinowitz, the girl who had rejected him. He'd tried to offer her extra food and a better job, but she showed him no interest.

"What is it with you, Lila? Why don't you like me?"

She'd sneered at him. "I love my husband. And a good-for-nothing thug like you could never hold a candle to a refined man like my Ben." That was when Caleb's hate for Benjamin Rabinowitz was born. He was not accustomed to women treating him this way, and he wanted to know what Benjamin had that he didn't. So he decided to find Ben and follow him. To Caleb's surprise and dismay, Benjamin reminded him of the rich Jewish boys he'd met when he was young, who had shunned him because his family was poor. These boys had a way of dressing and mannerisms that even now made Caleb feel inferior. And even though Benjamin was quiet, and Caleb didn't really know anything about him, the way Ben looked and carried himself reminded Caleb of a world that had shut him out when he was very young. Consequently, he despised Ben, but he also found himself obsessed with Ben and his family. When he made rounds walking through the ghetto, he always made it a point to pass the Rabinowitz's apartment.

One day he noticed Lila did not walk home from work at her regular time. He watched for the next three days, but he did not see her nor did he see the little boy who was always by her side.

Later Caleb learned that Lila escaped. It happened at the same time as the old Nazi guard, Werner, disappeared. For several months before the escape, Caleb saw Lila on the street talking to Werner, and now Caleb put two and two together as he remembered Ben's wife, the beautiful Lila Rabinowitz, with her platinum-blonde hair and blue eyes. He knew Lila had taken Moishe and escaped the ghetto with Werner, leaving Ben behind. But he didn't feel sorry for Ben; he thought Ben deserved it for being a pompous rich boy. Ben Rabinowitz became the personification of the privileged boys Caleb despised. But now here in the ghetto with Rumkowski by his side, Caleb had power. And with that power he could squash men like Ben Rabinowitz under the heels of the black leather boots that Rumkowski had given him as a gift.

Time passed, and Caleb worked hard to keep Rumkowski's friendship. He never questioned Rumkowski's orders or argued with him about anything. Caleb found Rumkowski to be a disgusting and despicable man, and he secretly despised him, but he made sure that Rumkowski thought he admired and loved him. In return, Caleb received better treatment. He was able to move to a larger apartment, which he did not have to share with anyone else. His food rations were larger, and he had some influence as to who was selected for the transports out of the ghetto to the work camps. Rumkowski was given a quota of Jews that he was expected to deliver to the transport office each day. Although Rumkowski never told Caleb where the transports were headed, Caleb heard rumors that the trains were being sent to a camp called Auschwitz. He wasn't sure what happened to the people who left the Lodz ghetto to go to the camp, but what he did know was they never returned.

Caleb had always loved a challenge. He could have easily sent Ben Rabinowitz right off to the camp, but he didn't want to win that way. He wanted Ben's girl to choose him over Ben. Caleb set out to win the heart of Zelda Lipman. The first thing he planned to do was get Asher out of the way. Asher was a violent man whose anger Caleb preferred to avoid.

Caleb went to Rumkowski and asked for permission to add Asher's name to the next transport list. Rumkowski nodded then he said, "Fine with me. Take someone else off the list, and add Asher Lipman. Doesn't make much difference to me. Just make sure the quota is filled. I don't want any complaints from the Nazis that we're short."

CHAPTER 8

When Asher Lipman received his "wedding invitation," which was what the ghetto inhabitants called the notices that were sent to let them know they had been selected for transport, he turned as white as an eggshell. Everyone knew that the transports led to somewhere terrible. The Nazis tried to convince the Jews they were being sent to work camps where they would be given jobs to do and better rations. But there were rumors in the ghetto that the Jews were being murdered. Asher was terrified. He read the notice twice, then he put his fist through the wall. He ranted and raved at his wife, striking her with his bloody fist and tearing the delicate skin of her lips. Blood poured down Zelda's face and mixed with her tears. Then Asher turned away from Zelda and his children, who had been watching wide eyed with fear, and walked out of the apartment, slamming the door behind him. Asher headed straight for Rumkowski's office. He arrived there to find a woman seated at the front desk. When she stood up to take some papers off a counter he saw that she was about four feet two inches tall, with short arms and legs, and a large head. Asher walked up to her and slammed his fist on the counter. She jumped. He glared at her, and in an angry growl he demanded an audience with Rumkowski. She told him to please be seated, and she would speak with Rumkowski. The woman walked away. She returned five minutes later and told Asher that Rumkowski refused to meet with him. Asher began calling the woman offensive names and yelling for Rumkowski. Caleb, along with two other policemen, came out of the back and escorted Asher out of the building.

Dejected and terrified, Asher went home to pack. When he walked inside, he looked at Zelda who was sitting at the kitchen table with a wet rag on her lip.

"I'm leaving in the morning," he said.

She looked down.

"I know I've been a lousy husband. I'm sorry. You know I didn't mean any of it."

"I know," she said, her voice hardly audible.

"If I die, I don't want to go to hell for being a lousy husband and father."

She didn't know what to say. She just shook her head, but she felt tears well in the corners of her eyes.

"I just wanted to say I'm sorry. I'm going to pack a few things. Listen. I don't have much, but I am going to leave my father's ring. Sell it if you need food for you and the children."

She stood up and put her arms around him. He pushed her away. "I've got to go," he said.

"Asher . . ."

"Yes?"

"I'm sorry too."

"For what?"

"For not being the best wife."

"You were the best, Zel. I just never knew how to show love."

In the end, Asher Lipman, the man who ruled his wife and children with an iron fist, was powerless. Like all the other Jews who had been given their wedding invitations, the next morning he was led to the train station where he was handed a small loaf of bread with a little jam, then Asher was forced onto the cattle car at gunpoint and sent away on the transport to hell.

After Asher was gone, Zelda was full of a mixture of emotions.

She felt guilty that she had such a strong sense of relief, and even though he'd been a terrible husband, her heart broke for him. Zelda no longer had to endure his beatings or fear that he might hurt one of the children.

It was hard for Zelda to accept the rumors she'd heard that the people who were sent away on the transports were being murdered. No one would kill perfectly good workers when they could use their labor for free. No, she didn't believe that the Jews were being sent away and killed. Zelda thought they were probably being sent to work camps where they were forced into hard labor. After all, they'd chosen to take Asher, and everyone knew that Asher was strong and capable of heavy, physical work. If he didn't return, it would mean one of two things—he'd either died from excessive, hard labor or from starvation. If he was alive, Asher would return. Asher was the sort of man who would never leave Zelda of his own free will. Sometimes when he was in a fit of rage and beating her senseless, he told Zelda that he owned her and that she was nothing but a possession to him. "I could kill you if I chose to. You are mine," he would say. And when she thought about those words, she felt her stomach knot. However, last night before he went to pack he'd said the kindest words he'd ever spoken to her. And she could not get those words out of her mind.

Sometimes when she was alone after Ben and the children had fallen asleep, she thought back on her life with Asher. Theirs had been an arranged marriage. At first she tried hard to please him. She wanted to love him, but it was not possible. As the years passed, Asher had turned any tender feelings she had toward him into hatred. Even now as she tried to remember the good things about their marriage, it was impossible to think of him without the memories sliding into that dark, hurtful, and violent place that was so much a part of their lives together. Still, she didn't want to think of him suffering. After all, he had been her husband since she was only thirteen years old. It was his face that she looked at each morning and his clothes she washed each week. He was the father of her beloved Sarah and Solomon. And her children were the only family she had left. When all the Jews had been rounded up in her neighborhood and taken to the ghetto, Zelda's parents refused to leave Poland. Her father, who had migrated to Poland from Russia, had sworn he would never face another pogrom. So when the Jews had to register in order to be identified as Jews, her father became frightened. He was certain there would be another pogrom like the one where he had lost his own father, when he was a child in Russia. Zelda's parents had not gone to register, and Zelda knew that if they didn't they would be in trouble, so she took both of her children and went to her parents' home to plead with them to register. The apartment was deathly quiet when she arrived, and as soon as she walked in Zelda knew something was not right. Holding Sarah and Solomon's hands, she explored the apartment where she'd grown up. The house, as always, was spotlessly clean. Zelda remembered the Hanukkah parties she'd had with her cousins, as they walked through the living room. She and her cousin Sadie had played dreidel for hours on this very floor. In the kitchen, her mother's favorite pot was on the stove clean and ready to make a batch of chicken soup. The Shabbos candleholders were lined up on the windowsill as they had been every day that Zelda could remember. Gently, she touched them and thought about the wonderful Shabbat dinners she'd enjoyed with her parents before her marriage.

"Stay in Bubbe and Zede's living room and wait for me," Zelda told Sarah and Solomon. That was because, although she didn't want to believe it, she already knew what she would find when she entered the bedroom.

"I'm scared, Mommy. I want to go with you," Sarah said.

"No, I'll be right back. I'm not going far, just into the bedroom. You stay here and hold Solomon's hand," Zelda said to Sarah, then she turned to her son. "Take care of your sister for a few minutes for me. You're a big boy; I can use your help today."

"Yes, Mommy," Solomon said, then he took Sarah's hand. "Don't be afraid," he told her. "I'll protect you."

Zelda took a heavy breath and forged ahead. She found them. Her parents. There they were, her kind and loving father, her sweet and capable mother, lying side by side on the bed holding hands. For as long as Zelda could remember they always held hands. They had the kind of marriage that Zelda only dreamed of. The two of them had always been best friends and lovers. Everyone who knew them knew they were very close, and now they were locked hand in hand, together for eternity. Lovers and best friends in death as they had been in life.

The days following her parents' deaths were hard days for Zelda. To make matters worse, she could not lean on Asher. He wasn't a warm and endearing man. When he found her crying on one of their first nights in the ghetto, he asked her what was wrong. She told him, "I miss my parents. I can't believe my parents are dead. I will never see them again."

"What's done is done," he said, his voice cold and hard, the stink of whiskey on his breath. "There's nothing you can do to change it."

She looked away. He'd walked over and tenderly caressed her shoulder. For a moment she thought that she detected a kindness in him, a quality that perhaps she might love. But as quickly as that kindness peeked out of the darkness, it disappeared. He shook his head, raised her face to meet his eyes, then he said, "If you're going to survive here in this hell, you'd better toughen up."

She nodded and felt her chin quiver. Tears fell down her cheeks.

"Stop it. That's enough," Asher said, and he walked out of the room leaving her alone to cope with her sadness. His cold heart had taught her how to be independent. She'd learned not to need him for anything.

When Zelda met Ben, for the first time she saw a man who was the polar opposite of her husband. Ben was gentle, educated, and soft spoken. Because Asher was so cruel, these were qualities she longed for in a man. She liked Ben from the first day the Lipmans had moved in to the apartment, although she would never have let him know.

As the weeks passed, her feelings for Ben grew leaving her scared and confused. He was always kind to her children, but when he'd stopped Asher from beating her son by taking him out for a drink, she realized she was falling in love with him. From that first time when he had touched her in the sacred place she'd reserved for her husband and no other man, something had ignited inside her. She found from that day on that she thought about Ben constantly. She wanted to make love to him all the time, and even though she felt guilty and shameful, she trembled with desire at the sound of his voice or the touch of his hand.

The day that Ben and Zelda became lovers, everything between Zelda and Asher changed also. Zelda tried harder to please her husband, probably out of guilt but also out of fear that if he suspected anything was going on between her and Ben, he would kill them both. She was always afraid of doing something that might raise his suspicions. Now he was gone. And although she didn't want to think about him suffering in a work camp, Zelda Lipman was no longer living in fear of her husband. She was free of him at last.

Ben was shocked when he found out what happened to Asher. He was sick to his stomach due to the guilt he felt over his affair with Zelda. But he still longed to be with her, to comfort her, and to provide the shoulder she might need to cry on to assuage her own guilt. The day after Asher left on the transport, Zelda met Ben after work to walk home with him as she always did. For several moments they walked in silence, but he could see by the dark circles under her red eyes that she had been crying. He waited for her to speak. When she didn't he took her hand. "How are you doing?" he asked, his voice soft and sympathetic.

"I feel guilty because of us."

"I know. Me too," Ben muttered, his voice barely above a whisper. "Do you want to end it with us?" he asked, afraid she might say yes.

She shook her head. "No, Ben, I don't. Except for my children, you have been my only joy in life."

"I am so glad you said that," Ben said, squeezing her hand.

"Do you think it's true?" she asked, looking down at the ground.

"What's true?"

"You know."

"No, I don't know what you're talking about. Please, tell me."

"You don't believe that they are killing the Jews that go away on the transports, do you?"

"Of course not," he said, not sure if he did or didn't believe it. "Why would anyone kill perfectly good workers? The Germans aren't fools."

"That's what I thought too."

"So Asher will probably be back . . ."

"Yes, probably. But for now, at least we don't have to worry about him," Ben said, then afraid he'd been insensitive added, "I mean, at least we can stop sneaking around." He hesitated for a moment. "This is all coming out wrong. I sound like a terrible person, but I am glad that we can be together without worrying about Asher beating you and my wanting to kill him."

"It's all right, Ben. I've thought about all of it. I, too, am guilty of being a terrible person because as much as I don't wish for him to suffer, I am still very happy he is gone."

"Perhaps you and I and the children should move out of our apartment. Maybe we should try and find a place where no one knows anything about us."

"How likely is it that we can find another place? Not very. Neither you nor I have any connections."

"I know," he said. "It was wishful thinking."

"I don't care what the other people, who live with us at the apartment, think of me. I know it's crazy, but my reputation isn't important to me anymore. We are living lives that are so unpredictable. Let them scorn me for being your lover; it doesn't matter. I've had so little happiness in my life that I am going to grab on to it while I can. With all the disease going around here in this ghetto, anything could happen. We could get sick and die tomorrow. I refuse to spend what little time I might have left on this earth worrying about what people say about me," she said.

"I'm glad you feel that way. I have never been a brave man. But

I find that life here in the ghetto is forcing me to find courage I never knew I had. I want us to be truthful with everyone about our being a couple. And I'm willing to take the flack."

"Yes, I agree. I don't think we need to make any announcements about our love affair, but we don't need to hide it from everyone either."

He nodded. "I will do anything to hold on to this happiness between you and I. I am going to hold it tightly with both hands, so it can never get away. And anyone who criticizes us for being in love can go straight to hell. I don't care." He kissed her and held her in his arms, feeling her heartbeat against him.

"Are you in love with me, Ben?"

He blushed and looked away for a single fleeting moment. "Yes, Zelda, I think I am," he said, smiling.

From that day forward, Ben and Zelda spent all their spare time together. A group of Jewish classical musicians gave a concert in the town square. They attended it together leaving Zelda's children with the thirteen-year-old girl and her mother, who lived in the apartment downstairs from theirs. At the beginning of the concert, Rumkowski appeared on the stage. He gave a speech, but neither Ben nor Zelda paid any attention to him. They were both so happy to be sitting together and openly holding hands that they didn't want to think about Rumkowski. He was going on, in a solemn but stern voice, about problems that he was having in keeping the Nazis happy. Zelda and Ben looked in each other's eyes instead of listening. If only for the few hours that this concert would last, they wanted desperately to believe that life was normal. They longed to get lost in the fantasy of themselves as a young couple in love and ready to embark upon a bright and hopeful future.

CHAPTER 9

ZELDA WAS ASHAMED TO ADMIT IT, BUT SHE HAD NEVER BEEN happier. Her marriage had been a disaster, and now for the first time in her life, she was alive with the excitement of each new day. She and her children were still always hungry. The constant threat of disease still hung like a dark cloud over the filthy and crowded ghetto, but even so, love changed everything. Zelda found that she laughed easily now even when she was scrubbing clothes until her fingers bled. Ben had changed her outlook on life and the future. Before they'd met, she would have accepted death easily, but now she wanted to live. While she was at work, she daydreamed of the end of the war, when she and Ben would move in to a small house along with her two children.

Sarah didn't like Ben. When Asher had been around, Sarah had openly feared her father; however, she still resented another man coming into their lives to take his place. Solomon, unlike his sister, had become friends with Ben. In fact, they'd been friends since the day the Lipmans moved in to the apartment. And now with Asher gone, Solomon's bond with Ben was growing stronger. Zelda dreamed the day would come when her little girl, Sarah, would come to love Ben as the kind and gentle father that Asher could never be. But every day, Sarah lay in her mother's arms crying for her father.

It was on a cold morning in early March of 1942 that Caleb first approached Zelda. She was standing in line shivering as she waited for her weekly ration of bread. Zelda was holding Sarah's hand while Solomon was jumping in puddles of slush.

"I thought your pretty little daughter might like to have a doll," Caleb said when he walked over to Zelda and her children. Zelda looked up at him. He was tall and very handsome in his police uniform, and since he wore a Star of David she knew he was one of the Judenrat police. It was obviously a used doll because the dress and face were dirty. For a moment Zelda wondered how he'd gotten it.

Sarah eyed Caleb skeptically, moving to hide behind her mother, but then she looked at the doll. She had never owned a toy. Her eyes lit up.

"May I give her the doll?" Caleb asked Zelda.

Zelda saw Sarah reaching out for the doll. She nodded. "Yes, that is very nice of you. Thank you," she muttered.

"Of course," he said, smiling. Then he added, "I'm Caleb Ornstein."

"Zelda Lipman. This is Sarah, and that's my son Solomon over there playing in the puddles. It's impossible to control him. He's at that age."

"I can see." Caleb laughed a little. "He's a typical boy. I was like that when I was young too."

She managed a smile.

"You're waiting for bread rations?" he asked.

She nodded.

"Wait here, I'll be right back." Caleb walked up to the front of the line and into the bakery. Within minutes he returned carrying a paper bag.

"Here is your bread and"—he smiled coyly—"something extra, something special for you and the children."

"Oh?" Zelda said, shocked. "Well . . . thank you," she stammered. "It's really very kind of you." Taking the bag, she grabbed

Solomon's hand and began to head home. *I wonder what the special something is*, she thought. *More importantly, I wonder why he is being so nice to me. He is the most handsome policeman in the Judenrat. Why is he interested in me all of a sudden? There are much prettier girls here in the ghetto. Girls without children. What does he want with me? Oh dear, this is flattering, but at the same time it makes me very nervous.*

As soon as they arrived back at the apartment, Zelda opened the bag. Inside she found two full loaves of bread and a large slice of strudel inside. Her mouth watered. She could have gobbled that strudel up right then and there, but she bit her tongue instead. She knew she would not eat even a bite of it; she would give it all to her children. They were far more important to her than her own selfish desires to taste sugar again. She cut the strudel in half for each child, but before she did, she dipped her little finger into the sweet filling and put it into her mouth. Zelda closed her eyes. It was so delicious that it brought tears to her eyes. But she would not eat even a morsel. Not even a crumb would she take away from the hungry mouths of her precious children.

It gave Zelda such pleasure to watch Sarah and Solomon as they enjoyed that strudel. They devoured it in seconds. Then Sarah took her doll and lay down on the floor to take a nap while Solomon went out to work for the afternoon.

"I'm leaving for work too," Zelda said to Sarah. "You be a good girl, and stay here until I get home."

"Can I go to work with Devorah? I can help sew the Nazi emblems," Sarah asked.

Devorah was their thirteen-year-old babysitter who lived downstairs. She worked sewing SS emblems onto uniforms for the Nazis. It hurt Zelda's heart that her children had to work at such a young age. But Sarah had gone to work with Devorah many times. And Zelda preferred that Sarah go with Devorah rather than staying alone in the apartment. Besides, if Sarah worked, she would be entitled to the afternoon bowl of watery soup that was given to anyone who was working, and she would earn a little money too. "Yes, I suppose so. Hurry though. It's late, and Devorah will be leaving her apartment any minute now."

"I want to hide my doll before I leave. I'm afraid that someone will steal her while I am gone."

"Yes, all right. Hurry though."

Zelda took Sarah downstairs to Devorah's apartment and knocked on the door. Devorah answered as she was getting ready to leave. "Can she come to work with you? She says that she can help by doing some sewing?"

"Yes, she does help me. I would love to take her with me," Devorah said.

"That's good. Thank you so much. I have to go. I don't want to be late for work," Zelda said.

As Zelda walked to her job she thought about Caleb. He was handsome, that was for sure. But she wasn't interested. She loved Ben. Ben was handsome too, just not as rugged or as capable of making a woman feel safe in this terribly unsafe world where they lived.

When Asher had first been arrested, Ben and Zelda still made a special effort to make love when they knew no one would be home. But in order to do that they both had to miss work, which meant that they had to forgo their luncheon soup. Food was so scarce that even the watery soup was better than nothing. They needed it to survive. But now Zelda's children began to accept that Ben and their mother were more than friends. Solomon had accepted it more quickly, but now that time was passing, Sarah seemed to be less preoccupied about her father's return. Zelda knew why. It wasn't that the child didn't miss her father, it was because Sarah was so hungry that she was fixated on food. She talked about it constantly, leaving Sarah feeling guilty, as a mother, she could not provide more.

At night Ben and Zelda would wait until they thought everyone was asleep, and then Zelda would slowly inch out of the bed she shared with Sarah and go to Ben's bed. They were as quiet as they could be as they embraced and made love during the night. However, they could never be certain that the others, including the children, had not heard them.

One warm afternoon in early July, Caleb walked into the shop where Zelda worked. He was wearing his Judenrat police uniform when he went to the boss and demanded to see Zelda Lipman. She had forgotten all about him. But when the foreman called her to the front of the room, her heart began to pound. Either Caleb had come to find her because he wanted to see her, or he was coming to arrest her. But even worse, in the back of her mind, was the fear that he might have come to bring her the dreaded wedding invitation. *If he is bringing the wedding invitation that will send me on the next transport, what will become of my children? I'll have to leave them with Ben. I am so terrified to get on that train. I don't know where it's headed. The rumors are terrifying*, she thought as she walked up to the front of the room trembling.

Caleb took her arm and led her out of the building and into the bright sunlight. Her heart was beating so hard she was afraid it might explode. There was an ache down her left arm, but she didn't say a word. She was too frightened to speak. Once they had walked for several feet, Caleb turned to Zelda and said, "I was hoping you would come and find me. But you didn't."

"I'm sorry, but I don't know what you're talking about."

"I thought perhaps you might have come to thank me for the doll for your little girl."

"Oh," she stammered. "Yes, the doll. Of course. But I thought I did thank you. You're right. I should have come. Thank you for the doll. It was very kind. I'm sorry, I didn't realize . . ." She was rambling.

"It's all right. I suppose I was just hoping that you would come to see me."

"Yes, come to see you . . . of course."

"You're afraid of me? Please don't be." Caleb's voice was kind and gentle.

"I should have thanked you. I thought I did. I'm sorry if I didn't. I meant to," Zelda said. She knew she was repeating herself, and she felt foolish, but she didn't know what to say.

"It's all right. That's not why I came by to see you today. I came by to invite you to a picnic."

She turned to look at him. *How can he talk of a picnic? He acts as if everything is normal when nothing is normal anymore. There is no food for my children. He has the power to get food, and all he talks about is a picnic. My little ones are starving. Our apartment is filthy and smells wretched because so many of the people in the building have contracted dysentery. My babies are so small and thin. If, God forbid, they got dysentery . . .* She was trembling. *The whole ghetto is overcrowded. I am afraid all the time: afraid for my children, afraid for myself, afraid for Ben . . .*

"What is it? Your face is so white that you look as if you've seen a ghost. Why are you staring at me that way?"

"You know that my husband was sent away on a transport?" she said.

"Oh, I am so sorry. I didn't realize," Caleb said. His tone was gentle and filled with concern.

"Yes, and I was afraid you'd come to send me next."

"No, why would we send you? The Nazis need strong men to work. You are not a strong man now, are you?" he asked with a sweet smile.

Trembling still, she shook her head.

"No, Zelda, I did not come to send you away. I am truly sorry if I frightened you. I only came to invite you to join me for a little picnic. I have some food for us to share."

Food. Just the word. Just the thought caused her mouth to fill with saliva.

"Are you hungry?"

She nodded.

"Well, let's see . . . I have a sausage, a jar of marmalade, and two loaves of bread."

A sausage, a jar of marmalade, and two loaves of bread? A feast. "I'd love to have a picnic with you," she said, wishing she could take the food home for her children instead of eating it herself.

"I am afraid that the only place we can go where we can be alone is my office."

Alone? What does that mean? I know what that means. But I am so hungry. And . . . a sausage. I can already taste it. It's probably horsemeat. But at least it's meat, and it's been so long since I've had meat . . .

"Yes, all right. I'll come to your office," she said.

They walked to his office together. He opened the door for her when they arrived and then began to set up the food.

Surprisingly, he was a perfect gentleman that entire afternoon. He didn't even try to touch her. He gave her half a sausage and one of the loaves of bread. Zelda took a bite. It was sweet, like horse-meat, but she'd been hungry for so long that her senses exploded with delight at the taste. She could have gobbled it down in seconds, but she thought of her children and asked, "I am very grateful to you for this food. But would it be too much to ask if I could take half my food home for my children?"

"Of course. I would expect nothing less from a mother. In fact, let me give you another half loaf of bread. If I remember correctly, you have two children? This will provide half of a loaf for each of them."

"God bless you," Zelda said, sighing. "This will mean so much to them."

"And to you? Does it mean anything to you?" he said, looking intently into her eyes.

"Yes, very much. I am very grateful to you."

Caleb smiled. "So come and see me more often, will you?"

She nodded.

"By the way, here is a children's book that I came across recently. Why don't you take it for your two children?"

"Are you sure?"

"Of course. I don't have children or a wife, so what am I going to do with a book of fairy tales?"

"Thank you."

"In case you forgot, my name is Caleb. Caleb Ornstein."

She nodded again. "I'll remember," she said, but she was thinking of Ben, and now that her stomach was full, she was feeling guilty for having spent an afternoon with another man.

CHAPTER 10

THROUGHOUT THE HOT MONTHS OF JUNE AND JULY, CALEB SHOWED up at Zelda's place of work at least once a week. Sometimes he brought gifts of food, toys, or clothing. Other times he would just ask her to take a walk with him. As they walked, he would tell her about his job and ask about her life. She kept her answers vague. But when Caleb reached for her hand and tried to kiss her as they walked through the park, she knew it was time to tell him the truth about her and Ben.

"I don't know how to tell you this, but I have not been entirely honest with you. I should not have been leading you on all of these months. You see, I have a boyfriend. We are in love. I am sorry. I shouldn't have taken all the things you have given me. It's just that the children were hungry, and they have so little." She looked down at the ground but continued, "Caleb, please don't think I am not grateful. I am. I am very grateful for everything . . ."

"A boyfriend?" Caleb asked. "I thought you were the devoted wife to the husband who went away on a transport?" His tone was full of sarcasm. He hadn't seen Zelda and Ben together in town since he'd started bringing her gifts. And he had started to believe that she had broken up with Ben for him.

"Asher was a hard man. I don't wish him any harm, but he was a terrible husband. When I met Ben, he was so kind and gentle that I fell in love with him."

"You never told me you were in love with another fellow. Do you think it was right of you to lead me on?"

"All I know is that I never meant to take advantage of you. But the things you brought made my children's lives so much better. And you have been so kind to me. Oh, Caleb, I'm so sorry. I never meant to hurt you."

"I see," Caleb said, then he walked away from her, leaving her standing alone in the street.

CHAPTER 11

CALEB KNEW HE COULD SEND ZELDA OR BEN ON THE NEXT transport if he chose to. Or he could force her to give in to him if he wanted it that way. But sex with Zelda was not his goal. He didn't need her to make love to him. He had plenty of girls who threw themselves at him in exchange for half a loaf of bread. No, that was not his goal with Zelda. His aim was to win her love, to take her away from Ben. He wanted her to choose him over Ben. And even though he had the power to put Ben on the next transport, that would have been a hollow victory. Caleb wanted Ben to see Zelda choose him. This was the only way Caleb could win the game he played in his head and finally smash that spoiled, educated, rich boy, the same way the rich boys had smashed him when he was younger. Even though Caleb didn't realize what he was doing, this game he was playing was his way of escaping the reality of the horrors all around him. Caleb wasn't sure how he was going to win Zelda, but he was enjoying the challenge and decided he would not send Ben away. Instead, he would wait until the right opportunity presented itself to him.

CHAPTER 12

Late August 1942

ON HER WAY HOME FROM WORK, ZELDA NOTICED A POSTER HAD BEEN put up on the wall next to the official ghetto calendar. It was an announcement that Rumkowski was going to be making another speech. The note warned that every person living in the ghetto was required to be present at this speech. It would take place in the open area that was located right in the middle of the square, the same place he gave all his speeches, early on Friday afternoon on the fourth of September. *Shabbas,* she thought. *It's bad enough we to have to listen to him. But why on Shabbas? Now I'll have to hurry and get in line to buy my food for Shabbas dinner as soon as he is done rambling, otherwise we won't be done eating before sunset.* She eyed the familiar ghetto calendar which included Rumkowski's five slogans, and she wanted to spit because she was sure that he spewed nothing but pure propaganda. She read Rumkowski's slogans aloud and shook her head. 1. Work, 2. Bread, 3. Care for the sick, 4. Supervision for the children, 5. Peace in the ghetto. *He pretends these things are important to him, but the only thing that's really important to Chaim Rumkowski is himself.*

Zelda Lipman hated Chaim Rumkowski. She, like many others,

had to keep silent because he ran the ghetto like a dictator. But she felt sure that since he'd become the Judenrat in the ghetto, he was probably happier than he'd ever been in his life. Everyone in the ghetto knew that Rumkowski had gotten married the previous winter to a young and beautiful lawyer. The girl's name was Regina Weinberger, and she could be seen walking through the ghetto now and then in her lovely new winter coat. Neither she nor her husband looked hungry like everyone else.

CHAPTER 13

THE FOURTH OF SEPTEMBER WAS A BRISK, ICY, BLUE-SKIED DAY. A chilly wind gusted out of the north as all the ghetto's inhabitants congregated in the square, pulling their coats tighter around their bony frames as they waited for Rumkowski to appear. They spoke to each other in whispers. Most were disappointed that they would be forced to forgo their soup lunch because they had not been able to work that morning. Others complained that they wished Rumkowski would arrive already so that they could leave and begin to prepare for the Sabbath.

Zelda and Ben stood side by side holding hands. Not far away, Sarah held her doll as she sat beside her brother, who was drawing in a pile of dirt with a stick.

Rumkowski arrived on time. He wore his gray-and-black wool coat with the Star of David on the right side of his chest. His white hair stood out on either side of his black hat. Squinting from behind his thick, black-rimmed glasses, Rumkowski smiled wryly out at the crowd of people who were talking among themselves. Then he waved to them, signaling them to quiet down.

Rumkowski removed his hat, then he stood with his head down looking very grave. He seemed to have aged since the last time

Zelda saw him. She pulled her coat tighter around her as she felt the chill of the wind whip through her clothes and penetrate deep into her skin. She shivered. Something was wrong. She could see it in Rumkowski's eyes. She felt it in the air. Zelda glanced over at Ben who looked frightened too. Then Rumkowski began to speak.

"A grievous blow has struck the ghetto. They are asking us to give up the best we possess—the children and the elderly. I was unworthy of having a child of my own, so I gave the best years of my life to children. I've lived and breathed with children. I never imagined I would be forced to deliver this sacrifice to the altar with my own hands. In my old age, I must stretch out my hands and beg: Brothers and sisters! Hand them over to me! Fathers and mothers: Give me your children!

"I had a suspicion something was going to befall us. I anticipated 'something' and was always like a watchman—on guard to prevent it. But I was unsuccessful because I did not know what was threatening us. The taking of the sick from the hospitals caught me completely by surprise. And I give you the best proof there is of this: I had my own nearest and dearest among them, and I could do nothing for them!

"I thought that would be the end of it, that after that, they'd leave us in peace, the peace for which I long so much, for which I've always worked, which has been my goal. But something else, it turned out, was destined for us. Such is the fate of the Jews: always more suffering and always worse suffering, especially in times of war.

"Yesterday afternoon, they gave me the order to send more than twenty thousand Jews out of the ghetto, and if not—'We will do it!' So the question became, 'Should we take it upon ourselves, do it ourselves, or leave it to others to do?' Well, we—that is, I and my closest associates—thought first not about 'How many will perish?' but 'How many is it possible to save?' And we reached the conclusion that, however hard it would be for us, we should take the implementation of this order into our own hands.

"I must perform this difficult and bloody operation—I must cut off limbs in order to save the body itself. I must take children because, if not, others may be taken as well—God forbid."

Zelda grabbed Ben's hand and squeezed it tightly. She swayed as if she might faint.

Rumkowski continued, "I have no thought of consoling you today. Nor do I wish to calm you. I must lay bare your full anguish and pain. I come to you like a bandit, to take from you what you treasure most in your hearts! I have tried, using every possible means, to get the order revoked. I tried—when that proved to be impossible—to soften the order. Just yesterday, I ordered a list of children aged nine; I wanted at least to save this one age group, the nine-to-ten-year-olds. But I was not granted this concession. On only one point did I succeed: in saving the ten-year-olds and up. Let this be a consolation to our profound grief.

"There are, in the ghetto, many patients who can expect to live only a few days more, maybe a few weeks. I don't know if the idea is diabolical or not, but I must say it: 'Give me the sick. In their place we can save the healthy.'

"I know how dear the sick are to any family and particularly to Jews. However, when cruel demands are made, one has to weigh and measure: who shall, can, and may be saved? And common sense dictates that the saved must be those who can be saved and those who have a chance of being rescued, not those who cannot be saved in any case . . .

"We live in the ghetto, mind you. We live with so much restriction that we do not have enough even for the healthy, let alone for the sick. Each of us feeds the sick at the expense of our own health: we give our bread to the sick. We give them our meager ration of sugar, our little piece of meat. And what's the result? Not enough to cure the sick, and we ourselves become ill. Of course, such sacrifices are the most beautiful and noble. But there are times when one has to choose: sacrifice the sick, who haven't the slightest chance of recovery and who also may make others ill, or rescue the healthy.

"I could not deliberate over this problem for long; I had to resolve it in favor of the healthy. In this spirit, I gave the appropriate instructions to the doctors, and they will be expected to deliver all incurable patients, so that the healthy, who want and are able to live, will be saved in their place.

"I understand you, mothers; I see your tears, all right. I also feel what you feel in your hearts. You fathers who will have to go to work in the morning after your children have been taken from you, when just yesterday you were playing with your dear little ones. All this I know and feel. Since four o'clock yesterday, when I first found out about the order, I have been utterly broken. I share your pain. I suffer because of your anguish, and I don't know how I'll survive this—where I'll find the strength to do so.

"I must tell you a secret: They requested twenty-four thousand victims, three thousand a day for eight days. I succeeded in reducing the number to twenty thousand, but only on the condition that these be children under the age of ten. Children ten and older are safe! Since the children and the aged together equals only some thirteen thousand souls, the gap will have to be filled with the sick.

"I can barely speak. I am exhausted; I only want to tell you what I am asking of you: Help me carry out this action! I am trembling. I am afraid that others, God forbid, will do it themselves.

"A broken Jew stands before you. Do not envy me. This is the most difficult of all orders I have ever had to carry out at any time. I reach out to you with my broken, trembling hands and beg: Give into my hands the victims! So that we can avoid having further victims, and a population of a hundred thousand Jews can be preserved! So they promised me: if we deliver our victims by ourselves, there will be peace!!!"

(At this point, there were shouts from the crowd about other options . . . some saying, "We will not let the children go alone—we will all go!!!")

"These are empty phrases!!! I don't have the strength to argue with you! If the authorities were to arrive, none of you would be shouting!

"I understand what it means to tear off a part of the body. Yesterday, I begged on my knees, but it did not work. From small villages with Jewish populations of seven thousand to eight thousand, barely one thousand arrived here. So which is better? What do you want? That eighty thousand to ninety thousand Jews remain, or God forbid, that the whole population be annihilated?

"You may judge as you please; my duty is to preserve the Jews who remain. I do not speak to hotheads! I speak to your reason and conscience. I have done and will continue doing everything possible to keep arms from appearing in the streets and blood from being shed. The order could not be undone; it could only be reduced.

"One needs the heart of a bandit to ask from you what I am asking. But put yourself in my place; think logically, and you'll reach the conclusion that I cannot proceed any other way. The part that can be saved is much larger than the part that must be given away!"

At first Zelda could not believe what she'd heard. Was it possible that she had not heard him correctly? Her mouth hung open in shock. It was as if she were in the middle of a nightmare, and nothing seemed real. A woman in the crowd, just a few feet away from Zelda, fell to her knees on the pavement and began to weep, crying out, "Please, no. Please, take anything else. Take my life but not my babies. Rumkowski, how can you be so heartless? How can you take our children?"

Rumkowski left the podium. Someone cursed Rumkowski as he walked by. "Gut zol oyf im onshikn fin di tsen makes di beste." God should visit on him the best of the ten plagues.

Another man called out, "Rumkowski, how can you expect this of us? How? Are you as inhuman as the Nazis? You are a monster. You should die a thousand deaths."

A woman with a kerchief yelled, "Have the Nazis gotten under your skin and turned you into one of them? You bastard."

A woman just a few feet away from Zelda, who was weeping,

yelled, "Your time will come, Rumkowski, and when it does, no Jew will be standing at your side. The Nazis will destroy you; mark my words. Mark my words, you devil of a man."

Zelda looked at Ben who was as pale as the silver sky. "What are we going to do? I can't give him my children. I won't give him my children." She fell into Ben's arms, her fists pounding into his side. "Help me, Ben. You must help me."

Ben stared at Zelda blankly. There was nothing he could do to save the children and he knew it. Solomon and Sarah were still at play; they were such innocents, completely unaware of the cruel destiny life had in store for them. He thought of Moishe and said a silent prayer. Even though he had no idea where Moishe was or what had become of him, at least Lila had given him a chance at life by taking him away. A new respect for Lila came over him. She did what he could not. He felt such shame that he could not help the woman he loved.

"I'm sorry. Oh God! I am so sorry," Ben said as he held Zelda in his arms. "Let's go home."

The children trailed behind singing together as Zelda and Ben walked silently back to the apartment. The crowd had been too large for Solomon and Sarah to see their mother weeping. Now Zelda wiped her face on the sleeve of her coat. She steeled herself with the knowledge that she had one chance to save her children. She knew only one person who might have the power to help her. She had never been courageous. But now that her children were in danger she was like a lioness: she would do anything for her babies.

When they got back to the apartment, Zelda went to work on making herself look attractive. She wet her hair then began to use her comb to define her natural finger waves. She used the black eyeliner that she saved for special occasions. She pricked her finger with a needle. Then she took a tiny drop of blood and rubbed it into her cheeks and lips to make them look red and healthy. Zelda didn't have many dresses, but she put on her favorite and left the first two buttons open to reveal the lovely porcelain skin of her décolletage. Ben watched her suspiciously. He wanted to speak; he wanted to tell her he loved her and wished she wasn't going to do what he believed she was planning. But he couldn't say a word. *How can I ask her not to do this when I know that I can't help her? I am worthless to her. The only man who can help her is Rumkowski.* Ben was so ashamed. He was convinced that Zelda was on her way to see Rumkowski, and from the way she was dressing, she was planning to offer him anything and everything she had if he would only find a way to spare her children.

Zelda couldn't look at Ben; she couldn't meet his eyes as she put on her coat and walked out the door. *This is exactly the same thing that happened with Lila. I couldn't save our son, and so she went to the man who could. Damn that bastard, Rumkowski. I hate myself because I am useless to every woman in my life. They share their bodies like whores in order to save their children, and all I can do is stand by and watch. I am less than a man. I don't deserve to be loved. I don't deserve anything worth having. I had two women in my life, and I lost them both in exactly the same way. The first one broke my pride, but this one . . . she broke my heart.*

Zelda walked as fast as she could without breaking into a run. She was on her way to Caleb's office. Her palms were sweaty, and she was sick to her stomach. But at least she'd never told Ben anything about Caleb. The last thing she wanted was for Ben to confront Caleb, and if he knew that Caleb had been pursuing her, he might have. That could have been disastrous. Ben didn't ask her where she was going when she left the apartment, and she was glad he didn't. But she knew he was upset about the children too.

Zelda pulled the heavy door to Caleb's office building. It swung open, and Zelda walked inside. "I am here to see Caleb Ornstein," she told the short woman at the desk.

"Is he expecting you?"

"No. I don't have an appointment, but I think he'll see me. At least I hope so."

"Who shall I tell him is here?"

"Zelda Lipman."

The receptionist slid off her chair, and as soon as she pulled herself up to her full height Zelda remembered that she was a dwarf. A wave of pity came over Zelda as she watched the woman go into the back offices. She returned a few minutes later and said, "Mr. Ornstein said he will see you."

"Thank you."

"By the way . . ."

"Yes?"

"There's really no need to feel sorry for me. I may not be tall or built normally. But I am very smart. That's why Chaim keeps me in his employ." The receptionist smiled.

Zelda was taken aback. How did the woman know what she was thinking? *Am I that easy to read?* she thought. *Well, it doesn't matter anyway. Right now, nothing matters except my children.* Zelda was trembling and twisting the handle of her purse as she walked toward Caleb's office. She hoped that he had forgiven her. And it would be very helpful right now if he was still interested in her, at least interested enough to be willing to help her in trade for what she would now offer him.

Caleb's feet were on the desk, and he was smoking a cigarette when Zelda walked into his office. A smile spread across his face as soon as he saw her.

"I won't pretend I don't know what brings you here," he said.

She nodded looking down at the ground, ashamed of what she was about to do. "Yes," she said, her voice barely a whisper. "I am afraid for my children, Caleb. I believe you can help me. I think you have some influence over Rumkowski. All I ask is that he leave my children with me and not send them away." Zelda twisted the fabric of her skirt as she spoke.

"And . . . why would you think I would help you? You rejected me. Why don't you get your boyfriend to help you?"

Tears welled up in her eyes. "He can't. You know that. He's not as powerful as you are."

Caleb laughed. "So you finally realized that? He's not as handsome either. But, of course, you didn't say that. I did."

"Yes, he's not as handsome," she added quickly. "You are powerful and handsome and desirable."

"Hmmm. Interesting how I've suddenly become so desirable."

She didn't know what to say. Words failed her now. Her entire body and mind were filled with desperation. The faces of her children flashed through her mind's eye as she began to unbutton her blouse. Standing before him exposed like a piece of meat, Zelda felt her stomach turn. She hoped to control the urge to vomit.

Caleb licked his lips, then he smiled and stood up. He walked over to her and took her into his arms. "You're cold," he said.

"I'm sorry," she stammered.

"Do you want me?" he asked.

She swallowed hard and nodded her head.

"Say it."

"I want you."

"Say, 'I want you to fuck me.'"

Tears ran down her cheeks. "I want you to fuck me," she repeated as she felt bile rise in her throat. *Don't throw up. You must not throw up. Think of Sarah; think of Solomon.* She swallowed the bile back down. It burned her throat.

"Good. I like the sound of that," he said. "Get down on the floor," he continued as he undid his pants.

Don't vomit. She repeated to herself as he pushed himself inside her. *Don't vomit.* She was bone dry, and it hurt. It felt like he was splitting her in two, but he didn't seem phased. He just continued to pound into her. Then he pulled out and looked at her face.

"Put it in your mouth."

No, please. I will throw up for sure. She just lay there looking at him wishing that somehow he would change his mind. Intercourse was bad enough, but this? She didn't think she could do it without puking.

"What are you waiting for?" he said.

She shook her head. Her skirt was still up over her waist. The tears still stained her cheeks. Zelda sat up and leaned over him. *My children. My babies. I must save my babies,* she thought. Putting his erect penis into her mouth, she gagged.

"Bitch," he said. "Do I make you sick?"

"No, it's just that I've never done this before," she lied.

"Then just do it."

She did as he asked. But when he finally released his thick mucus-like fluid into her mouth, she vomited on the floor. "I'm sorry," she moaned. "Forgive me, please."

"Get out of here. You've insulted me twice now. First you reject me for that good-for-nothing boyfriend of yours. Now you puke all over the floor of my office."

"I told you that I have never done this before. I am begging you to help me. I am afraid for my babies. I need your help. I will do anything. I will do this again as many times as you want me to. I promise you I will get used to it. Please, let me keep my children. They are so young; they need their mother."

"Why should I? You were the lousiest lay I've ever had. Go home. Go back to your worthless boyfriend. See if his wealthy and educated background means anything now. Go on, and see if he can save your children."

"Please, I'm begging you. For the sake of decency. I am pleading with you." She was sobbing as she pulled her skirt down to cover herself and began buttoning her blouse.

"I said, get out," he said, walking away from her and turning to look out the window.

CHAPTER 14

When Zelda returned to the apartment and Ben saw her red eyes and tear-stained face, he took her into his arms. He assumed she'd been to see Rumkowski. He figured she'd begged him, probably offered herself to him. She didn't say a word about where she'd been or what she'd done, and he didn't ask. He just held her.

Zelda was beside herself with fear. She couldn't eat or sleep. Her mind was racing, but she could not find clarity. Then at three in the morning, as she lay beside Ben, with her heart racing, she got an idea. Nothing about this new plan that was forming in her mind was ideal, but it was better than the alternative. She jumped out of bed, her mouth sandpaper dry with anxiety, and ran to the bed where Sarah and Solomon slept. She watched them breathe for several precious seconds, knowing she would never be able to do so again. They were so young, so innocent. How could she let them go away from her all by themselves? But what choice did she have? Either way, they were leaving her in the morning. Was she making the right decision? Where are the Nazis sending these children? Could it be a better place? Am I making a mistake by what I am about to do? My motherly instinct tells me I am not. Every bone in my body is demanding for me to get them out of here before Rumkowski can put them on that transport. Thank God, at least my son is street smart. With God's help, he will be able to find a way to protect himself and his sister.

"Solomon," she whispered, knowing that the sooner she awakened him the more time he and Sarah would have before daybreak. Gently, Zelda shook his shoulder.

"Mama?" he said, his eyes opening slowly. "Are you all right?"

"I must speak to you. I know you're only a child, only nine years old, but you must listen to me, and you must remember what I am about to tell you. Are you awake enough to listen?"

"Yes." He sat up, puzzled.

"You must take your sister, and get out of the ghetto. I know that sometimes you leave here through cracks in the ghetto wall to make trades with the Polish men on the black market. You do this, don't you?"

He didn't answer.

"It's all right, Solomon. I know you have done it many times."

He nodded and shrugged. "I hope you're not angry with me."

"No. I need you to get out of this ghetto and away from the Nazis. Use the same crack in the wall that you have been using. Tomorrow morning the Judenrats are going to be rounding up all the children and sending them on a transport."

"To where? To where Father went?"

"I don't know, but I don't trust them. I don't trust the Nazis. I am afraid for you and for Sarah. You must take your sister and run. I am going to give you a ring that your father left me. It's gold. Sell it through the black market, and use the money to buy whatever you two need to survive."

"Mother?" She could see the shock and fear on his face, and she wanted to cry. He looked so small and helpless "Then what? Then where should we go?"

"Have you made any friends with the men in the Polish black market?"

"Yes, I have."

"Ask them to help you. Beg them to help you."

"What about you?"

"I'll be here with Ben. I'll be all right. But you must never return to this place. Don't worry about me. Watch out for your sister. Take care of her. Promise me you will."

"I promise, Mama," he said. But when she put her hand on his shoulder he was trembling.

"I am going to give you all the of the food that I have to take with you. Eat it sparingly. Make sure to share it with Sarah."

"Of course I will."

"Now get dressed. Hurry. There is not a lot of time left. Get as far away from this ghetto as you can, and do it as quickly as you can. Watch out for the police . . ."

"I know, Mother. I've moved through the shadows avoiding the police for a long time now. I'll get us out, and I'll take care of Sarah. And after the war is over, I'll bring Sarah back here, and we'll find you again. I promise you."

"I love you, Solomon, my little man. My brave, little man." She hugged him as the tears rolled down her cheeks. Then she awakened Sarah and told her what was happening.

Sarah began to cry, but Solomon took both of her hands in his. "Don't you worry. You're my sister, and I won't let anything bad happen to you. I'll take good care of you."

Ben heard the noise and woke up as Zelda was kissing her children goodbye.

"Be good, and be careful." She handed Solomon a towel that she'd filled with all the food they had. Then she put the ring Asher had left into Solomon's palm. "I love you both with all my heart. My babies. My sweet, precious babies. Dear God, please, I beg you. Watch over my children," she said, then even though her face was covered with tears, she gave them a smile. "Go now. Hurry," she said.

Solomon took Sarah's hand, and they left the apartment. Zelda and Ben ran to the window to watch them. But Solomon was so savvy that he and Sarah disappeared into the shadows within seconds.

Zelda fell into a fit of weeping as Ben held her in his arms. "I wish there was something I could do. Oh, Zelda . . ."

"Just hold me, Ben," she said.

The following morning, Ben went to work. Zelda was getting ready to leave for work when Caleb arrived at her apartment. He demanded she give him her children.

"They're not here," she said boldly.

"Oh?" Caleb turned to the other policeman who was helping with the roundup and said, "Search this apartment, and find this woman's two children."

They searched but found nothing. Caleb was so angry with Zelda that he searched the entire building. Still, there was no sign of Sarah or Solomon. So he grabbed Zelda's arm roughly and walked her to the transport.

That morning, Caleb, along with the other Jewish ghetto policemen took thousands of children under the age of ten to the transport. But unlike the other mothers who were left behind in the Lodz ghetto, Caleb pushed Zelda onto the train car that was filled with crying children.

"You think you've outsmarted me, don't you? Now you will go instead of your children. You will take their place," Caleb said. Then he spit at Zelda. The children all around her were weeping.

Even though he spit at her, Zelda begged Caleb one more time. "Please, I'll do anything you want. Anything at all. Leave me in the ghetto." But he just walked away from her. The train car was slammed shut, leaving Zelda the only adult in an entire boxcar filled with terrified children. She tried to look out through an opening in one of the slats still hoping she might find some way to appeal to Caleb. But she didn't see him. It wouldn't have mattered anyway. She knew that he was never going to help her.

Ben was at work when Zelda was taken. When he arrived back at the apartment, he received the news from the others in his apartment building that Zelda was gone. *No one ever returns from those transports*, he thought. Rumors spread through the ghetto that the people who were on the transports were being murdered. Until now, Ben had doubted the truth of it. But somehow as he thought about

Zelda and all the little children from the ghetto, he knew it was true. They were doomed. A small voice in the back of his head warned him that he would never see them again.

Ben walked out of the apartment in a rage. He'd been so consumed with anger and fear for Zelda that he'd not even taken the time to put on his coat. It was cold outside, but he didn't feel it. He had no concern for his own welfare. His face was blood red, his fists clenched at his side as he headed for Rumkowski's office.

"May I help you?" the small woman at the desk asked.

"I must see Rumkowski," Ben said.

"I'm sorry. He's very busy today. He's unavailable to see anyone."

Fueled by anger, Ben pushed past the woman and stormed into Rumkowski's office.

"You bastard," Ben said. "You filthy, good-for-nothing bastard. You sent my girl away on a transport. She might well be on the way to her death. I ought to kill you with my bare hands."

"Help!" Rumkowski yelled, his eyes wide with fear. "Help me!"

Two of the Jewish ghetto policemen came rushing into Rumkowki's office. One of them was Caleb. A smile flashed over Caleb's face as he grabbed Ben's arms, then Caleb's smile vanished as quickly as it had appeared.

The two policemen held Ben tightly and tried to pull Ben away, but before they did, Ben looked into Rumkowski's beady eyes and said, "I will kill you one day. Mark my words. One way or another I will find you, and I will kill you." Ben had never been so bold in his entire life. But he had lost so much and suffered so deeply that he was no longer the same gentle man he had once been.

Rumkowski laughed. He was bold and confident now that his two policemen were holding Ben tightly. "How dare you threaten me, you son of a bitch. I've got news for you. You're going on the next transport out of here. Once the Nazis get their hands on you, I highly doubt you will have a chance to do anything to anyone."

CHAPTER 15

BEN SPENT THAT NIGHT IN A CELL IN RUMKOWSKI'S OFFICE. IF HE had been able to get out, he would have tried to kill the man, would have strangled him with his own two hands. But Ben was locked in, and even if he screamed through the entire night no one would hear him.

In the morning, Ben was taken out of his cell by two of the ghetto policemen. One of them Ben recognized as the same handsome, Jewish man who had held him off of Rumkowski the day before. There was something in the young man's eyes that sent a chill down Ben's spine. He looked at Ben with disdain, and Ben had no idea why this man would hate him so much.

The two policemen held Ben tightly as they led him to the transport station. Try as he might to fight his way out of their grasp, Ben knew it was no use. There were two of them, and even one was much stronger than he. When they got to the train station, the police still held Ben in a tense grip while the train was being loaded. All the others who were being sent away were given half a loaf of bread with jam.

"No bread and jam for you," the handsome one said.

"Why not just give it to him, Caleb?" the other policeman said.

"He's going on the damn transport. Might as well give him the food."

"He threatened Rumkowski," the one called Caleb said. "He doesn't deserve it."

The other policeman shrugged. "Sorry, fella," he said to Ben.

Once the train was overloaded with poor souls, Caleb pushed Ben forward. Before he forced Ben into the boxcar, Caleb whispered into Ben's ear, "My name is Caleb Ornstein, and just so you know, I fucked your girlfriend."

Ben turned to look at Caleb in shock just as the steel door of the train car slammed shut, sealing Ben's fate forever.

CHAPTER 16

THE TRAIN CAR THAT BEN WAS LOADED ONTO WAS NOT THE SAME one as the children. This one was full of adults who were packed so tightly that they were forced to stand. There was no water and soon the little bit of food that the other's had been given was gone. The smell of feces and urine mixed with the odor of sweat and fear permeated the air. It was pitch dark except for the light that came through the few cracks in the wooden planks. A hot and airless tomb. Many times, Ben felt dizzy as if he might faint. Every so often someone asked where they were going, but no one knew the answer. Sometimes, the sound of someone praying or weeping broke the silence in the death car. And occasionally, one of the prisoners spoke to another, but Ben remained silent.

At first, the words that Caleb had whispered in Ben's ear filled him with so much fury that he thought he would burst. It had been cold for the last week, but today it was hot for September. It was like autumn was belting out her last song before she gave way to the murderous winter cold that waited just around the corner. It stayed warm for several days making Ben think that the cold would have been more tolerable. But he found as the days passed, and the heat and the thirst overtook him, his rage at Caleb began to fade. He was weak, too weak to feel anger. There was a terrible ache in his head, and he felt dizzy and nauseated.

Ben no longer felt the burning hunger that he'd come to accept as a part of life. He wasn't hungry at all and that worried him. He began to wonder if he might be dying, and he began to believe that he could easily be dead before the end of this trip. He was fairly certain that the woman who was standing next to him had died. Her body remained in a standing position but only because the other people were sandwiched in so close to her that it kept her from dropping to the floor. He'd tried twice to speak to her, had even gone so far as to shake her shoulder. There'd been no answer. Ben couldn't say exactly what killed her. But everyone knew that death lay around every corner, and it seemed obvious that the chances of dying were far greater than those of living.

Held up by the man on Ben's left and the wooden boxcar on his right, Ben began to drift off to sleep. He tried to make himself believe that he was headed to a better place, a place where he and Zelda might be reunited. Perhaps it really was a work camp. Perhaps they really would receive more food. Perhaps he could hold her in his arms again. He was exhausted, spent.

Ben's eyes closed, and he saw a vision of Zelda smiling at him when the train came to a sudden and abrupt halt. Everyone was hurled forward. Ben lost his footing; his heart began to race as the metal door was unlocked and flung open. The light of day stabbed his eyes. He'd been in the darkness so long that he could hardly see as he was forced out of the rail car in a rush of prisoners. His knees and legs were shaky, and he almost fell several times as the guards prodded the prisoners forward with their guns. "Shnell, you Jew swine," they yelled; the vicious-looking dogs they held on leashes growled and barked. "Run! Run!" the guards yelled. As he ran, Ben saw skeletal-looking men in gray-striped uniforms with large, dark, and empty eyes standing on the sidelines of the crowd who were arriving. These men were crying out in languages he didn't understand. There was a terrible smell, even worse than the smell in the train car. It made Ben feel like he might vomit, but there was no time to stop even as the bile rose in his throat. Ben swallowed hard, then he gagged and almost choked, but he kept running as the guards pushed him into a line. It felt like a horrific nightmare that Ben could not escape from.

A man in a black SS officer's uniform, with hair as black as a raven's, was pointing to each prisoner. "Left, right, left, right."

"Yes, as you say, Herr Doctor," one of the guards said, addressing the man in the black uniform.

An old man, who was ahead of Ben in line, was sent to the left. Ben was sent to the right.

"That's Dr. Mengele," someone said. "He's a sadistic bastard."

Ben didn't say a word. His eyes scanned the crowds in hopes of finding Zelda and the children. But there were so many people, and every time he stopped to look around for even a second, a guard either prodded him with a gun butt or hit him.

The next several hours were broken down, in Ben's mind, into moments of terror. He was smeared with a slimy, green fluid then told, "You are being sent to shower where you will be deloused. That's because you're filthy swine. All Jews are. Take off your clothes; fold them nicely, and leave them in a pile, then follow the line."

"They are going to kill us," one of the men said.

"Why would they do that? They need us to do their work," another said.

"Don't you smell that odd and horrific odor that's everywhere in this place? That's the smell of burning bodies."

"Shut your mouth and move. You're wasting time. Faster, I said. Faster!" the guard roared, hitting the man in the face with his rifle. The man's face ran with blood.

"Remove your clothes, and fold them neatly," one of the guards announced in an official tone, "then put them on the bench. Be sure you remember where you left them."

Ben removed his clothes and laid them on the bench as he was told. There were prisoners who were walking, collecting the belongings of the men who were being herded into the showers. These prisoners wore yellow Stars of David sewn on the chests of their gray-striped uniforms. Ben recognized one of the men who was gathering the clothes as someone he'd known briefly from the Lodz ghetto. It was a young, muscular man of about twenty-five years. He couldn't remember the prisoner's name, but he saw kindness and sadness in the young man's eyes.

Naked, Ben followed the others into the line. The guards were busy tormenting a cantankerous man who was refusing to cooperate. When the young man, whom Ben recognized from the ghetto, walked by, Ben felt it was his opportunity to ask a few questions. There were only a few seconds for Ben to speak up, and although he was terrified of the answers he would receive, Ben said, "Excuse me. You look familiar. Were you in the Lodz ghetto?"

"Yes, I recognize you. You're Ben Rabinowitz, aren't you?"

"Yes, I'm sorry I don't remember your name."

"Jake Aaronstein."

"Jake, I know you are probably not supposed to tell me anything, but please, I have to know. Are the Nazis going to kill us now? I heard someone say that the showers are not really showers. They said that the people who go in never come out alive. But if that's true, then why would the guards tell us to fold our clothes and remember where we put them."

"The Nazis are full of tricks and lies. I can tell you for sure that you won't get your clothes back. Look around. Don't you see that me and the other fellows are busy collecting them? The Nazis take everything of value that is brought in here, but from what I have overheard, this transport is one of the lucky ones. You won't die today. They need the men from this transport to fill various jobs. So you will be sent to work."

"Have others been killed here? Is it true? Do people go into the showers and not come back alive?"

"They have killed people here. The first time I saw it happen, they murdered an entire transport of Soviet prisoners with some kind of gas in those showers. And since spring of this year, I have seen them sending more and more of the transports of Jews that are coming in to be gassed. Like I said, Rabinowitz, you're lucky. You came at the right time. They need workers in the rubber factory, so from what I've overheard, this group of men who came in today is going to be spared."

"My God," Ben said.

"Yes, it's true."

"What are you two standing around and talking about? This isn't a lunch date at a beer garden," a young guard said. "You get in line." He pointed to Ben, then he glared at Jake and said, "And you get back to work."

Jake nodded.

Ben walked into the line feeling a little better but wondering if Jake had told him the truth or spared him out of pity. Perhaps they were not really spared. Perhaps they were on their way to being gassed.

The men stood packed so closely they could smell each other's rank breath. It was a dimly lit room with showerheads above them. A hundred thousand hours seemed to pass, although in reality it was only a few minutes. The smell of sweat and filth filled the area. The prisoners stood together trembling, not knowing if they were going to be cleansed or murdered. Ben heard men crying. He heard men praying. Then there was a noise, a rattling of the pipes, and his heart nearly burst with fear. For a single second he thought this might be his last breath, but then water rained down on him, and he began to laugh and cry at the same time.

CHAPTER 17

November 1942

ON BEN'S FIRST DAY IN AUSCHWITZ, FOLLOWING HIS SHOWER, A shaving of his head, and a painful visit with a tattoo artist who scribbled a number into the flesh of his arm, he'd been ushered by a guard into a room that was lined with wooden cots and told he must find room for himself. Each bed was already overfilled with men. It was so crowded that they were forced to sleep on their sides to make room for each other. Ben searched the room, frantic to find a place to sleep before the guard returned. As he passed each of the bunks the men turned away from him. He knew they weren't being intentionally cruel. There was just no room. Sweat formed on the back of his neck. If the guard returned and he hadn't found a place for himself, he was sure he would be severely punished. As he walked to the end of the long aisle of beds, a young man walked up to him. "Follow me; there is room over here," he said.

Ben followed. Someone called out, "Watch out, he's a fagela." Several of the men started laughing. *He must be a homosexual*, Ben thought, but he ignored the warning and continued to follow the man.

"Here's where I sleep. I have a little room on the other side. You could sleep there. But I think you should know that everyone avoids sleeping by me because I'm a queer. When I first got here I thought the Nazis would kill me on the spot. Instead, they gave me this lovely pink triangle to let everyone know what I am." He pointed to the triangle on his uniform. "I guess the men are afraid of me. I'm not an animal. I won't try to do anything to you during the night. You're perfectly safe here. But I thought you should know everything about me before you decided if you want to sleep over here. We all sleep like this," he said, showing the way they would sleep. "We have more room by sleeping this way. I will sleep with my feet at the foot of the bed. You'll sleep with your feet at the head of the bed. Do you see?"

"Yes, I understand. And thanks for explaining. Now maybe you can tell me your name too?"

"Joshua Greenspan. I am a Jew," he said. "I want you to know that just because you're sleeping beside me doesn't mean I have designs on you. Actually, you're not my type." Joshua smiled.

"You're rather outspoken. I'm Ben Rabinowitz. I'm a Jew, but I'm not a fagela. However, I don't hold it against you either," Ben said, smiling. "Thank you for sharing your bed with me."

"I'll show you around this lovely palace, and I'll help you to master our routine here at the grand and glorious Auschwitz." Joshua winked.

"Some palace," Ben said.

"It's horrific, I know. But listen to me. Just do whatever they tell you. Keep your head down, and with a little luck you'll make it through."

"I can't help but wonder how people can treat other human beings this way. This place looks like it might have been a stable at one time. It's hardly big enough for all the people they have stuffed in here. And to make matters worse, it stinks like shit."

"That's because a lot of the prisoners in here are very sick. They have constant diarrhea. Try not to be the last person to get to the toilet because if you are you will be expected to empty the pot. That's a tough job. Sometimes, because it's so crowded, and so many people are sick and running to the bathroom, you'll find that you won't be able to make it to the pot in time. That's when you'll have to urinate or defecate in your food bowl."

"Oh my God. My food bowl? I can't imagine that," Ben said. "I could vomit just thinking about it. I have to tell you the truth; I don't know if I'll survive here."

"No one knows for certain if they will be able to endure. But you have to keep believing that you will. If you let yourself fall into a depression, it's just a matter of time before you'll be dead. I've seen it happen in here plenty of times."

"How can I not be depressed? I don't know what happened to my son, or to my girl and her children. They could all be dead for all I know."

"Everyone here has a story. Everyone here has a family and friends and loved ones. We are all worried about their safety. But you can't dwell on it, my friend. If you do, it will eat you alive. You want a suggestion?"

"Yes, I need all the help I can get."

"We all need a reason to go on. What I find works well is thinking about someone you love. Don't let yourself wonder if they are alive or dead because that will drive you mad. Just make yourself believe that they are alive. Talk to them in your mind. Make them so real to you that it feels as if they are standing right next to you."

"Is this what you do?"

"It is."

Ben nodded. "I'll try," he said. "I was going to ask my friend Jake, who works as a sonderkommando, if he could find out if my girlfriend is here."

"You can ask, but you might not want to know the answer. If you find out she's dead, it will crush your spirit. And right now, Ben, the only thing that separates life from death for each of us is our spirit."

"Now there are a few things you are going to need to know. Stay

81

far away from the fences. If you touch the fence, you will die instantly; it's electric. You will learn that you need to find ways to exchange favors with the other prisoners. That's how we survive. Do you speak German?"

"Yes, not very well, but I do. And I completely understand it."

"That's good. Most of the language spoken here is a mixture of German and Polish. You'll pick up more German as the time passes."

CHAPTER 18

AT FOUR THIRTY EVERY MORNING, BEN PULLED HIMSELF OUT OF THE filthy, wooden bed where he slept. He never slept well and was still exhausted. He folded the thin blanket he'd been given. His entire body was covered in large red welts, bedbug bites, that itched and then burned when he scratched them until they bled.

Still half asleep, Ben raced to get in line for the bathroom so that he would have a chance to relieve himself before the whistle sounded, signaling that all prisoners must report for roll call. One of the first things Joshua warned him about was that being late or absent for roll call was cause for severe punishment. "There are two roll calls—one in the morning and one at night. Sometimes they have one at noon too. Make sure you're on time," Joshua said. "If you are late, our entire block could be punished. Last year it was the middle of winter, cold as hell, and one of the men in our block had dysentery. To make a long story short, the poor fellow couldn't get off the pot. Because of him, we all had to stand outside in rags for the entire night. It was freezing. Five men died that night. They just fell over and died."

Ben stared at Joshua. He was quiet for several minutes. Then Ben muttered softly, "That could happen to anyone."

"Yes, it could. But don't let it happen to you. Because when we were finally back in our block, the other men beat the hell out of the fella who caused us to be punished. They beat him so badly that he couldn't walk. The next day the Nazis sent him to the hospital. He was never seen or heard from again. I'm sure they killed him there. That's another thing: if you're sick, don't let them know it. That hospital is a death sentence."

"You didn't participate in the beating, did you?"

"Nahh. I don't have the heart to beat anyone up. But I sure was angry with him. It was a truly miserable night we had standing out in the cold practically naked. I remember shivering; my teeth were chattering so badly I thought they would fall out."

Joshua was a violinist by trade. Before he was arrested and sent to the camp, he'd played with an esteemed orchestra in Berlin. Now he played with the camp orchestra standing outside and playing songs by Wagner as the overworked, starving prisoners fell into line during roll call.

Ben followed the rest of the men from his block as they took their places in the roll-call line. He glanced up and shot Joshua a quick, wry half smile.

The guard, with his clean, pressed uniform and black, shiny boots walked in front of the prisoners eyeing them with disdain. Then he began roll call, not by name but by number. Each man, including Ben, had a number. It was the same number that had been tattooed into his flesh the day he'd arrived.

"Three-four-eight-seven-two-zero-nine," the guard said.

"Here," Ben answered.

Once everyone was accounted for, the prisoners were given a quick breakfast of bitter ersatz coffee. Then another whistle was sounded, and Ben got into another line. A guard then escorted him to his work detail.

Ben was assigned to a work detail at the rubber factory, which was built near the camp in order to make it more convenient for the use of slave labor. For eleven long hours he stood over large vats of boiling liquid. And by the time he returned to his block he was shaking with exhaustion. Joshua was concerned. He knew that Ben was too delicate of a man for the rigorous work in the rubber factory. That was one of the hardest jobs in the camp, and it had been known to kill stronger men.

When Joshua was not playing his violin with the orchestra, or practicing, he worked in the kitchen. This was one of the better jobs a man could have at the camp. It sometimes gave him access to extra food if he had a quick hand and was able to steal. Joshua had been given kitchen detail because he'd been lucky enough to make friends with one of the guards, SS Sturmmann Alarich Wolff. Wolff was repressing his own homosexuality. When Joshua saw the way the guard looked at him, he knew that Wolff was a latent homosexual, and he came up with a plan. A risky plan at the time, but it worked out well. That same day, when no one was around, Joshua approached the guard and discreetly offered Wolff what he secretly yearned for. At first Wolff was angry, and Joshua was sure he'd made a terrible mistake. But then Wolff reconsidered, and the two went to Wolff's private office. Joshua swore to Wolff that he would never say a word to anyone. And he kept his promise. A year passed, and Wolff became so attached to Joshua that he grew protective of him. At the time, Joshua was playing his violin with the orchestra rather than working in the camp hospital. Wolff was afraid the hard work and exposure to disease in the hospital would be too much for Joshua, and since he didn't want Joshua to die, he took him out of his job there and sent him to work in the kitchen.

Joshua hated all Nazis, but he knew how to exploit the power he had over Wolff. The next time Joshua and Wolff were together, he told Wolff that he was worried about Ben. "This job he has in the rubber factory is too hard for him," Joshua said.

"You like him, perhaps. You sleep beside him." Wolff raised his left eyebrow.

"I like him, but not in that way," Joshua said, smoothing the hair off Alarich's face, "not in the way I like you. There is no one else like you, Alarich. You are my lover, but he is a friend. And I'd like to help him, if I can."

"What do you want me to do?" Wolff asked, softened by Joshua's caresses.

"I want you to get him a job with me in the kitchen."

"It's a lot of trouble for me to go through for a man who means nothing to either of us."

"I didn't say he meant nothing to me. I said he was a friend not a lover. I want you to help him," Joshua said. "Do this for me? Please?" Joshua put his hand around Alarich's manhood. Then he lowered his mouth over the erect shaft. Alarich sighed. Joshua stopped. "Will you do it for me?" he asked.

"I could command you to finish."

"You could, but you know it wouldn't be as good as if I did it because I wanted to."

"You are a little minx." Alarich laughed. "Very well. I'll arrange for your friend to work in the kitchen."

"And I'll take you to heaven in exchange for your trouble," Joshua said.

CHAPTER 19

BEN WAS TERRIFIED WHEN THE FOREMAN CALLED HIS NUMBER THE
following day at the factory. "Three-four-eight-seven-two-zero-
nine," the man shouted. "Three-four-eight-seven-two-zero-nine,
come to the front."

Wringing his hands together as he ran, Ben almost tripped and
fell in a pool of liquid someone had spilled. He felt a muscle twist in
his back, but he dared not stop When he got to the front of the
room his back was aching, and he was so nervous that he felt a
strong urge to urinate. "Three-four-eight-seven-two-zero-nine, show
me your number."

Ben pulled the sleeve of his uniform up to reveal his tattoo. The
foreman nodded. "Follow me, Jew," he said.

Ben wished he knew where the foreman was leading him, but he
dared not ask. He clenched his teeth. They walked outside into a
gust of cold wind that penetrated right through Ben's thin uniform.
He shivered but didn't slow down.

"Ech, it's too cold out here for me," the foreman said, turning to
one of the Nazi guards who was standing at the side of the building,
smoking a cigarette. "You shouldn't smoke, you know. Our führer
doesn't approve of smoking." The guard nodded at the foreman

trying to hide his disdain. But he threw the cigarette on the ground and put it out with the toe of his boot. "I need you to take this prisoner to the kitchen. I got a message from your superior officer. This man has been transferred."

Transferred? Transferred? To the kitchen? Could it be possible? Ben's heart leapt with joy. *The kitchen. I am so afraid to let myself be hopeful. And yet I can't help it. Is it really possible? Oh dear God, working in the kitchen I might even find a way to get my hands on a little extra food. And it certainly would be much easier than working in the rubber factory.* He knew the kitchen would be hot but not as miserably hot as the rubber factory. And the smell of food would be far more pleasant than the smell of rubber and the heavy odor of sulfur that was always present in the factory. Sometimes he found that odor made him sneeze uncontrollably until his nose and eyes ran, and he could hardly see in front of him. Ben was so filled with joy at the possibility of working in the kitchen that he wanted to shout out loud, "Thank you," to God, to the guard, to every ray of sunlight, to the wind, to everything, and everyone around him, but he knew better. Instead, he followed quietly behind the Nazi as they walked back through the large fence that read Work Makes You Free and then into the warmth of the camp kitchen.

Joshua nodded at Ben when Ben arrived.

"Show him what to do," a heavyset Nazi, with a dirty, white apron over his uniform, said to Joshua.

Joshua nodded, then he walked over and started teaching Ben the work that needed to be done. From that day forward, Ben was no longer required to attend roll call in the morning. He got up earlier than the others and went directly to the kitchen where Joshua met him as soon as he'd finished playing the violin at roll call. The work was hard but not nearly as hard as the rubber factory. The days were long: eleven, sometimes twelve hours without a break, but if they didn't get caught, they could sometimes sneak an extra bite of bread or a raw potato.

On Sundays, there was no work for most of the prisoners. However, the kitchen help were required to work. Still, every Sunday, after Ben and Joshua finished cleaning up after dinner, Jake came to their block to visit with them. He'd stolen a deck of cards from the pants pocket of a prisoner whose things he was collecting to take to Kanada. Kanada was the name that had been given to the sorting area where all the valuables taken from the prisoners were stored.

Ben, Joshua, and Jake spent the final hours before bedtime on Sunday nights playing cards. They sat around the single fire, where all the prisoners gathered trying to forget the hunger that churned in their bellies and the cold that chilled their bones.

One Sunday night after Jake had just dealt them each a hand of poker, he picked up his cards, but he was not able to concentrate. Instead, he turned to his friends and said, "The mass murders of the people who come in on the transports are increasing. I've overheard the guards saying that they've started using a gas called Zyklon B. They pile the people into the showers then drop the gas. They're sadistic bastards, most of 'em. They watch the gassings through a little window. I don't know how they can stand to watch such terrible things. After it's all over, they send me and some other sonderkommandos to clean up. It's hard. really hard. I've never seen anything so horrible in my entire life.

"Lately, they have us burning bodies in pits too. And the worst part about it is, I see these fellas when they first come in. I see them get undressed and carefully fold their clothes. I can see the hope in their eyes, and it breaks my heart. Worst part is that sometimes they talk to me. Thing is, I can't tell them anything. Not that I would want to. What good would it do them to know what was in store. It'd only be worse. Then the next thing I know I am carrying their bodies out and scrubbing blood and feces off the walls and the floor. I keep wondering how long it will be before it's my turn to be gassed." Jake held the cards so tightly that he was bending them in half. "As of right now I'm still working inside the little red house collecting the belongings of those who are going to the showers. It's a terrible job, but at least it's warm. The Nazis have decided to dig up some of the mass graves and burn the bodies. Last week they transferred a bunch of the sonderkommandos outside to do the digging. It keeps getting colder and colder out, but these poor fellows are still working outside in their thin uniforms. I am afraid I am going to be transferred outside soon. And the smell. Oh, the smell. Well, all I can tell you is it's overpowering."

Ben shuddered. "I assume the stuff that looks like snow that is constantly falling all over the place is ashes from the burning of the bodies," Ben said.

"Yes, it is. It's all over me, all the time. It's in my hair and in my eyes. I taste it when I eat or drink," Jake said, shaking his head.

"I wonder how long any of us has left. Sometimes I think that we're all destined to die here," Ben said.

"Stop it, right now, both of you." Joshua grabbed each man's wrist. "Look at me. Look at me. Look straight into my eyes and listen. If we keep thinking and talking about all the misery all around us, we're as good as dead. We have to force ourselves to remember the good things and hold them close to our hearts. Somehow, we have to believe. We have to make ourselves believe that we are going to survive this, that our lives can and will be good again."

"Do you believe it?" Jake asked Joshua.

"I do. I must. I hold on to hope. After all, things are looking better, aren't they? America has entered the war, and there are some Germans who think that Germany is losing," Joshua said.

"Are you sure of this? How do you know?" Ben asked.

"I just know. I have a friend who told me."

"Who?" Jake asked.

"That's none of your business," Joshua snapped. He didn't like what Wolff stood for, but at the same time he would not go back on his promise to him. He would not reveal his source. "You just have to make yourself believe. Because the minute that you start accepting that you are going to die here, you will."

"He's such a philosopher," Ben said, patting Joshua on the back.

"Not a philosopher. Just a man who is hopeful," Joshua said. "Why don't we talk about good things? Tell me, Ben, was your mother a good cook?"

"She was. And I'm embarrassed to admit it, but I was a mama's boy when I was a youngster. I had trouble breathing. Asthma, the doctors called it, and so I was never strong enough to play sports with the other boys. I would sit at home and read. I was always trying to help my mother in the house. And in turn, she tried to prepare my favorite foods whenever she could get her hands on the ingredients."

"Like what?"

"She baked a strudel that was so delicious it melted in your mouth."

"I thought you told me you were married, or did you have a girlfriend. Sorry, I can't remember," Joshua said.

"I was married to a headstrong woman who left me. She took my son. In all fairness, she was trying to do right by our boy. She got him out of the Lodz ghetto. I have not seen or heard from either of them since."

"I'm sorry," Joshua said.

"I'll tell you what . . . she was a lousy cook," Ben said, laughing. Then all three laughed. "Her name was Lila; ours was an arranged marriage. She was very beautiful, and I came from a financially comfortable home. That's why she was interested in marrying me. My father was in the garment production business. We owned a small factory. I attended a university for a few years. I was going to study accounting. My parents thought education was important; they insisted on accounting. I really wanted to teach and maybe, someday, even write a book. When Lila's father approached my father with the possibility of a match, my father presented the idea to me. I met her and was smitten by her looks. So I agreed to the marriage. Shortly after, Lila got pregnant and gave birth to my son, Moishe. But then a year later, the Jews were no longer permitted to attend any university, so my parents just assumed I would take over the family business."

"Did you love her?" Jake asked.

"I don't know if you would call it love. I cared for her, and I miss my son. But the real love of my life was a girl I met in the ghetto after Lila left. Her name was Zelda. That's the girlfriend you remember me telling you about." Then he went on to tell his two friends all about what happened with Zelda, her children, and Rumkowski. "But you know what's kind of funny? Before

Rumkowski sent Zelda away, I was never the sort of fellow who could stand up for himself. But when I went to see Rumkowski that day when I got home and found Zelda gone, I found a strength in myself that I never knew was there. Would you believe that I told him that someday I would kill him? I can't believe I had the courage to say it, but I did. Me—Ben Rabinowitz." He gave a short laugh. "I've always been such a nebbish and a coward. I guess love changes a person. God, I miss Zelda."

"Rumkowski was a real bastard. I'm just waiting for the transport that brings him in here," Jake said, "because you know that the Nazis aren't going to spare him, don't you? They'll throw him in here just like the rest of us when he is no longer of any use to them."

"What did he do to you?" Ben asked.

"He had one of the idiots whom he hired as his policemen throw my parents on a transport while I was at work one day. He's a real son of a bitch. Only a real son of a bitch would collaborate with the Nazis the way he did. I think he thought he was one of them. But believe me, they'll turn on him. To them Chaim Rumkowski is nothing but another Jew. The only difference is that he hasn't got a friend in the world except maybe his policemen. But all the other Jews from Lodz hate him." Jake's face was red with anger.

"I don't know how a man can turn on his own people the way Rumkowski did," Ben said.

"I didn't know the man. But extreme situations reveal a person's true nature," Joshua said.

"What do you mean by that?" Jake asked.

"I mean that being put into a position of power by the Nazis gave Rumkowski an opportunity to save himself. He could have tried harder to help the others in the ghetto but he didn't. Deep down the man was a coward. He was self-serving. Now I'm not saying that we aren't all self-serving to a point. But just how far a man will go to save himself tells you a lot about his character," Joshua said.

"What would you have done"—Jake looked at Joshua earnestly —"if you'd been in Rumkowski's position?"

"I don't know. I'd like to think I would help my fellow Jews. But it's hard to say what one will do when confronted with danger and possibly death."

"Jake, I have agonized over whether I should ask you this or not," Ben blurted.

"Ask me what?"

Ben took a long moment, and then he sighed. "Ask you if you know anything about what happened to my girl. Her name, as I told you, was Zelda: Zelda Lipman. Do you recall anyone by that name passing through the showers . . . or, God forbid, the gas chambers?"

"Oh!" Jake nodded slowly, then he looked away. "I wish I could help you find your Zelda. I wish I could confirm that she is safe. But I don't remember anyone by those names. There have been so many people who have come through here, people whose names I never knew."

"It would have been a day or maybe a couple of days before I arrived."

"I honestly don't remember them," Jake said.

"Well"—Ben bit his lower lip—"that's good. That's good news. Perhaps they are still alive."

"Yes, perhaps they are," Joshua said, patting his friend's shoulder.

"What about you, Josh? Did you have someone special in your life?" Ben asked.

"It's different for us, homosexuals I mean. It's harder to meet someone and form a lasting love affair. I had a childhood friend. His name was David; I was in love with him, but he never knew." Josh smiled. "I never told him. And then he left Germany with his family in thirty-six. His father was a scientist of some kind. I'm not sure where they went. I've always believed that had he known how I felt about him he would have declared his love for me too. I could see it in his eyes when we talked. But neither of us had the courage to speak the words. Anyway, I'm glad he got out. I'm glad he never had to come here to Auschwitz."

"Did you ever tell your parents that you were a homosexual?"

"It was just me and my mother. But no, I never told her. I never knew my father. My mother was an independent type of woman. She was an artist, a brilliant artist. She had one dramatic love affair after another. Maybe it was because she was painfully beautiful, and men found it hard to resist her. But she was also very moody, and her love affairs never worked out. She suffered terribly from depression. When she was in the throes of one of her deep dark spells, she would lie in bed for days at a time without eating or speaking to anyone, even me. I was just a child, and it terrified me. But when she was happy, she was as bright as the sun. She sang to me in her lovely soprano voice and took me to the park and to the zoo. I thought she was the most beautiful creature on earth, and I wanted to be like her. She was so graceful, so lovely. When she walked down the street everyone's head turned."

"She was taken by the Nazis, I assume," Jake said.

"Not my mother. Oh no. The Nazis didn't have to kill her. She did it herself," Joshua said, shaking his head. Then he took a long hard breath. "I came home from school one day and found her dead of an overdose. I don't know if it was accidental or intentional. It didn't matter which it was. The only thing that mattered to me was that she was gone."

"I'm sorry," Ben said. "Maybe we should stop talking about our past."

"No, it's good to remember. I don't have much to hold on to, but when I get out of here I am going to go and look for David, and maybe I'll even tell him how I feel. You want to know something crazy?"

"Sure," Ben said.

"The more I think about him, the more I believe that he loved me too. But it's hard for a person to admit to himself that he might be a homosexual. So I think we both hid it from each other. I could be wrong. I could be very wrong. But the idea that he loved me too is what keeps me going in here."

"I guess if we're all telling stories about our past, I'll tell you mine," Jake said. "I grew up poor in a rough part of town. When you're a Jew in a poor German neighborhood, full of unemployed drunks, you'd better learn to fight. And that's what I did. I was a prize fighter. I spent hours lifting weights and training every day. I don't know if you realize this, but most men only last a few months working as sonderkommandos. That's because they aren't physically strong enough to take the job. I am different. I have known harsh treatment all my life."

"What did your parents say?" Ben asked.

"My parents weren't around. I ran away from home at fourteen. I lived on the streets. It was better than watching my father waste away from drinking while my mother was constantly whining and begging him to stop."

"Did you have a girl?" Joshua asked.

"Plenty of girls. I never wanted a steady girl. And now, I'm glad I never had one. Love makes you vulnerable. As long as I don't have to worry about anyone else but me, I can survive this place. But if I had someone I cared about, I'd be worried about her constantly, and I think that might break me."

Later that night after Jake left and the men were all in bed trying to sleep, Ben whispered to Joshua. "I never told this to anyone. But on the day I was transported, one of Rumkowski's policemen shoved me into the train car, but before he did, he said that he had sex with Zelda."

"Rumkowski the Judenrat in the Lodz ghetto, who we were talking about earlier?"

"Yes. And this fellow who said this to me was one of his henchmen. He was young. Couldn't have been more than thirty. Handsome too. I've been sick about it ever since. I keep asking myself what happened. Did he and Zelda have an affair? And why did he feel the need to tell me? I think about him all the time. He told me his name was Caleb Ornstein. I have gone over it and over it in my mind. I am sure I didn't know him before all of this. So why did he want to hurt me so badly? I can't figure it out."

"The more you dwell on it, the longer it hurts you. And the longer it hurts you, the more this Ornstein character poisons your mind. Stop thinking about him and what he said. It can't do you any good."

"I wonder what happened to him. I know this is crazy, but sometimes I wonder if he somehow escaped because he hasn't shown up here. I wonder if he got away."

"His last name was Ornstein?"

"Yes, Caleb Ornstein. He whispered it to me as he pushed me on the train."

"That's a Jewish last name. He's a Jew."

"Yes he was. All of Rumkowski's policemen were Jews."

"Then Ornstein could not possibly have escaped entirely. He might have run away. And I can't tell you what his personal hell looks like, but I can promise you that the Nazis have found a way to make his life miserable. Even if it's only through guilt or memories."

"You're probably right."

CHAPTER 20

December 1942

On the second Sunday in the month of December, Jake arrived at Ben's block early in the morning before the first roll call. He was trembling with anxiety. His breath was shallow, and his face was so gray it almost appeared to be a sickly shade of pea green.

"What's the matter with you?" Joshua asked as he got ready to go to work in the kitchen.

"Some of the sonderkommandos tried to escape from here. I hear that as punishment they plan to gas all of us."

Ben walked over to his two friends. "What's wrong? You look terrible. Are you sick?" he asked Jake.

"He's terrified and rightly so," Joshua said. "Listen to me carefully. You have to find a way to make yourself useful if only for the next few days. I will do what I can to help you."

"What can you do? You're in the same position as the rest of us," Jake said.

"Yes, that's true. But let's just say I have a friend who might be able to help," Joshua said, thinking of Wolff.

"Who is your friend? You never told me about any friend you had," Ben said.

"How do you think you got transferred from the rubber factory into the kitchen?"

"You asked this friend, you are talking about, to have me transferred?"

"Yes. But you must not tell anyone else about this. No one needs to know."

Ben nodded.

"You too, Jake. Promise me."

"I promise," Jake said softly.

After work that evening, Joshua disappeared. Ben assumed he'd gone to find his friend who Ben also assumed must be a Nazi. He was afraid for Joshua. After all, he'd learned that a Jew could call a Nazi a friend one minute and the next minute, find himself in line to be gassed by the same Nazi friend. They simply could not be trusted, and he was worried. He'd come to love Joshua and Jake like brothers. They were his best friends, and although they were not his blood, he considered them family.

Joshua didn't return to the block until late that night. Ben was still awake.

"Are you all right?" he asked.

"Yes, I'm fine. Everything is going to be all right. Jake will still work in the gas chambers, but he will be spared from death. It was the best I could do."

"Do you think you can trust him?"

"I am pretty sure I can. Of course, there are no guarantees, but I'd be surprised if he didn't keep his word. My friend values the secrets he and I share, and he values my friendship for various reasons. So, although I wouldn't exactly say we are in a position of advantage, I would say things look good for Jake."

"He could kill you to keep you quiet. Have you thought about that?" Ben asked.

"Yes, of course, I have. But then who would scratch his unspoken itch? He doesn't want to lose me. So he'll help me if he can. And I don't think this will be very difficult for him."

"Thank God. And thank God for you, Josh. You saved Jake's life," Ben said.

"Let's hope so. I only did what I believe any of us would do for each other if we had the chance."

"Yes, I would do whatever I could for either of you. And I think Jake would too."

"I believe that," Joshua said, yawning. "Get some sleep. It'll be morning before you know it, and then we'll have another long day of work ahead of us."

"But at least we're pretty sure that Jake won't die tomorrow."

CHAPTER 21

Fall 1943

A POWERFUL COLD FRONT CAME THROUGH THE CAMP IN LATE November 1943. It penetrated the thin fabric of the prisoners' uniforms. All night long the prisoners in Ben and Joshua's block coughed and sneezed.

By Christmas, Joshua was very sick. His head was heavy with fever. Still, he forced himself to get out of bed and go to work. "If I don't work, it's just a matter of time before I'm going to be shot or sent to the gas."

"Why don't you ask your friend if he can find a way to get you a little time off from work so you can recover?"

"I'll be all right," Joshua insisted. But his face was flushed, and his hands and feet were cold to the touch. As they lay in bed at night, Ben could feel Joshua shivering. By the third day, Joshua was having trouble breathing. He told Ben that his chest ached.

Not only was Ben worried sick about losing his best friend, but because Ben had been diagnosed at an early age with asthma he was also concerned that whatever Joshua had might be contagious. And Ben did not think he would survive any kind of lung disease.

Three weeks passed with no word from SS Sturmmann Alarich Wolff. He usually sent for Joshua at least once a week. And although Joshua, who was deathly ill, had finally told Ben the SS Sturmmann's name, Ben had not yet gone to see Wolff. He was afraid to go to Wolff and tell him that he knew about his friendship with Joshua. But he would have to do so if he was going to save his friend's life. There was no doubt in Ben's mind that Wolff would not take kindly to him giving even the slightest indication that he was aware of the relationship between Wolff and Joshua. In fact, he was afraid that if he even attempted to talk to Wolff, the guard might have both Joshua and him executed in order to keep his secret safe. Every day Joshua grew weaker, until one morning he could not get out of bed. Ben felt his heart race in panic. The hospital, with the monsters that were referred to as doctors, was known to be a death trap for any prisoner unfortunate enough to find their way there. Rumors came from the inmates who worked in the hospital that the doctors performed unnecessary, and painful, experiments on the patients for nothing more than their own sadistic pleasures. Every prisoner Ben tried to ask for advice, about how to help Joshua, shuddered with fear at the mention of Dr. Clauberg and Dr. Mengele. They referred to Mengele as the angel of death. Ben had never met Clauberg. He'd only heard horror stories about him. However, he remembered Mengele. Josef Mengele had been present when the transport that carried Ben to Auschwitz first arrived at the camp. He didn't know it at the time, but he later learned that Mengele was the attractive, young, dark-haired SS officer who had been standing in the selection line deciding which prisoners were fit to live and who deserved to die. It stood out in Ben's mind how nonchalant Mengele had been as he made his decisions. He'd been so casual he might have been deciding what to have for lunch instead of the fate of the poor souls who stood at his mercy.

That night when Ben was serving dinner, he saw a friend he knew who was in charge of cleaning up the hospital. He told the man that Joshua was very sick and asked him what he thought Ben should do.

"Well," the prisoner answered, "the hospital is a little different than the rest of the camp. Men and women are separated at the camp but not in the hospital. And let me tell you, Rabinowitz, the women patients are terrified of Clauberg. The bastard is working on efficient, but not necessarily humane or painless, methods for sterilizing woman. From what I have seen, he's using some form of radiation. It's terrible. The women he works on cry and cry, both from pain and from losing their ability to bear children. The sounds of their weeping and moaning fill the rooms all day and night. I don't think anyone could rest there even if the two bastards weren't sadistic excuses for doctors. Mengele isn't interest in women. He has this morbid and sick fascination with twins, especially children. He has no conscience. I've seen him take healthy children and make them violently ill."

Ben shook his head. "I don't know what to do."

"But not only that, Mengele is a cruel and heartless man who enjoys confusing and torturing the children. I saw him once give out candy to a group of Gypsy children and put his arms around them. Call me uncle, he told them. They were laughing and playing. But then Mengele turned toward the guard and told the guard to gas them."

"My God!" Ben said.

The very idea of these evil men having control over Joshua, who was sick and weak and at their mercy, terrified Ben. Then two days passed with Joshua barely able to move. Ben lugged his friend out of bed and practically carried him to work in the kitchen. Then when he was certain the guards were busy, he risked his own safety by stealing food. If he'd been caught, Ben knew the penalty would be death. But to bribe the kapo, to cover for Joshua, he needed the food. As long as he was able to supply food, the kapo would not tell the Nazis that Joshua was too sick to work.

Joshua grew weaker with each passing day until he was awake all night hacking and coughing. In the morning the straw where Joshua had laid his head was covered in mucus and blood. There was no denying it, Joshua was dying. And if something wasn't done very quickly, he would be gone.

Ben went to work, but his mind was on his friend. He didn't know how long he had left, but if Joshua was still alive at the end of the day, Ben decided he had no other choice but to risk speaking to Wolff.

CHAPTER 22

His legs were unsteady as Ben made his way through the camp. He was headed to Wolff's office. Several times along the way he thought of turning back, but he forced himself to go on.

Ben entered the building. He was surprised that he was able to enter so easily without anyone stopping him. Although he'd never gone into the offices before, he was sure that in the past this had not been as easy. Looking around him and hoping that no one would stop him, Ben walked down the hall where he found the door to Wolff's office half open. Peeking inside, he saw another man sitting at Wolff's desk doing paperwork. There was a large, black dog lounging on a rug by the man's side. *I should go,* Ben thought. *I should leave here right now and go back to my block before I get in trouble.* He stood paralyzed in the doorway, his palms sweating as he watched the man in the office. *I want to run away from here but I can't. I have to find Wolff. He is the only person who might be able to help Joshua.*

"Pardon me, SS Sturmmann," Ben stuttered. "I was coming to speak to SS Sturmmann Wolff. Do you know where I can find him?"

"What do you want with Wolff?" The man sat back in his chair and eyed Ben suspiciously.

"I was told he wanted to see me about something having to do with my work in the kitchen," Ben lied.

"Hmm, I see. Well, it couldn't have been very recently. He's been transferred. He's not here anymore. So go on back to your block. I'm busy." The SS officer went back to his work.

"He's been transferred out of Auschwitz?" Ben asked, his heart pounding like a bomb ready to explode in his chest.

The Sturmmann looked up from the papers he was sorting and stared at Ben, clearly annoyed. "I said he's not here. He's not at Auschwitz. You're trying my patience. Now go before I get angry."

Ben stumbled out of the administration building and walked back to his block feeling defeated. *I waited too long. Now there is nothing I can do for Joshua. His fate is in God's hands.*

Joshua did not leave his bed that evening to have dinner.

"I brought you some food," Ben said.

"I'm not hungry." Joshua's voice was scarcely audible.

"You have to eat. If you don't eat you'll die," Ben said. He'd just returned from the evening meal with a piece of hard bread in his pocket. It was his ration for the next day, but he tried to break off pieces and put them into Joshua's mouth.

"I'm sorry. I can't eat. I can't swallow," Joshua said. "You've been a good friend to me. I've loved you. Don't worry, you didn't disappoint me. I always knew that you were not the way I am . . ." Joshua smiled a sad and wry smile. "I had no expectations."

"But I do love you, Josh. You can't go and leave me in this hell all alone. You have been the only light in here. Everyone else is drowning in their own misery. Me included."

Joshua smiled. "You have Jake. Stick by him. He too is a good friend."

"Don't you go dying on me . . ." Ben shook Joshua's shoulders, who felt almost weightless in Ben's hands. Tears ran down Ben's cheeks. "You can't die. I won't let you."

"I have something to tell you," Joshua said. "Remember when I told you that story about David, my childhood friend who I was in love with?"

"Yes, I remember. Think of him. Stay alive so you can see him again. You have to tell him how you feel. You have to tell him that you love him."

Joshua laughed softly, then he began to choke. Blood ran from his lips. "That's what I wanted to tell you. I lied to you and Jake. I told you both that I never told David that I loved him. I said that I believed he loved me too. Do you remember?"

"Yes, I remember."

"Well, it wasn't true. I told him. One day, he and I were alone on the beach and I told him. I said, 'I love you,' and then I tried to hold his hand. He pushed me away. He got up and ran across the beach. He never spoke to me again. I tried to go to his house to see him, but he wouldn't see me. Then I heard that his family had left. So my dream of declaring my love and him returning it? That was nothing but a dream, a fantasy. Wishful thinking from a pathetic queer."

"Don't call yourself that. Don't, please. I love you."

"But not in that way. You love me as a brother, as a best friend. I've never been loved in the way I've always longed to be loved." Joshua moaned

"I love you in every way. Please, Josh, don't die on me here in this place. Please don't."

"Let me go, Ben. I'm in pain, and I'm dying. It's for the best. If I go now I can die making believe that someone like you could be in love with me, even if it's not true."

"I do love you. I can't give you what you want. I have always wished I could for your sake because you've given me so much. But it's just not in me. If only there was something I could do to make you more comfortable, something that would bring back your will to live," Ben said. He was crying now. He knew Joshua loved him. He'd known it for a long time even though Joshua had never told him.

Joshua smiled wryly. "Yes, my will to live," he said. "I'm so very tired. I need to sleep. But tell me again, Ben; tell me one more time, please. Say you love me."

"I love you," Ben said, and he knew that not only had he just fulfilled a dream for his dear friend, but he had also just said goodbye.

CHAPTER 23

In the morning, Ben carried Joshua's lifeless body out to the pile of corpses. As he laid what was left of his friend down on the ground, he had to keep reminding himself that Joshua's soul had already left his body. Tears welled up behind his eyes as he went to work. Life in Auschwitz was hell, but it was even worse without his dear friend by his side.

That evening, Ben told Jake that Joshua was dead, and the two of them sat together reminiscing.

"He was one hell of a fella, that Josh. He kept me from giving up," Jake said. "No matter how bad things got, he always knew what to say."

"Yes, I know. I feel the same way. Now we have to find our own strength," Ben said. "And I've never been a strong man."

"I have, and believe me, this place can break any man. Even the strongest."

The following day, another transport came through the already crowded camp. The man who came to take Joshua's sleeping place beside Ben was more of a boy than a man. Ben thought he could be no more than seventeen.

"Hello, I'm Isaac," he said. Then he looked down at the straw and saw the dried blood. "That's a lot of blood. What happened?"

"My good friend died here," was all Ben could muster.

"I'm sorry," Isaac said, turning the straw. "I'd find another place to sleep, but there's nothing else open."

"I know. It's all right," Ben said. Then he got up and walked outside. He didn't feel much like talking.

A few minutes later, the whistle blew, and Ben was forced to go to bed. He lay there for several minutes thinking about Joshua. Tears fell from his eyes onto the dirty straw, and sleep finally overtook him.

Ben dreamed of Zelda. He was holding her in his arms. They were dancing. It was their wedding day. She was radiant. He wore his skull cap and a beautiful tallit that she'd hand embroidered for him. Moishe was there too. He was laughing and playing with the other children. Joshua smiled at him. Joshua, his best man, looked healthy, strong, and handsome. And the food . . . oh, the food. There was so much delicious food. Ben could taste the sweet applesauce and the crisp latkes. The brisket melted in his mouth. He dipped the mandel bread into his coffee and put it into Zelda's mouth. "Delicious," she said.

"I love you," he whispered.

"And I love you with all my heart."

The morning roll-call whistle jolted him awake. There was no food. Joshua was dead. Zelda and Moishe were missing. And Ben was alone.

CHAPTER 24

Summer 1944

THE HEAT OF SUMMER DESCENDED UPON THE POLISH TOWN WHERE
Auschwitz was located, bringing its own form of misery. Not only
was the heat unbearable during midday, but the bedbugs were worse
in summer than winter. All five crematoriums were working at full
capacity all day long. They were burning bodies. The smell was
overpowering in the summer heat. And the shower of ashes was a
constant reminder to the prisoners that someday they might be
burned, and their ashes could mix with the others in the constant
death rain.

Ben and Isaac became friends. However, Ben never allowed
himself to become as close to Isaac as he'd been to Joshua. He
didn't want to care for another person only to lose him. However, he
was still very close to Jake and often feared that if Jake died, he
would be alone in the camp, without anyone. He found this idea
terrifying, but in a strange way it was also freeing. Loving was
dangerous in this place. It could cost a man dearly. The pain of loss
had the power to strip away his will to live. It had almost done so to
Ben when Joshua died. Sometimes he thought about Zelda or

Moishe, and his heart ached so badly that he found it hard to get out of bed. So Ben forced himself to push everyone and everything he had ever loved out of his mind.

The Sunday evening card games continued, but now Isaac took Joshua's place. And Ben found he looked forward to them less and less. He was tired, worn out from starvation, loss, and overwork, and if it would not have been a terrible disappointment to Jake, he would have preferred to be alone. All he wanted to do, if he had a spare moment, was lie down.

One hot night at the end of July, Ben returned from work to find Jake waiting for him in his block.

"What's wrong? Why are you here?" Ben asked.

"Nu? Something has to be wrong?" Jake asked. "I can't just come to see you?"

"It usually mean's there's a problem when you come during the week. So what is it?"

"You'll never guess who arrived here on the transport this afternoon."

"Zelda?" Ben's heart leapt. "Is it? Or Moishe? Lila?"

Jake turned away. "I'm sorry. I didn't mean to get you excited. No, it's not Zelda, Moishe, or Lila. Rumkowski arrived here today."

"Oh," Ben said, unable to hide his disappointment. He was disappointed that he would not see a beloved face. But he was also glad that no one he loved had arrived in this terrible place. As long as they were not in Auschwitz, he could hope and believe that they were alive and safe in a much better place.

"You know there are other fellows from the Lodz ghetto who work with me in the sonderkommando. They know Rumkowski too. And, like you and me, they want to see Rumkowski suffer. So we were all talking today."

Ben wanted to see Rumkowski pay for his crimes but not nearly as badly as he wanted to see Zelda and Moishe safe and alive. "Yes," he said.

"We want to trap him and bring him into the crematorium on a Sunday when no one is there and then . . ."

Ben nodded. He was still thinking about Zelda. *Rumkowski is here.*

So we'll all have our revenge. But I still don't have my son or my girl. Revenge is not nearly as sweet as holding someone you love.

"What's wrong? You don't seem happy about this," Jake said.

"I hate him. And I'm glad that he'll finally pay for all he's done to his fellow Jews. It's just that, for a moment, I thought that you might be talking about my Zelda being here. And as much as I'm glad she's not here, I sure would rather see her than Rumkowski. My love for her is stronger than my hate for him. I don't even know if she's alive."

"I know."

Ben nodded. Then he added, "All right, then. You might as well tell me the plan. What are we going to do to Rumkowski?"

"Good. So you're in?"

"I'm in," Ben said, remembering the threat he'd made to Rumkowski the day that Zelda was sent away.

CHAPTER 25

A FEW NIGHTS LATER, RIGHT AFTER ROLL CALL, JAKE, BEN, AND SIX other sonderkommandos, who had also been in the Lodz ghetto, gathered outside one of the blocks to make plans. They all quickly introduced themselves to Ben.

"I'm Matthew."

"Samuel."

"Paul."

"Lev."

"Ruben"

"Ethan"

"Jozef."

"Salmen."

"It's a pleasure to meet all of you. I'm Ben Rabinowitz."

They all nodded.

"Now, down to business. We don't have much time before the whistle will sound and we have to be in bed. So let's get going with the plans," Jake said.

"We have to lure him into the crematorium," Jozef said, nodding at Jake, then he continued. "Then we should all be waiting there for him."

"But how? What would make him come with us? I'm sure he knows that all of us hate him," Lev answered.

"Are we sure he knows that?" Ben said. "He knows I hate him because I told him. I promised him that one day I would have revenge for what he did to my girl, Zelda, and her children. But is there anyone here among us who never had any contact with him?"

"I have never had direct contact with him." Ruben bit his lip. "I just remember that speech he gave about the children and what a son of a bitch he was to everyone in the ghetto."

"I never knew him personally either, although I'm sure he was responsible for my wife, God rest her soul, and me being sent here." Salmen shook his head.

"So how about this?" Ben said. "Let's say one of you two fellows, that he never met, start to befriend him now."

"I'll do it," Lev said.

"Good."

"So what do I do? Tell me exactly." Lev leaned against the building and listened intently.

"All right. Here's what you do. Make sure you get behind him in the food line tomorrow. Then casually start talking to him. Take it real slow. If you take your time, he'll never suspect that you have a motive. Don't tell him you know who he is. Tell him you were in the Warsaw ghetto, not Lodz. Get him to talk about himself. Listen to him. In other words, do whatever it takes to make him trust you. Then once he does, tell him that you stole some valuable things from prisoners on transports. You tell him that you hid these things in the crematorium. Ask him if he can help you fence the stuff. He has connections. I'm sure he'll have an idea of what to do to sell things. Then once you tap into his greed you tell him he has to come to the crematorium to meet you on a Sunday evening because that's when the crematorium is shut down. "

"You think he'll come?" Lev bit his lip. His right eye twitched.

He reached up to rub his eye, and Ben saw that he had a slight tremor in his left hand.

"Yes, I believe it will work, but only if you come across as sincere. You have to make him trust you," Ben said. "Now since I work in the kitchen, I'll do my best to steal some extra food. I'll give it to you, Lev, so you can share it with him. By sharing food with him, it will make him believe that you really consider him a good friend. In his mind, he will see the two of you building a bond. Not that you could ever really trust him, but it will never come to that."

"Extra food? You're going to give him extra food." Lev licked his lips. "All of us are starving. There isn't a man here who couldn't use some extra food. I hate to give it to that bastard."

"Yes, we could all use extra food. There's no doubt about that, but if we want revenge on Rumkowski, we're going to have to use the food as a lure," Ben said.

"I'd rather eat it," Samuel said. "Sometimes I feel like I'm starving to death. Who the hell cares about Rumkowski?"

"I care. He took the love of my life away from me. I hate him. I want to see him pay for what he did, not only to my Zelda and her children, but to all those children he sent away from the Lodz ghetto." Ben spit the words out.

"You're right," Samuel said with conviction. " Even though I sure would like the extra food, it's worth the sacrifice. Rumkowski deserves to suffer. He hurt all of us. He hurt every Jew in the Lodz ghetto."

"So, Lev, will you do it?" Jake asked.

"Yes, I'll do it. I'll start tomorrow morning. It might take a few weeks for me to build his trust."

"We have time." Ben nodded. "Maybe. If they don't kill us all first."

The prisoners all laughed at Ben's attempt at a joke. But the roots of the laughter were embedded in deep pain.

The next day, Ben saw Rumkowski for the first time since he'd left Lodz. The sight of the old man made his blood boil. Lev fell into line two men behind Rumkowski and easily started a conversation with the two others and Rumkowski. After they'd gotten their food, Lev followed Rumkowski and sat beside him, continuing the conversation.

Well done, Ben thought. And although he was happy to see his plan progressing, as far as Rumkowski was concerned, he still felt a dagger in his heart when he thought about the man who had told him his name was Caleb Ornstein. Up until now, Ben had not mentioned Caleb to Jake. He decided the next time he and Jake were alone, he would tell Jake everything, including what had happened with Ornstein. Then he would ask Jake to find out if anyone new had heard of Caleb Ornstein, and if they knew what had happened to him.

After the card game on Sunday, Ben walked Jake back to his block and told him how Ornstein had pushed him into the train car and said he'd been intimate with Zelda.

"I don't know him," Jake said.

"He's a tall, handsome fella."

"I'll see if I can find out any information about him. He may not be here."

"I don't attend roll call because of my job, so I can't say I've ever seen him there. And I haven't seen him at meals either," Ben said.

"You want revenge," Jake said. It was more of a statement than a question.

"I want revenge, yes. I burn with the hatred I feel for him. The need to see him pay for what he did aches in my heart and in my belly. But I also want to know what happened between him and Zelda. I want to know if Zelda was his lover during the time that she and I were together. I want to know why he felt the need to tell me what he told me. I need answers."

"It might not be the best thing for you to hear what he has to say. What if he tells you that your girl was cheating on you. How is that going to make you feel?"

"At least I'll know."

"I'm not sure you want to know everything. I've found that sometimes it's better not to know the truth. Especially now. What good will it really do you, Ben? Just between you and I, I wonder if this revenge on Rumkowski isn't going to be a hollow victory. Sometimes, I find, revenge hurts the revenge seeker more than it hurts the one who is supposed to be paying. But if it's what you want, I'll do what I can to find out if Ornstein is here," Jake said.

"Yes, please find out what you can."

CHAPTER 26

THE FOLLOWING WEEK, JAKE TOLD BEN THAT HE COULDN'T FIND
anyone who knew what happened to Caleb Ornstein. Several of the
men he spoke to, who had been in the Lodz ghetto, remembered
him. But no one knew what had happened to him.

Ben just nodded with disappointment. Then he gave Jake a
chunk of stale bread. "This is for Lev to share with Rumkowski."

"Good. Try and get more if you can."

"I will. I'll do what I can," Ben said, then he asked, "So what's
going on with the plan for Rumkowski?"

"I talked to Lev. We've set a date three Sundays from today."

"Three Sundays," Ben said, salivating and wishing he could take
just one bite of the bread before they gave it to Rumkowski.

"Yes. The Nazis are running out of fuel to run the crematorium.
They've been closing early on Sunday." Jake shook his head; his
voice was angry and bitter. "So we'll all meet inside the crematorium at six in the evening. Then if all goes as planned, Lev will
bring him in."

"And then what?"

"And then we lay into him. We make him pay for everything we've lost."

"We're not going to kill him, are we?"

"No, just show him a little muscle. Get out some of our aggression," Jake said. "That's what everyone wants to do. So I'm in."

"I have to tell you the truth. I hate violence. But I am so damn angry, Jake. And this bastard deserves it."

CHAPTER 27

THE FOLLOWING DAY, ONE OF THE PRISONERS, WHO WAS WORKING IN the kitchen, was caught stealing food. The guard saw the prisoner stuff five pieces of potato peel into his pants.

"Direkthilfe? What's this?" the guard said as he pulled the peelings out of the man's pants. "You Jews are so disgusting. You're such filthy pigs. Who, but a dirty swine, would put food in their pants and then eat it?" the guard said in mock anger. He was toying with the prisoner.

"I'm sorry. I was starving. Please have mercy on me."

"Mercy? Mercy? When you take advantage of the German people by stealing food? The German people who work hard and pay good money for your keep? We have to pay to feed you, and this is how you show your gratitude. Not only are you subhuman rats, but you're unappreciative."

The prisoner was trembling. Urine ran down his leg forming a puddle on the ground.

"And look at that. You have the audacity to pee in the kitchen?" The guard took his rifle and shot the prisoner in the head at close range. Blood and brains sprayed across the kitchen, some of it landing in the miserable excuse for soup that would be the men's dinner. No one said a word, but Ben thought he heard someone gag. Then the Nazi pointed at Ben and another prisoner. "You two swine, clean up this mess."

Quickly, Ben and the other man dragged the body out to the pile of bodies and laid it on top. Neither of them said a word, but both of them looked into each other's terrified eyes.

That night as Ben lay in bed, he shivered as he thought about the food he'd stolen to lure Rumkowski. He could have been caught and shot, and his brains could have ended up on the floor of the kitchen. He'd been so driven by his hatred for Rumkowski that he'd been blinded by rage. What a despicable man Rumkowski was. But was revenge worth dying for? Still, how could Rumkowski have taken children from the arms of their mothers to save his own worthless life? Ben took a deep breath, then he thought about Zelda and how much he missed her. He thought about her two children. Would those two little ones ever have an opportunity to grow up, or were they already dead? The very idea that those two vibrant children might have been taken out of this world made him feel nauseated. And what about Moishe and Lila? Where were they? He still believed Lila had bribed Rumkowski somehow, in order for him to look the other way when she escaped with Moishe. It had hurt him to think that his beautiful wife had lain naked under the old, disgusting Rumkowski and probably Ornstein too. At the time he was angry with Lila. Hurt, so hurt. But looking back now, he was glad that Lila was strong willed, and that she had the courage to do whatever needed to be done in order to save their son. Moishe: he prayed that Moishe was still alive. His own precious son.

CHAPTER 28

WHEN BEN ENTERED THE KITCHEN TO GO TO WORK THAT MORNING, he looked at the calendar. It was August 27. His mind was on the ambush on Rumkowski that was to take place that night. All his life, violence had made him feel sick to his stomach. He'd never started a fight. Every fistfight he'd been forced into, he'd lost miserably. Now he was going to go and beat up on a man who was unsuspecting and defenseless. There was no doubt in his mind that Rumkowski deserved it. Even so, the more he thought about it, the more the idea was unsettling for Ben. Although he'd seen plenty of blood since he'd been transported to Auschwitz, and even before in the ghetto, the sight of it still sickened him.

That evening after Ben finished work, he walked quickly toward the crematorium, hiding from the watchful eyes of the guards as he made his way.

The others were already there waiting for him when he arrived. It was dark, damp, and eerie in the stone room where so many bodies of innocent people had been burned like trash. There were ashes still on the floor. Ben wondered whom they belonged to—

someone's father, someone's mother, someone's lover, or someone's child. He shivered when he thought of the children. Every person who died here in Auschwitz had a past; they had a family; they had a story to tell.

Ben had been at Auschwitz for a while now, and he had long since gotten used to the smell in the camp, but being inside the crematorium, the odor was more powerful, stronger than it was in the rest of the camp. He felt himself gag.

The men all waited in silence for Rumkowski. Each of them lost in their own thoughts, consumed with their own memories. In the stillness, Ben felt that he could almost hear the voices of those who had been sent here and murdered because of Rumkowski. Was Zelda one of them? He shivered slightly as he heard the voices of Lev and Rumkowski outside. They were about to enter the building. It was about to begin, and as much as Ben believed Rumkowski deserved to be punished, he wished he could run away from all that was about to happen.

And then Lev and Rumkowski were inside. From that moment on, everything was very unreal for Ben, like a nightmare.

The prisoners, who had been waiting, came out of the shadows all at once.

"What's going on here?" Rumkowski asked, his voice controlled, but there was an undercurrent of fear and panic.

"Do you remember me? I'm Joseph Bitterbaum."

"How about me, Rumkowski? I'm Samuel Greenberg."

Rumkowski turned and tried to run away, but Lev grabbed him and pulled him back. Two more of the prisoners held him as Rumkowski fought to get away.

Then each stated their name.

"Ben Rabinowitz. Remember Lila Rabinowitz? Or how about Zelda Lipman? She was my girl. She had two children. Solomon Lipman and Sarah Lipman, whom she sent out of the ghetto in the middle of the night. They were just babies, but she had to send them all alone to protect them from the fate you had planned for them. How could you do it, Rumkowski? How could you allow the Nazis to take all the children who were under ten on transports?"

"It wasn't my fault." Rumkowski was like a wildebeest cornered by lions. His nostrils flared with the sense of danger. His voice was no longer confident. He began to plead for mercy, the mercy he'd denied so many others. "The Nazis forced me to do it. I was only trying to keep as many Jews alive as I could. They demanded that I send them ten thousand people. I only sent the children and the elderly because they couldn't work. I was trying to do the best for our people. I believed that if the Jews could work, they would be useful to the Nazis, and at least some of us would have a chance."

"So you sent them babies. Children under ten? And old people whose lives you felt were worthless? Were they murdered, Rumkowski? Were they all murdered?" Ben asked, trembling. He walked over to Rumkowski and began shaking him hard.

"Yes, probably," Rumkowski said, hanging his head.

"How can a man take children away from their mothers and send them to a camp where he knows they'll be murdered. How?" Lev asked. "You sent my two young sons. You did that to me. You sent my children to be killed. What kind of a monster are you? And you sent my wife. A good woman. A pious woman, who lived only to help others. You had her killed. Her blood is on your hands." Lev was breathing hard. "And you know what? When I went to befriend you, you didn't even recognize me. You didn't even remember, that's how little their lives mattered to you. You son of a bitch."

"Rumkowski, you killed my poor, old mother. She didn't have a mean bone in her old body. She was always doing things for everyone else. If somebody was sick in our shul, she was the first person to bring them food. Someone needed help with a sick child, she went to their aid. And just like that, Rumkowski, you wrote her name on a piece of paper that sent her to die. You should be ashamed," Ruben said.

The men each told their stories while Rumkowski struggled to get away. He tried to fight, to kick, to pull his arms free. But Jake was strong, and although Lev, Ruben, and Samuel held on to Rumkowski too, Jake was strong and could have easily restrained the old man by himself.

"Take off your clothes," Jake said to the other prisoners. "If we are going to do this, there's going to be blood. And if there's blood on your uniform, the Nazis will know you were involved."

The prisoners took off their uniforms and stood naked surrounding Rumkowski.

"Oh no, please, have pity," Rumkowski said. He was on his knees now. "Don't do this. I beg you."

"Get him," Jake said. "Now."

Then the naked prisoners fell upon Rumkowski like a pack of wild dogs. They beat him with their fists, with tree limbs, and with rocks. They kicked him in the stomach, in the chest, in the face, and in the head. Lev smashed his skull over and over with a rock. They were consumed by hatred and rage, like wild demons whose hunger for revenge would not be assuaged. Ben hated Rumkowski, but he couldn't hit him. He ran outside and vomited.

He wanted to run away and go back to his block. If only he could erase that terrible scene from his mind, but he couldn't. He knew he would carry it with him until the day he died. On his knees he looked up at the stars. Guilt and self-loathing washed over him. God was watching. *I have to go back in there. I am a part of this. I know it's wrong, and someday I will pay dearly, but I cannot leave and turn my back on the others.*

Ben forced himself to stand up. He felt God's eyes upon him, and he was terrified, but he walked back through the doors and into the crematorium.

The sound of the whistle that signaled the prisoners were to go to bed, reverberated throughout the camp. It was only a sound, yet Ben felt as if the earth had begun to tremble. He imagined it was the voice of God saying, "Vengeance is mine." He shivered at the thought.

The whistle was sobering. It brought the prisoners back to reality. They stopped and looked at each other. In the darkness, all that could be seen were the whites of their eyes.

Rumkowski lay still in a pool of blood. His face unrecognizable.

"He's dead," Jake said.

"Are you sure?" Ben asked, but he knew Jake was right.

"Leave him here," Paul said. "Let the Nazis find him. No one but us will know what happened in this room today. Are we all sworn to secrecy?"

Everyone said yes.

"Then quickly get dressed, and let's get out of here before someone comes," Jake said.

The men didn't say a word. Each of them dressed in their uniforms and left the area quickly.

There was a full moon that night. Staying out of the light, Ben ran quickly back to his block. If he were seen by one of the guards in the towers, he would be shot. When he arrived at the block, he quickly got into bed.

"Where were you?" Isaac asked.

"Never mind."

"I was worried."

"I'm sorry. Go to sleep," Ben said. It wasn't long before Ben heard the sound of Isaac's slow and steady breathing. Ben was glad that Isaac was asleep. He didn't want to talk about what happened.

A ray of moonlight drifted through the window. Ben caught a glimpse of his hand. *I didn't strike a blow, but I was a part of this murder. I gave them the food that lured Rumkowski to his death. So I, too, am responsible for his murder. I have killed a man*, he thought. *He was a bad man. But nevertheless, I've killed another human being.* Then Ben began to sob. His body trembled. But he wasn't crying for Rumkowski. He was feeling sorry that he had been capable of such a horrific act. Ben was mourning the man he used to be: a tender, loving, and gentle man, and at the same time he was weeping for the man he'd become.

CHAPTER 29

Autumn, A Party in Vienna, Austria 1944

ADOLF EICHMANN WAS SITTING AT A TABLE SIPPING A GLASS OF WINE when his eyes fell upon the petite blonde who was standing on the other side of the room. She looked elegant, almost like a movie star, as she tossed her head back and laughed at something her companion, Dr. Josef Mengele, was whispering into her ear. Eichmann knew Mengele rather well. They'd met on several occasions where he'd been introduced to Josef and his wife, Irene. *Well, this girl is certainly not Irene. Irene was immemorable, but I would never have forgotten a girl like this. She must be his mistress.*

The blonde looked his way, and her eyes caught his. She gave him a suggestive smile then turned her attention back to the doctor.

Eichmann watched Mengele lead the beautiful woman out onto the dance floor. As she moved gracefully in Mengele's arms, Eichmann felt his manhood stir. Then as Mengele pivoted his partner, she looked Eichmann's way again. Eichmann was too far away to see the color of her eyes, but they were dark and sensual with mascara. Her lips were full and blood red with lipstick. He wanted her, and he was a man who got what he wanted. *I am certain that she isn't Mengele's wife*, Eichmann thought, *so there can be no harm in walking over to Josef and saying hello.*

After the couple returned to their seats, Eichmann approached them.

"Dr. Mengele," he said.

"Obersturmbannführer. How are you?" Mengele smiled.

"I'm doing fine. Thank you for asking. You're looking well," Eichmann said.

Mengele smiled. "Would you like to join us?" he asked.

"Yes, thank you." Eichmann sat down. "And who is the lovely lady?" he asked.

"This is Ilsa Guhr. She is a guard at Ravensbrück."

"A pleasure to meet you," Eichmann said.

"The pleasure is mine, Obersturmbannführer." She smiled, lowering her eyes.

"Please call me Adolf."

"Adolf," she repeated. "I've heard people talk about you."

"Good things, I hope."

"Yes, actually. I've heard that you are the expert on all Jewish questions."

Mengele let out a laugh. "I don't know how commendable that is."

"Well, Josef, someone has to be an expert. Someone has to give the rest of us direction. We all know how dangerously tricky the Jews are, now, don't we?" She smiled, then she winked at Eichmann flirtatiously.

Mengele scoffed and began looking around the room. Ilsa knew he was getting bored of the situation. She'd known him long enough to realize that unless all eyes were on him, very little kept his attention for long. They had been lovers on and off for years, and she knew he could be very cruel. In fact, there was a time when he'd spurned her, breaking things off between them. He'd chastised her for being too perverse for him. *Too perverse for him, really now, that's absurd. With all the ghastly experiments he has performed on children and twins, he had the nerve to call me perverse.*

Mengele stood up and smiled charmingly. "If you two will excuse me, I see an old friend," he said, then nodding his head, he walked away.

Ilsa glared at him as he sauntered toward the bar stopping beside a girl with auburn hair caught up in a bun with a diamond clasp. Mengele touched her back. The girl whirled around, and then they both laughed. "Josef!" Ilsa heard the girl say. Ilsa was humiliated. Once again Mengele had spurned her. But this time he'd embarrassed her in front of Eichmann, a high-ranking official whom she needed to impress. Turning to Eichmann, she smiled nervously trying to appear casual as if she didn't care what Mengele did. Eichmann touched her hand under the table, then with his other hand, he took her chin and gently turned her head so he was able to look in her eyes. "Mengele is a fool; he's always been a fool. Any man who could leave a woman as beautiful as you alone for even a moment . . ."

She put her hand over his lips then whispered, "Thank you."

"Would you like to come for a walk out on the terrace with me? It's a beautiful night," Eichmann suggested.

"Yes, I would, very much," she said, getting to her feet.

He took her elbow and led her outside. They stood overlooking the yard. It was a starless night, and the new moon was just a sliver of silver in the dark sky. The small, twinkling lights from the chandelier in the ballroom hardly stretched to illuminate the outside terrace.

"I would like to get to know you better," he said in a husky voice.

"Would you now?"

He nodded. "I find it hard to believe that I have never seen you at one of these galas before tonight."

"I've been to a few, but we must have missed each other."

"And what, if I may be so bold as to ask, is the relationship between you and the doctor?"

"Nothing serious. We've known each other for years. But we are really no more than friends at this point."

"Well, then, we must not waste any more time standing here and talking. Would you like to come to my room for a nightcap?"

She nodded. "Yes," she said, her voice as soft as the autumn breeze.

He smiled. "Then shall we go?"

CHAPTER 30

THE NEXT THREE DAYS WERE LIKE A WHIRLWIND ROMANCE BETWEEN
Adolf Eichmann and Ilsa Guhr. They did little other than eat, make
love, and sleep.

One afternoon, famished, they went to an outdoor café. Autumn
leaves covered the ground, and although the weather was growing
cooler, the sun shot golden rays down to the earth.

"How long are you staying in Vienna?" he asked her.

"I have to go back to Germany to work next week," she said,
sipping her wine.

"Do you like your job?"

"Sometimes, I suppose. Sometimes not. Do you like yours?"

"It is difficult sometimes; I must admit, but I like being good at
my job. Do you know what I mean?"

"Yes, of course," she said, not wanting to tell him about the
perverse night games she played on the prisoners to amuse herself.
She was not sure how he would take it if he knew that she had sex
with the female prisoners, tortured them, and then murdered them.
Mengele had not cared that she was a sadist or a murderer, but he'd
been repulsed by the homosexual acts she'd engaged in, especially
with prisoners. She didn't want to lose the obersturmbannführer's

interest. He was too important to her future. So far, everything was working according to her plans. In fact, the real reason she'd convinced Mengele to bring her to this party was so she could meet Eichmann. She'd heard rumors that Eichmann had connections to ODESSA, the secret organization of Nazi sympathizers who were already in place to help the SS escape if Germany were to lose the war. And the way things were going for Germany, Ilsa felt fairly sure she was going to need a way out.

"Well, I have heard some things about you," she said, then she ran her tongue over the rim of her wineglass.

"Oh? And what have you heard?"

"I've heard that you are so important that even the führer listens to you when it comes to the Jewish question."

He laughed and waved his hand as if to brush her off, but he was flattered. "You have heard this, huh?" he said.

"I have." She batted her eyelashes.

He smiled.

"Adolf?" She called Eichmann by his first name now that they were lovers.

"Yes, dear?"

"I know you are married. I mean, of course, everyone knows that. And . . . of course, I've seen photographs of you and Veronika. So I was wondering if . . . once we leave Vienna . . . will I ever see you again?"

She seemed to really care, and the look in her eyes was melting his heart. "Of course we will meet again," he said.

"I mean, you know how these things are. We are lovers here in Vienna for a moment. Then we return to our lives, and it is as if all of this never happened."

"I could never forget you."

"I understand that. But you do have a wife . . ."

"And you should know that I do not plan to divorce my wife. There is too much stigma attached to divorce, and it would not be a good career move for me."

"Of course not. And I would not expect you to. I will always be discreet about us. Your wife need not know anything," she said.

"You can trust me. When our time here ends, I just don't want this to be goodbye."

He smiled at her. "What a delight you are to me. And I promise that I will try to come to Ravensbrück to visit with you."

"Will you?"

"Of course," he said, then he patted her hand. "And then perhaps we might be able to get away for a week together as well. Perhaps a week in Munich? I'll see what I can arrange. This is only the beginning of us, my dear. Not the end."

"I am glad to hear that. I was afraid this would just be a quick affair, if you know what I mean."

"I do. But you're far too pretty to worry about anything like that. Alas, I can't promise you marriage because of my wife and my responsibilities to the party. However, I do vow that we shall be very good friends for a long time to come."

"Let's take a walk," she said, a little disappointed by his answer. Ilsa was used to men falling at her feet. Except for the insensitive Dr. Mengele, she had all of them eating out of her hand, doing whatever she asked. There were plenty who were more than willing to divorce their wives if she would consider marrying them, but not him—not Adolf Eichmann. He said he was content to be an occasional bed partner and a friend. That was a little hurtful and insulting. She frowned. "It's too cold to sit still. I would much prefer to continue walking." *Don't be a fool. Don't let your pride get in the way. You need him. It doesn't matter if he isn't mad about you. All that matters is that he agrees to help you.*

"Whatever you would like, my dear."

He slipped his arm through hers, and they walked for several streets until they came upon a park bench. He led her to the bench, and in spite of what she said about preferring to walk, he sat down. She sat beside him. Inside she was fuming. He had gotten the better of her. He won. His will prevailed over hers. He preferred to sit and so they sat. But she could not let him know that she was angry. This was her opportunity to secure a safe future for herself. She must not let anything so petty get in the way.

An oak tree with a thick trunk and mane of leaves in muted fall colors stood only a few feet away. A symphony from a mismatched orchestra of songbirds filled the air. For several minutes the couple sat without speaking. He took a deep breath and sighed, smiling.

Then Ilsa took Adolf's hand and brought it to her lips. She placed a soft kiss on his palm, then she ran his hand across the side of her face.

"I have something that I need to talk to you about," she said. "It's very important."

He nodded.

"And I am afraid . . ."

"Of me? You are afraid of me?"

"What I am about to ask of you might well sound like treason. I have to trust you because I am so afraid."

"Please go on," he said. "Of course you can trust me, Ilsa."

"Adolf." She hesitated. "I know it is treason to say that there is a possibility that Germany might not be victorious in this war. But . . ."

"Yes, I know. It's all right. I understand what you are trying to say. Things don't look good for us especially on the Russian front."

"Exactly," she said. Then choosing her words carefully she continued, "And, well . . . I don't know if the world will be kind to us if we lose the war. We can't be sure they will understand all of the good we tried to do. By us, I am speaking of you and me, and all of us who worked so hard to rid the world of undesirable elements in order to make it a better place for future generations of Germans."

"I have thought of that too." An automobile honked in the distance, and Ilsa jumped. Adolf put his arm around her shoulder and gently squeezed. Then he lifted her chin so he could look into her eyes.

"I am afraid that if the Allies get ahold of us they will torture us." She shivered.

"I can help you," he said.

Ilsa was thrilled. Everything was falling into place. This was why she'd come to the party in Vienna. This was why she'd seduced Eichmann. She needed a way to guarantee her own safety should the Reich come to an end. And here he was falling right into her trap. *Don't look overeager*, she told herself. Then she lay her head on his shoulder so that he couldn't see her eyes.

"Of course, I am hoping that the tide turns and that Germany will win the war. I long for our dream of a thousand-year Reich, but just in case," she said, but she had lost all hope. She knew the end of the Nazi era was near. Ilsa had known for some time that things were turning bad for Germany, so she'd made her own plans. She'd saved plenty of money from the stolen goods she and her friend Hilde had taken from the prisoners at Ravensbrück where she worked. And she knew she could continue to trust Hilde to keep on stealing for her because she had information on Hilde's adopted son that would ruin his life. Except for Hilde and Hilde's husband, Axel, who were both Nazi guards at concentration camps, Ilsa was the only living person who knew the truth about their son, Anatole. She knew Anatole was a Jewish child whom Axel had stolen from the Jewish children's camp.

It all began when Hilde had a miscarriage, which sent her into the throes of a deep depression, leaving Axel feeling powerless to help her. But as he later admitted to Ilsa, an idea came to him as he was passing through Ravensbrück one morning when he eyed a blond-haired, blue-eyed, Aryan-looking little boy in the children's camp.

Ilsa had been passing by. She stopped to watch from a hiding place, and she saw him steal the boy. Axel then took the child home. They called the boy Anatole. But Ilsa looked deeper into the situation and learned the child's real name was Moishe Rabinowitz.

At first Axel lied to his wife, Hilde, telling her that Anatole was a Polish child whom he'd taken from a Polish woman who was a single mother unable to take care of him. However, Ilsa knew the truth, and she told Hilde because she needed Hilde's help with her own plans. As Ilsa expected, Hilde already adored the little boy, so she begged Ilsa to keep Anatole's secret safe. In exchange for Ilsa's silence and also for Ilsa conveniently ridding Hilde of Anatole's mother, Hilde agreed to steal from the Reich and give all her stolen goods to Ilsa.

This was over a year ago. And during that time as the Reich was falling, Ilsa was gathering a large collection of valuables, which she would use for her escape when the time came.

"What you are asking of me will cost you. I'm afraid it will be expensive. There are many people who must be paid off. Not in reichsmarks, but in diamonds and gold. Do you understand me?"

"Yes, I understand," Ilsa said.

"And you can pay?"

"I can," she said.

He nodded and bit his lower lip. "Good," he said. "Then you have no reason to be afraid. I have connections who are very willing to help."

"But where will I go?"

"I think the best place will be South America. Peron is very sympathetic to our cause. And for the right price, one can start life over in Argentina. And you have already said you have some gold?"

"Some, yes," she said.

"Then I will arrange what I can for you."

"But . . ."

"Yes?"

"I would prefer to go to America, if it's possible," she said.

"America?" He rubbed his hand over his chin. "Really?"

"Yes, I would."

He let out a laugh. "Anything is possible . . . if . . ."

"If?"

"If you have enough gold, jewels, etcetera."

"I'll get them."

"If you can get them, I'll do what I can to see that the arrangements are to your liking."

She threw her arms around his neck and planted a kiss on his lips. He smiled. "So perhaps I will make a trip to Ravensbrück next month to see you."

"I would like that."

CHAPTER 31

THREE DAYS LATER, ILSA WAS SITTING IN THE DINING CAR OF A TRAIN headed back to Germany. She had just finished her evening meal when a distinguished-looking man approached her. "May I join you?" he asked, his voice thick with an accent she did not recognize.

"Yes, of course."

He sat down but did not introduce himself. Instead, he waited until the waiter came to place his order.

"What can I get for you, sir?"

"Nothing, thank you," the man said. After the waiter left, he took a cigarette out of his pocket. "Would you like one?" he asked.

"Yes, thank you." She took a cigarette, and he lit it.

"What is your name?" he asked. She was trying to place his accent; it was not German or Austrian. Perhaps it was Spanish?

She stared at him. "Why do you ask my name?" Then in a huff, she added, "What is your name?"

"My name is of no importance. But I am going to need to see your papers before I talk to you."

She didn't trust him. "I am not going to show you my papers."

"Indeed," he said, taking a puff from his cigarette. "Let's just say that we have a mutual friend. His name is Otto."

. . .

"Otto? I don't know anyone by the name of Otto," Ilsa said, puffing on her cigarette.

"Perhaps you know him by Adolf? Adolf Eichmann?"

"I know him," she said. Her eyes opened wide.

"Well, he asked me to meet you here on this train. However, it will be necessary for me to see your papers before I go any further."

Ilsa showed him her papers.

He nodded. "Come to my private cabin, number thirty, in ten minutes."

Then he stood up and left.

Ilsa sat back in her chair and watched the man walk down the hall. He'd mentioned Eichmann. That could mean he was someone Eichmann had sent to help her with her escape. Or this man could be an enemy of the Obersturmbannführer's who might use her as a means of revenge. It was a bit risky to go to a strange man's cabin, but she had no choice. After she paid the waiter for her dinner, she walked down to Cabin 30. She knocked.

"Who is it?"

"Ilsa Guhr." Once she was inside, he locked the door.

"Sit down," he commanded.

She did as she was told.

"I am with a secret organization called ODESSA. Eichmann gave me your name and told me to take this train in order to find you. He's instructed me that you are looking for aid. Someone to help you leave Germany if it so happens that you need to leave."

"You mean you are the person who will help me get out if there is no doubt that Germany is losing the war, and those of us involved with the camps need to get out quickly?"

"That's exactly what I mean."

Ilsa nodded. " Would you be able to get me to America?"

"That is not for you to know right now. Right now, you should be grateful that you will be able to get away. I predict things are going to be very bad for those of you who were high up in the party," he answered sharply. "I will need an address for where you can be located, and I will need gold and or diamonds."

She expected as much. "I have diamonds and gold. But I don't have them with me."

"Where can I send someone to collect payment?"

"Ravensbrück Concentration Camp. I am a guard."

He nodded. "Good."

"What guarantee do I have that I will ever hear from you again once I have paid?"

"None. You have no guarantee. You will just have to trust me."

"Hmm." She bit her lip. "I don't know."

Then his voice grew warmer, and he smiled. "Don't worry. There are plenty of Nazi sympathizers who are just waiting to help you escape if you need to."

"For a hefty price," she said.

"Of course. There is a price for everything, my dear. Nothing in life is free."

She nodded. "I will expect someone to come and collect payment."

CHAPTER 32

AFTER WORK ONE NIGHT WHEN ILSA WAS GETTING READY FOR BED, A man knocked at the door of her room. She knew instantly who it was. He identified himself. "I'm here to collect your payment," was all he said.

She had already prepared a box of jewels for him. She knew that it had better be a sufficient amount, or ODESSA might keep her payment but never deliver on their promise. So she divided all she had into quarters and placed three quarters of the jewelry into the box, leaving a little for herself. In the back of her mind she planned to have Hilde increase the stealing so that she could replenish what she'd just given away. There was a large three-carat diamond among the things she'd taken, that she truly fancied. She held it up to the light and marveled at how it shimmered. *I don't want to give up this beautiful diamond, but I am going to have to put this in the box if I want to be taken seriously.*

She handed the man the box. He did not open it. He thanked her, then turned and walked back out into the night.

She wondered how he'd gotten in and out of the camp. *He must be working with other guards here who let him come and go as he pleases,* she thought. *So there must be plenty of others just like me who are also looking for an escape route.* It was treason to discuss Hitler's possible defeat, but Ilsa was beginning to believe that it was probable, probable enough to have given a stranger a bag of gold and diamonds.

After the strange man left, taking her payment, Ilsa did not hear from anyone concerning her plans. She was disappointed that Eichmann didn't call or come to visit either. And she began to fear that she might have been taken. If she was, there was no one to complain to. The goods she'd given the stranger were stolen from the Reich, and then she'd used them to engage in treasonous activity. So if she never heard from any of them again, she would have no choice but to bear the loss in silence.

CHAPTER 33

September, Auschwitz

ON THE MORNING FOLLOWING THE MURDER WHEN EVERYONE WAS AT roll call, the Nazi guards announced that they found Rumkowski, the old Judenrat from the Lodz ghetto, beaten to death in the crematorium.

Ben kept his eyes glued to the ground as the guards walked through the lines of men trying to look in their eyes and see if they could determine who was responsible. But for some reason, unbeknownst to Ben, that was the end of it. There was no further investigation. A month had passed since Rumkowski's murder. With the exception of Jake, Ben never saw any of the other prisoners who'd been involved in the incident, again. And although he and Jake had grown closer since that fateful night, neither of them ever spoke of what happened. They remained good friends and continued to play cards with Isaac on Sunday. Occasionally, someone in the block would mention something that had happened with Rumkowski back when they were in the Lodz ghetto and a brief look would pass between Jake and Ben. But it was only a momentary connection that was gone as quickly it had appeared.

Sometimes there were quiet whispered conversations among the prisoners in the block at night. They'd heard rumors that the Nazis were losing the war. Ben often wondered if there was any truth behind these claims or if the poor prisoners were just wishfully thinking. He'd heard that America had entered the war, and that Germany had suffered great losses on the eastern front. Some of the prisoners had given up, but there were those who held out hope that the Americans were on their way to liberate the camps. He wished, with all his heart, that it would happen. Sometimes he would have dreams of American soldiers bursting into the camp and shooting the Nazi guards. But in the morning, when he opened his eyes, he was still starving and still wearing his striped uniform, and the bedbugs were still leaving itching and burning welts all over his emaciated body.

As he'd promised Ben, Jake had tried to find out if Zelda was in the women's camp. He'd asked everyone he knew, who had any contact with the women's camp, to check and see if they could find out anything about Zelda Lipman. But no one had heard of her. Ben was disappointed and worried. He hoped she'd been sent somewhere other than Auschwitz, somewhere better. However, deep in his heart, he was certain that she'd probably been sent to Auschwitz and gassed when she arrived. The thought of her and the children dying so young tore at his heart, and sometimes he wanted to give up. He'd entertained thoughts of running toward the barbed wire. In his mind he could see and hear the guards in the overhead tower shooting him down. *At least if he were dead, this would be over.* But something inside stopped him. Something told him that things would get better if only he would just hold on.

On a Sunday in late September, Ben returned from work to find Isaac hunched over and weeping as he sat on their bed.

"Are you sick?" Ben asked Isaac, who was sitting on his cot slumped over.

"No, it's Jake."

"Where is he? Is he sick?"

"He didn't come here tonight to play cards. You know how he usually gets here a couple of hours before you get off of work. So I walked over to his block and asked one of the other prisoners who worked with him if they knew where he was." Isaac was trembling. His hands lay on his lap. There was no flesh on his hands; they were just bones covered with a thin layer of skin like the hands of a skeleton. The prisoner I talked to told me that the Nazis gassed a whole group of sonderkommandos this morning. Jake tried to run. He didn't go into the showers willingly. He tried to get away. But they shot him. He's dead."

"Oh my God," Ben said. "Oh my God." He walked away from Isaac. Unable to catch his breath, Ben went outside. Standing alone in the semidarkness he looked up into the sky and cried out, "Why, God? Why have you taken everyone and everything away from me? And yet you don't take me? Why? Why do you let me go on living to suffer alone?" Then he fell to the ground, and with his face in the dirt, he wept.

CHAPTER 34

September 1944

SOMETIMES, EVEN THOUGH BEN WAS EXHAUSTED, HE WOULD WAKE UP in the middle of the night sweating and crying. *I should have given up all hope by now. I should be an empty shell with no feelings left inside me, just waiting to die. So many of the other people in here are that way. And yet I am still haunted by a tiny spark of hope, still praying that Zelda and Moishe might be alive. I am still longing to believe that all this will end, and things will get better. The human spirit is so strange, the will to live so strong, so desperately, miserably strong.*

One night during dinner, Ben was ladling out the watery soup when Paul held out his bowl.

"Do you remember me?" Paul asked.

"Yes." Ben nodded.

"Move along," one of the prisoners from the back of the line said in a testy voice. "We're hungry, and at this pace there won't be time to finish before the whistle sounds."

"I'd like to talk to you. Can you meet me in Crematorium Three tonight after you finish work?"

"Yes, I'll come," Ben said, wondering if perhaps Jake had

mentioned Caleb Ornstein to Paul before he died, and perhaps Paul had some information on Caleb.

After work, Ben quickly went to meet Paul who was waiting outside Crematorium III. "Come, let's take a short walk. What I have to say is for your ears alone. I don't want to risk anyone else hearing us."

Ben nodded and fell into step beside Paul.

Paul said, "You remember that I work as one of the sonderkommandos? I was a good friend of Jake's. He always spoke very highly of you."

"He was a dear friend," Ben said. "I miss him every day."

"Yes, so do I. And because Jake trusted you, I feel that I can trust you too."

"What is it that you want to tell me?" Ben kicked a stone with his shoe.

"You must swear that you will not tell anyone what I am about to tell you. Because if one thing goes wrong with this plan, the entire scheme will fall apart, and everyone involved will be executed."

"Go on. What plan are you talking about?"

"Swear that you will not tell a soul."

"You have my word."

"All right, then. I'll tell you. Do you know the Nazis have been killing off the men in the sonderkommandos?"

"Yes, I know. Just like they did to poor Jake."

"Exactly. The men in the sonderkommandos believe that the Nazis plan to execute all of them."

"I wouldn't be surprised. Nothing they do surprises me anymore," Ben said in a somber voice.

"We, those of us in the sonderkommandos, are planning an uprising. "

"An uprising?"

"Yes, we've had enough. I had to dispose of the bodies of my father and sister. I was forced to sort through their possessions. I thought I would die when I had to put the pocket watch that I gave my father into a pile for the Nazis—my own father, my own sister. For God's sake, after they were dead, I was forced to shave my sister's hair and remove my father's gold tooth. I want revenge. I want to spill some Nazi blood."

"How many of you are there? I thought they were killing everyone in the sonderkommandos."

"Yes, they've been killing us off, and there aren't as many of us as there were. But we've joined with a very strong group of nineteen Soviet prisoners of war who are going to help us. We need men who can be trusted and who will be willing to take great risks to help us with this uprising."

"And you want me to help?"

"Yes."

Ben reflected for a moment. "What do you want me to do?"

"We need weapons. Do you receive the dirty trays from the women's camp?"

"Yes."

"Can you get direct access to them?"

"Sure. All I would have to do is ask for clean-up duty," Ben said.

"We have a connection with some of the girls who work at the Weichsel Union Metallwerke."

"That's a munitions factory, isn't it?"

"Yes. These women have been smuggling explosives in the bottom of their food trays, but the fellow they were working with in the kitchen recently became ill. He's been taken to the hospital. We have no doubt he'll never be seen or heard from again."

"Was it Simon Lebowitz?"

"Yes, you knew him?"

"Not really. I knew who he was, and I knew he got sick. I never knew he was working on something like this. May I ask how long you have been preparing for this?"

"Since June."

"From the size of the trays, I'd assume these will be very small amounts of explosives," Ben said..

"You're right, but they add up. Like I said, we've been working on this for a while now. Are you with us?"

"I'm with you," Ben said. "For Jake."

"Good. Very good. You'll start tomorrow at dinner. You'll have to be very careful and very discreet. Make sure no one knows what you are doing, and be sure to check every tray. Even if you think you can trust a fellow, don't tell him. These girls are putting their lives at risk to smuggle these explosives to us. Make sure you don't miss anything."

The whistle sounded. "What do I do with the explosives once I have them?"

"Bring them here to me each night as soon as you've finished work."

CHAPTER 35

THE FOLLOWING DAY AFTER WORK, BEN BROUGHT FOUR SMALL collections of powder, each of them folded carefully into a tiny piece of paper.

"There should be another one," Paul said.

"This was all I found."

"There is no room for error, Rabinowitz. Like I told you before, the women are going to great lengths to get this stuff out to us. You must not overlook even one. Do you understand me? Be more careful. Please."

"I'm sorry," Ben said. He was angry with himself, although cleanup was not his favorite job because it posed no opportunity to steal an extra potato skin or bit of carrot. After all, no one ever left a thing on their tray. And he had to be so careful that no one noticed him searching through the trays. However, the very idea of an uprising had somehow breathed new life into him. It had given him a reason to continue to fight to live another day.

"We believe that there will be opportunity for escape during the uprising. The guards hardly expect any of this of us, and so everything will be very chaotic."

"Do you have any other weapons besides the ones I am collecting? Guns?" Ben asked.

"We have hammers, axes, things that some of the prisoners have been able to steal from their jobs."

"It all sounds very ambitious. I am hopeful that we can pull it off. But to be honest with you, I don't know where I would go if I were able to get out of here," Ben said. "I have no home, no family left."

"None of us do. If you can get out, run like hell until you can get into the forest. Then search until you can find a group of partisans."

"If I don't, then I will starve to death alone in the forest," Ben said.

"But you'll starve a free man, yes? If you stay here, eventually the Nazis will murder you. So, I say, if you must die, it's far better to die on your own terms than to be murdered by these bastards."

Ben nodded. "You're right." Then he added, "Do we have a date yet when this uprising is to take place?"

"Not yet."

CHAPTER 36

October 1944

ON AN OCTOBER AFTERNOON, BEN WAS WORKING IN THE KITCHEN peeling carrots when he heard a loud noise followed by gunshots and shouting. Then he saw several groups of prisoners running, followed by guards. More shots rang out. Prisoners fell.

"What's going on?" Josepf, one of Ben's coworkers asked.

"I don't know," Ben admitted.

There was a loud blast that sounded like a bomb. The ground shook as if God had struck it with an angry fist.

Ben and Josepf looked at each other.

They tried to sneak outside to find out more information, but as soon as they left the building, two guards with rifles herded them into a line of prisoners who were being held at gunpoint.

"Does anyone know what is going on?" Josepf asked.

"The crematorium exploded," someone said.

"Exploded?" a prisoner said, his mouth falling open in shock.

"I think that one of the sonderkommandos blew it up with a grenade."

"Where the hell would they get a grenade?" another prisoner asked.

Ben knew where they would have gotten a grenade. They would have made it out of the explosives he had been collecting. But why wasn't he told that the uprising was going to take place today?

"I heard it started because one of the sonderkommandos attacked a guard with a hammer in Crematorium Four. Someone said that this morning the sonderkommando found out that the Nazis were planning to liquidate all of them."

"Oh my God. So there has been a revolt?" Josepf asked.

"Shut your mouth. There will be no talking here." One of the guards nudged Josepf with the point of his rifle.

Ben felt his heart sink as he watched the prisoners run by him. Ever since he'd spoken with Paul, he'd been thinking about the possibility of making an escape. And he'd decided that freedom was worth the risk of dying. So he had been waiting for the chance to try and run away when the uprising took place. But, now, as he stood at gunpoint with the rest of this group, he knew the opportunity had passed him by. In the distance, he saw a few of the prisoners getting out by cutting the barbed wire. But many more were being shot down or electrocuted by falling into the fence as they were running.

Over the next few hours, Ben learned that the revolt had indeed started in Crematorium IV and then had spread to the rest of the sonderkommandos. But before the men in Crematorium III and Crematorium V knew what was happening, the SS arrived and stopped them from joining the others in the uprising.

That night, the sound of barking dogs sent terror through the hearts of the prisoners in Ben's block. They knew the SS had sent them out to find the escapees and tear them to shreds.

The results of the uprising were not promising. Only two SS officers had been killed, one beaten to death, another thrown into a furnace. But two hundred fifty prisoners had died including everyone who had been involved in organizing the revolt.

Three days later the whistle blew, and the voice of one of the guards came over the loudspeaker demanding that everyone leave their jobs and come outside to line up as if this was a roll call. The prisoners ran to the roll-call area and fell into their regular place in line. Twelve dead bodies of the men who had tried to escape hung in full view of the prisoners.

"Good afternoon, you disgusting swine," an SS officer said as he walked up to stand in front of the group. He was a handsome man, healthy and robust. His shoeshine-black hair matched his well-polished, black boots. The death-head symbol on his hat glistened like a false idol in the sunlight. "Take a good look at these bodies hanging here." He shook his head mockingly. "These vermin were foolish enough to think that they could rise up against the SS and escape. And now? Well, you can see what's happened to them." He barked a harsh laugh.

"As I'm sure you know, a few of the prisoners decided to act up here a few days ago. Let me assure you that no one involved in this fiasco will go unpunished. If you happen to know of a man who you think escaped that day, please be assured that he did not get away. There was a group of men who got out of here and were hiding a few miles away in a barn. Such ingrates they were. But we knew what to do. We sent the dogs after them. The dogs sniffed them right out. How could they not? Jews have a stench, after all. Anyway, their hiding in that barn made things really rather easy for us. We just set the barn on fire, and they were burned alive. You should have heard the screams. And for those of you unfortunate enough to have a wife or a girlfriend who was involved in all of this, perhaps a sister or a daughter, any one of your lady pigs, who we discovered stealing explosives, well, rest assured that she will face torture and execution. Let this be a lesson to any of you who would dare to try and cause chaos here. It will not be tolerated."

CHAPTER 37

January 1945

On a frigid afternoon in mid-January, Ben was at work in the kitchen. There was not much to be thankful for these days, but he was thankful to be working in the kitchen, especially in the middle of winter because it provided a little more heat than any of the other jobs in the camp. He was cleaning out the large soup cauldron when a group of guards came racing in. They tore through the kitchen and began to divide the food among themselves. But a few of them actually gave a morsel or two to the prisoners.

Ben received a huge hunk of bread from a guard he knew well. He was glad to receive the extra food but worried. Something was happening.

"Line up outside in rows of six across," one of the guards demanded. "Go now and mach schnell!"

Ben left the kitchen and followed the rest of the prisoners outside. His uniform was thin and hardly protected him from the cold. He shivered as he stood in the lineup feeling as if he might freeze to death if he had to stand outside much longer. Shivering at

154

the sidelines stood three guards in warm coats, with their guns pointed at the prisoners.

A tall, slender man with dark hair and deep-set, sunken, dark-rimmed eyes walked to the front of the group and began to speak. "I am SS Oberscharführer Wilhelm Boger. Today we will be leaving Auschwitz. You will follow orders. Each of you must stay in this line just as you are now. We will travel on foot to our destination in an orderly fashion. Each of you will be given three potatoes and two pieces of cheese. Don't be foolish and eat it all at once. This food must last you for the entire journey. You will not be given anything more for a long time, so use this gift from the German people wisely. You will be required to pull the handcarts that contain the luggage of the SS officers. Make sure that you are very careful with these possessions. You will be responsible for their safe arrival. Any damage to these things will cost you dearly. Those of you lazy swine who lag behind or try to escape will be shot on sight. Let's go. Mach Schnell. March."

Ben looked up to see the placement of the sun. He determined it was probably some time around four o'clock in the afternoon as the prisoners were led out of the gate that read Work Makes You Free.

It had snowed the night before leaving the ground covered in a blanket of freezing, white powder that found its way into Ben's ill-fitting wooden shoes and treacherous patches of ice hid buried under the snow. Sliding on the ice in their wooden shoes, the prisoners tried to keep up with the rest of the line. They knew if they lost their footing it could cost them their lives. Some fell behind and were shot by the guards. One of the men who walked on the left side of Ben slipped several times. Ben grabbed him, holding him steady, but still walking, not losing his place with the rest of the group.

Dead bodies lay in ditches on the side of the road. These were reminders of what would happen if a man fell and could not get back up before he was seen by the guards. Ben felt his stomach turn as he lumbered past the dead. The bodies lay in the snow, with blue lips and parchment-paper-gray skin. Dried blood stained the white blanket crimson. It was growing painstakingly difficult for Ben to continue, but he knew that he must. Hunger burned in his belly, and there was a throbbing behind his eyes that made him feel dizzy. *Two potatoes left*, he thought, but even though he was frightened, he was starving to death, but he was afraid to eat them. If he did, he had no idea if or when there might be more. And yet all he could think of was the potatoes. The way the starch would taste against his tongue and the crunch of it's raw white meat. *Walk. Keep walking. Don't think about food.* His eyes teared from the cold, and the tears froze on his eyelashes and cheeks. His nose ran and dripped down the front of his thin uniform. His parched throat ached. Quickly, Ben reached down and grabbed a handful of snow and pushed it into his mouth. It was so cold, so very terribly cold, but the wetness of it soothed the scratchy pain in his throat as it melted down into his belly. Night fell, and Ben was exhausted. Each step he took was a battle, but he willed his feet to keep moving. His ill-fitting shoes cut into the flesh of his feet. And, now as the sun was setting, the wicked, icy wind felt even colder. The man beside Ben collapsed. Ben tried to pull him back up, but he was dead weight.

"Leave me," he said. "I can't go anymore."

"No," Ben insisted. Suddenly saving this man was the most important thing in the world to Ben. "Get up." Ben was pulling hard on the man's uniform shirt. In the semidarkness, Ben could see the man shaking his head. And then one of the guards came over.

"Get back in line," the guard said to Ben.

Ben was shivering. He was crying too. For some reason, even though he didn't know this man, he could not leave him dying in the snow. He pulled at the man's shirt again. The man would not move.

"I'm losing patience," the guard said. He was almost apologetic. For a mere second Ben thought he saw pity, a human quality that was rarely found in the guards at Auschwitz. "It's cold out here. We have one more mile before we will stop for the night. Get back in line."

"But this man . . ." Ben stammered.

Before Ben could finish speaking, the guard set his rifle on the prisoner who lay in the snow. He fired. The man's blood and brain matter splattered Ben's clothing. Ben looked at the guard. For a single second he didn't comprehend what had just happened.

"Get up, and get back in line, or you're next."

Ben did as he was told. *I was mistaken*, he thought. *This man's not human; he's a monster. They're all monsters.*

By the middle of the second day of the march, Ben began to feel a terrible stabbing pain in his toes. He wanted to sit down and rub them. They were so cold; he needed to make them warm. But there was no stopping not even for a second. And by the third morning, his toes were numb, and he felt certain they were frostbitten. He was tired; his entire body ached with exhaustion. His eyes began to close, and he wanted to lie down in the snow and let go. But he didn't. He willed his eyes to stay open and willed his feet to take one more step. At eighty pounds, the bones of his ribs and arms rubbed against the thin fabric of his uniform. One of the men, who had been pulling the cart that was carrying the possessions of two of the guards, died during the night. Ben was put in his place. The weight of the cart was too much for him. He began to weep. *I don't have anything left to live for. Even if the war is really ending, where will I go; what will I do? I don't know where my son is or if he is alive or dead. And poor Zelda. I am afraid to think of what happened to her. It would be easier to die than to go on fighting for life. It would be so much easier to just sit down in the snow and let these bastards shoot me.* Ben stopped walking and sat down. The snow was at least three feet deep. It soaked into the back and bottom of his uniform. The icy chill stung his skin.

"Get up," a thick, heavyset guard, with a red face and a double chin, growled at him.

Ben shook his head and stared down at the snow ready and waiting, waiting for the bullet through his temple that would end the misery that had become his life. But, instead, an arm in a gray-striped uniform lifted him and began to push him forward. When he looked into the prisoner's eyes, he saw the face of a man he hated: Caleb Ornstein.

Caleb pulled him along, holding him up.

"Do you know who I am?" Ben said, struggling with the words.

"Of course, I know. You're Ben Rabinowitz."

"You're Caleb Ornstein, aren't you?"

"Yes, I am."

"Get away from me."

"I'm sorry for what I did. Please, I beg you to forgive me. I've thought about you every day since I got here to Auschwitz. I owe you. I had no idea what I had done to you by sending you here. I didn't know until I got here myself. Please, forgive me. I was wrong. I made mistakes. I can't change the past, but give me a chance to change the future. We need each other. It's impossible to survive this place without friends. I need you."

"Go to hell," Ben said. "You should have left me there in the snow."

"I couldn't. I've changed. Auschwitz had changed me. I'm not the same man I was in Lodz. I've been through plenty. And I'm sorry. All I can say is that from the bottom of my heart, I am so very sorry."

Ben looked into Caleb's eyes. "Where did you come from? How did you get to Auschwitz? I haven't seen you since I left Lodz, and I've looked for you here at Auschwitz. The truth is, I wanted to kill you."

Caleb sighed. "I know. I don't blame you."

"And why the hell are you helping me now?"

Caleb let out a deep breath that formed a white cloud around his face. "Because I owe you. Because I am haunted by everything I did to you and Zelda. I was a fool. I was jealous of you because you were born rich, and I was from a poor family. But I learned the hard way that in the end you and I are the same—we are both Jews. The Nazis taught me that. And being in a death camp teaches a man a lot about himself. I didn't realize what I had done to Zelda or to you until I got to Auschwitz. Then I knew, and it was too late. The guilt of what happened to all the kids, all the people that I helped Rumkowski shove on to those trains." Caleb hesitated. He shook his head, then he continued. "I got here the same time Rumkowski arrived. I know what happened to him. I'm not sure who did it, the sonderkommandos, I think. But there was no doubt that he deserved it. I probably deserved the same fate."

"No talking," a guard, who walked by them, commanded, hitting Caleb with the butt of his rifle. Caleb winced, but he keep moving.

The guard stayed close by, and so they walked in silence for almost a half hour. Ben was stunned by all that Caleb had told him. He should be angry. He should tear Caleb apart with his bare hands, but he didn't. He was too weak to fight and too weak hold on to any anger.

A man who looked old but was perhaps, in truth, about forty had been walking in front of them. He slipped on a patch of ice and fell, his shoe flying off. He struggled to stand up but couldn't. He kept slipping like a marionette as he tried to get his feet back under him. One foot twisted awkwardly. It seemed as if he'd broken a bone in either his foot or ankle.

The guard, who had been watching over Ben and Caleb, was instantly upon the fallen prisoner like a hungry wolf.

"Please, have mercy," the man said, still trying to get back on his feet.

While the guard was busy with the man, Caleb began to speak to Ben. This time he spoke in a whisper. "I want to help you, so listen to me. I've been thinking about this for a long time. When I was in the Lodz ghetto, I saw a man filling these big metal milk containers with important papers and artwork, then he buried them. I asked him what he was doing. He said he was planning to come back for them after the war was over. That's when I got this idea. You see, at the time, I had access to valuables I could steal. So I filled a couple of the milk containers with money and jewelry, then I buried them in several different places. I might just survive this, so I can't tell you where all of them are. But I am going to tell you where you can find one. Do you remember where I worked? Where Rumkowski and I worked?"

"Of course. How could I ever forget?"

"All right. The milk container is buried on the west side of that building, the one where I worked with Rumkowski."

"Why are you telling me this?"

"Because I want to make peace with God just in case I die. I feel like I have to do what I can to pay back what I owe you. I know money won't bring back your girl. We can only hope that she's alive. And believe me, I pray for it every day."

"Me too. And the two children as well," Ben said.

"All the children. All the children that Rumkowski had us put on that transport. I wish I had the power to go back and change that. I would never have done the things I did. I'm scared, Rabinowitz. I'm scared I am going to die here and end up in hell for eternity."

Ben looked over at Caleb. He was not the handsome, suave man Ben remembered: he was thin and sickly with pockmarks on his face, but he looked sincere. And in spite of all he'd done to Ben, Ben felt sorry for him."

"I am hoping that you will live through this, and when you go back to Lodz to dig up that milk container, the stuff inside will help you start your life over again."

"I never knew you were such a God-fearing man. I wouldn't have believed it of you."

"I wasn't until I got to Auschwitz. The man who slept beside me was a Hasidic Jew. I told him everything I did. We talked about you, and Zelda, and all the children. I confessed everything. He listened without judgment, then he gave encouragement as I prayed, and I begged for God's forgiveness. He brought me back to God."

"Is he still alive?" Ben asked.

"No. He's dead."

Ben nodded solemnly.

For three days, Ben and Caleb walked side by side. Then they were loaded onto an open train car where they were packed so tight they were forced to remain standing. But because of the close proximity of all the people, it was much warmer than walking.

"The war is ending," one of the prisoners in the train car whispered, "The Nazis are scared; that's why they are taking us away."

"Are you sure? I've heard that before," someone else said.

"No, of course not. No one is sure of anything."

Almost three days later, the train stopped in front of Buchenwald, and the prisoners were unloaded. Caleb walked beside Ben. Ben's eyes scanned the camp. His head ached with hunger, his limbs felt rubbery and unstable. *Are they planning to kill us?* he thought. *Have they brought us here to kill us?* His heavy eyes searched for a gas chamber or crematorium. There was none. *Perhaps they have a more efficient and quicker method to murder us at this place than they did at Auschwitz.*

The prisoners were driven like cattle, forced to run as fast as they were able, into large barracks. The room was filled with sickly men laying on bunks and on the floors. The smell of feces, urine, and unwashed bodies was even stronger than it had been at Auschwitz.

Ben couldn't forget what Caleb had done, but he began to forgive. And slowly his anger faded away. He needed a friend. He searched everywhere for Isaac, but he was unable to find him. Caleb was all he had now.

During the transport, Ben lost his two little toes, but other than that his feet were still functional. Caleb was not as fortunate. His wooden clogs had cut into his toes on his left foot and now the cuts were hot, red, swollen, and oozing pus.

"Your foot is infected," Ben said.

"It'll be all right."

Ben helped Caleb clean the open wound with snow: a thick, ill-smelling pus still seeped from the wound.

"I'm glad I got to know you," Caleb said.

Ben nodded.

"You still don't forgive me, do you?"

Ben shrugged. "I suppose I do. I just wish you hadn't done what you did."

"It wouldn't have changed things. If it hadn't been me, it would have been some other fella. Believe me, I regret it every day. Every day. But no matter what I would have done, we all would have ended up in Auschwitz anyway."

Ben didn't answer.

"Listen to me. This is important. It's something you should know."

"Go on."

"I have a cousin who works in the diamond district in New York City. That's in the United States of America. Anyway, in case I don't make it, I mean in case something happens and I die, I want you to contact him. Tell him you were my friend. Ask him to sponsor you. His name is Levi Mansky. Here, take this." Caleb handed Ben a dirty, yellowed scrap of paper with Levi's address scribbled on it.

"You'll survive," Ben said, trying to sound reassuring.

"Take the paper. Please . . ."

Ben nodded and took the paper.

"I wish you would forgive me. What can I do?"

"I do forgive you, Caleb. I don't hate you anymore. I'm too tired and hungry to hate. All I can think about is food. If I fall asleep, I dream about food," Ben said.

"Maybe I don't believe you could forgive me because I can't forgive myself."

It had been two days since they'd each received a raw potato. At Auschwitz they'd been starving, but at least they'd received ersatz coffee each morning, a watery soup at midday, and a piece of bread at night. Here at Buchenwald, days could pass before they got anything to eat. Then Ben continued, "I've even considered eating pieces of flesh from the dead bodies. God forgive me."

"I understand," Caleb said. "The thought of it is disgusting, but I know how you feel."

That night after everyone was asleep, Caleb got out of bed and snuck into the kitchen. He was going to see if he could find some food for Ben and himself. The throbbing in his infected foot was so great that the foot cramped up and he fell, knocking over a pile of empty, wooden containers. A rat who'd been nestled inside one of the boxes ran out and scampered across his head. The noise alerted a guard who came rushing in.

"What are you doing here? You don't belong here." Then the guard surveyed the situation. He glared at Caleb. "Stealing, no doubt! You filthy Jew."

Caleb cowered, huddling into the boxes that he'd knocked over.

"Stand up. Now!" the guard commanded.

Caleb tried to stand, but his foot was paralyzed with pain. He let out a small scream of agony. He'd overcompensated and sprained his other ankle when he fell, and now it was too twisted for him to straighten it out.

"I said get up. How dare you defy me?"

Gripping the side of a box, Caleb pulled himself to his feet. Sweat poured down his brow. Holding on to the box, he tried to stay on his feet. His breathing was labored.

"Show me what's in your pockets." The guard was toying with him.

Caleb showed the guard his empty pockets.

"Hmmm . . ." The guard shook his head. "I don't like the way you look. You look like a thief to me. But then what can one expect from a Jew, right?" He pulled out a black pistol and aimed it at Caleb. "Goodbye, Jew," he said, smiling, and fired the gun.

There was only an instant before Caleb's entire body surrendered to death, and in that instant he thought, *God forgive me for all I have done.*

CHAPTER 38

A FEELING OF DREAD LODGED ITSELF DEEP IN THE PIT OF BEN'S
stomach when he awakened the following morning and Caleb was
not in bed. He got up and immediately began to search for him. But
it was not long before one of the other men, who slept in the same
barracks and knew Caleb, came to tell Ben that Caleb's dead body
was on top of the pile of dead bodies outside the building.

Frantic, Ben rushed out to see if Caleb might still be alive. A
sudden need came over Ben. He wanted Caleb to know that he was
truly forgiven. But it was too late. Ben returned to his block alone.

A month passed. Ben grew so thin and weak that he found it
difficult to get out of bed. He had no friends left. Everyone he'd
known was gone. And he began to feel like he was waiting to die.

Something was happening with the guards. They were no longer
the enthusiastic sadists he knew them to be. They'd stopped imple-
menting roll calls. They huddled together in groups, speaking to
each other in whispers. It seemed they'd lost all interest in the
prisoners.

Then on a morning nearing the end of April, the old familiar
whistle sounded. It had been months since there had been a roll call.
Over the loudspeaker came a voice: "Report for roll call."

One of the other prisoners in Ben's block tried to help Ben to get on his feet. Ben turned over in bed. He shook his head and refused. "I'm not going," he said. "Let them shoot me. I don't care. I'd rather be dead than go on like this."

All the men in Ben's block left Ben and ran outside. Lying in bed, barely strong enough to move, Ben waited for a guard to come and inspect the block. He hoped the guard would shoot him and finally put an end to his misery. But no one came.

A loud air-raid whistle reverberated through the camp. The sound was so deafening that it hurt Ben's ears. Prisoners came running back into the block. They threw themselves on the floor and covered their ears.

"What's going on out there?" Ben asked.

"I don't know," one of the men answered.

Then there was a thunderous roar. The ground shook. Then it happened again.

"We're being bombed. I think the Allies are here," someone said.

Ben felt a wave of strength course through him as he forced himself to rise from his bed and walk to the door to look outside. The prisoner was right. They were being bombed. The guards were running for shelter, scattering across the camp. Dead bodies flew like black bats through the air. Fires erupted in angry bursts of red-and-orange flames.

One of the other prisoners grabbed Ben and pulled him to the ground. "Stay down," he said.

The bombing continued through the night. By some miracle, the block where Ben lay on the dirt floor was not hit or burned.

The night's activities left Ben too weak to move. As the sun peeked her golden head through the gray, smoke-filled sky, Ben still lay coughing. Then one of the prisoners came running into the block. "They're gone! All the guards, all the Nazis, they are gone!"

Gone? Ben thought. Then he closed his eyes. *The war must be over and I am dying. How ironic.* He wanted to laugh, but he was too weak. His eyes began to close. But before he drifted off, two thoughts went through his clouded mind. *A milk carton is buried somewhere near the building where Rumkowski worked in the Lodz ghetto. It's filled with valuables. And somewhere in New York City, America, lives a man named Levi Mansky who just might be willing to sponsor a friend of Caleb Ornstein's. If I can just live through this . . . I might be able to start over.*

CHAPTER 39

Heidelberg, Germany 1927
Ilsa

ILSA GUHR SAT HUDDLED NEXT TO THE FIREPLACE IN THE SMALL cottage where she lived. Her stomach was in knots as she gripped the doll her mother had made for her out of rags.

"I'm sorry, Hans," the small-town doctor said in a somber voice. "It's too late. We did everything we could for her."

"I don't know how I am going to go on without my wife. I can't take care of the child alone. What does a man like me know about raising a six-year-old girl? I have a farm to tend to and no sons to help me."

Ilsa could hear the despair in her father's voice. He had always been a cold man but nonetheless a man she both feared and admired. Her body trembled. She was unsure of what all this meant. Ilsa's mother had been ill for over a week. Every day she'd sat at her mother's bedside waiting for her mother to speak, but her mother had not said a single word. And only once during that entire week had she reached out to hold Ilsa's hand. If only her father would come and hug her. If only he was warmer and she could somehow feel as close to him as she felt to her mother. Ilsa desperately needed someone to talk to, someone to ease all her fears, but her father was not ever going to do that for her. He was a quick-tempered man who was frugal to a fault. And his love for money had prompted him to wait to fetch the local doctor. He had been hoping that her mother would get better on her own.

"I'm sorry," the doctor said.

"It's not about missing my wife. It's about the harsh reality of living on a farm. Once my wife fell ill, things got very tough around here. I've been exhausted trying to do her share of the work as well as my own. This little girl needs cooked food. She needs to be disciplined. I can't do it all."

"You might consider putting the child in an orphanage for a while: at least until you get on your feet."

"I could, but I need my daughter's help. She does some of the farm work. She feeds and milks the cows. She churns the butter. It would be a mistake to send her away."

"You will find a way to make this all work, Herr Guhr. Little Ilsa might be able to do more than you think."

"Possibly. But I could marry again. It might be the best thing to do."

"Might be too soon for that," the doctor said sympathetically. Then he continued, "Perhaps you might want to hire someone to help you."

"There's no money for that," Hans said as he came walking out of the bedroom. Then he turned to Ilsa who stared at him with wide eyes. "I'm sorry," he said, but his voice was cold. "Your mother passed away this morning."

Ilsa began to cry, but no one came to comfort her. She wiped her tears on her doll's dress.

CHAPTER 40

TWO MONTHS AFTER ILSA'S MOTHER DIED, HER FATHER HITCHED UP their horse and wagon and drove into town leaving ten-year-old Ilsa with the neighbors. As she watched the little wagon disappear down the dirt road, she felt lost and alone. The neighbor lady was nice enough, but she was not Ilsa's mother. And she had three children of her own. If her father did not return, she felt sure that she would end up in an orphanage. The neighbor's ten-year-old daughter, Margret, secretly taunted Ilsa, telling her that if her father did not return, Ilsa would be an orphan. Margret and her two siblings made up terrifying stories of witches who ran the orphanages. They told Ilsa that they'd heard tales of how badly these witches treated little girls who were unfortunate enough to fall into their clutches.

"And eventually, after the witches are done torturing the children, they eat them," Margret said.

Ilsa felt terror strike her through her heart.

"Do you remember the story of Hansel and Gretel? Well, they're the same witches who run the orphanages."

It was a week before Ilsa's father returned. He had a woman with him, who was younger than Ilsa's mother had been but not nearly as pretty.

"This is your new mother. Her name is Adelle. We got married in town," her father said.

Ilsa cowered in the corner.

"What's the matter with you? You're acting like a half-wit. Come over here and say hello," her father commanded.

She was too old to suck her thumb yet she did. Ilsa was unable to speak. She stared at the woman with fear.

"Didn't you hear me? You idiot. I said to say hello," her father demanded. He was getting impatient with her.

"Hello." Ilsa choked the words out. *This woman is not my mother. No one can replace my mother.*

"You'll mind Adelle, and do whatever she tells you to do. I don't want to hear of you giving her any trouble. Do you understand me? If she tells me that you aren't minding her, I'll take my belt to your backside."

Margret was standing in the corner. She giggled.

Ilsa stared at the woman named Adelle. She was slender with a nice figure, but her face was plain, her eyes too small, her chin too pointy. "Yes, Father. I'll do as you ask," Ilsa managed.

The woman looked Ilsa up and down, then she shook her head.

"Come on, let's go home," Ilsa's father said.

Ilsa followed her father and Adelle. They sat in the front and she in the back.

That night, when Ilsa's father went outside to wash before dinner, Adelle turned to Ilsa and said, "You're fat and sloppy, and I have to admit I'm ashamed to say you are my daughter. You will just have to stop eating so much, and clean yourself up."

Ilsa's feelings were hurt, but she just nodded. She hadn't kept herself clean since her mother passed away. And her hair was a mass of knots because there was no one to help her comb it.

"I'll bet you don't have many friends in school, now, do you? Being fat and slovenly like that? I would have to think that your mother was just like you."

"Don't talk that way about my mother," Ilsa said. It hurt her when Adelle said cruel things about her. But when Adelle made nasty comments about her mother, Ilsa was willing to risk a beating to stand up to her.

"And what are you going to do about it? Tell your father?" Adelle sneered. "If you do, I'll tell him that you are just being difficult. I'll tell him that you refuse to do your chores. And you know what that will mean, now, don't you? He'll beat you until you can't stand up."

All through dinner, Ilsa watched Adelle as she charmed Ilsa's father. He seemed so pleased with her cooking and her soft voice. But Ilsa knew the truth. The woman was mean and hurtful. However, she dared not tell her father; he would never believe her anyway. He would take Adelle's side.

After dinner, Adelle told Ilsa to clean up. Once she'd finished, Adelle inspected the kitchen. Pleased, she nodded.

The following morning when Ilsa awakened, her stepmother was waiting. She was given a slice of bread and a glass of milk for breakfast. Ilsa glared at her stepmother. This was far less than what she had become accustomed to eating. "This is not enough food. I'll be hungry," Ilsa said.

"I have to cut back on the amount of food you eat. You are just too fat, Butterball," Adelle said. Once she'd finished, her stepmother said, "Now get outside, and start churning the butter. Make yourself useful."

Ilsa did as she was told. But once she was alone in the barn, she sat down on a pile of hay and began to cry. She hated this woman, and she hated her father for bringing her into their home.

A half hour passed.

"Ilsa, hurry up and churn that butter," Adelle yelled out to her from the porch. "And don't eat it all, please. I'm sure that eating that butter is what's turned you into a fat, little butterball," she scoffed.

With tearstained cheeks, Ilsa began to churn the butter. She was a chubby, little girl, and it had always been a sore spot for her. Her mother had been kind. She'd promised Ilsa that Ilsa would grow out of it. Now her mother was gone.

The weeks passed. Ilsa felt so alone that when she went to sleep at night she wished she would die before the morning came.

In school Ilsa was withdrawn and painfully shy. In her worn-out clothes that were too small, and dirty, broken shoes, she looked a mess. Her hair was always matted with dirt and knots, and it made a strong contrast to the other girls whose mothers curled or braided their hair. Instead of being kind, the other girls teased her mercilessly.

To add fuel to the fire, every Sunday in church, Adelle called Ilsa "Butterball." She used the nickname loud enough for the other girls to hear. Ilsa was already an outcast, so the nickname stuck. It followed her to school where, to make matters worse, she'd never been a good student. She struggled with her studies while her classmates made up cruel singsong verses about her that they sang while jumping rope.

Ilsa, Ilsa, fat little butterball
Ilsa, Ilsa takes a fall
Ilsa, Ilsa so fat she blocks the entire hall

Ilsa was not a pretty child. Her pale skin and chubby body made her an easy target for the school bully. Her family owned a dairy farm that made and sold butter, among other things. So her dirty, tangled, yellow hair made it easy for them to compare her to a round, yellow ball of butter. The name Butterball stuck. And every time Ilsa heard it she cringed.

The other girls her age, who lived on the neighboring farms, walked home from school together. But they made it clear that they didn't want Ilsa to walk with them. And when she passed them, they would call out to her.

Poor little butterball fat as can be
If she tried to swim she would drown in the sea
But I'd better watch out because she might eat me
Butterball, butterball fat as can be

Their teasing cut deep, but Ilsa refused to let them see her cry. Instead, she waited until she was alone, and then she wept hard and long. She had never been a popular girl, but at least when her mother was alive she had a friend. Now she was alone in the world and very depressed. Sadness began to turn to anger and hatred. Ilsa blamed her stepmother for her hideous nickname. And although she had no idea how she would do it, she swore to herself that someday she would punish her stepmother.

When Falk, Ilsa's stepbrother was born, Ilsa's father demanded that she help her stepmother with the baby. Her father adored his young wife, and now that she'd given him a son, his affection toward her was even greater now than before. Ilsa did as she was told, but she was only waiting.

CHAPTER 41

June 1934

ILSA WOULD ALWAYS REMEMBER THE YEAR 1934 AS THE MOST significant year in her young life. In June, she started menstruating, and with the onslaught of puberty her body began to change. Instead of looking like a giant ball with spindly legs and arms, she began to see hourglass curves forming. Her breasts and hips became full, and her waist slimmed down. She was short, but her legs were shapely. At the same time, the school she attended implemented a new program called the Jungmädels. Ilsa joined. She'd never been a part of anything before, but her group leader was firm in her insistence that the girls bond together. Teasing was not tolerated. Even though there was no trace left of the butterball Ilsa had been as a child, she was still very insecure, and whenever people whispered to each other, she was sure they were making fun of her.

The boys, whom she'd known since she was very young, who had once called her names and laughed at her, were now paying attention when she walked into a room. She saw the admiration in their eyes. They tried to walk home from school with her. One boy left a piece of candy and a note on her desk telling her how pretty she was. This was new for her. When no one was looking, she winked at the boys in church. They smiled as their faces grew red with embarrassment. Ilsa had never felt pretty before, and she was having a lot of fun with all this.

As she walked home after school one day, Klaus, the boy whose family owned the farm directly west of hers, caught up with her.

"May I walk you home?" he asked.

Ilsa nodded. "Sure." She was still a little socially awkward, so she walked alongside him quietly. It was easy to smile and wink across a crowded room. It was much harder to make conversation one on one.

"I have a deal of sorts to make with you," he said, confident in his proposition.

She looked up at him.

"I'll give you my mother's quill pen if you show me what's under your dress."

Ilsa blushed and turned away. "Never," she said, shocked.

Klaus pulled the pen out of his breast pocket. It was made of ivory and had a black plume. Ilsa thought it was the most beautiful thing she'd ever seen. "Here, why don't you take a look at it?" he said, handing her the pen.

It felt cool in her fingers.

"It's nice, isn't it?"

She nodded.

"It's been in my family for generations."

"Wouldn't you get in trouble if it was gone?"

"No." He laughed. "My mother would think she had misplaced it."

Ilsa held the pen up to the sun and looked at it more closely. Even though her father had a fairly successful farm, she'd never owned much of anything. Her clothes were secondhand, and the only doll she'd ever had as a child was the one her mother made for her from rags.

"All right." She wanted that pen. She wanted it badly, so she nodded. Her voice was trembling as she said, "All right."

"Come with me. There's a little private area down by the creek."

Ilsa followed Klaus. She held the pen in her hand and thought about running away with it, but she was not very athletic, and she was afraid he would catch her and hurt her. She thought about giving the pen back to him, but she wanted it so badly.

When they got to the creek, Klaus turned to her and smiled. "Take off your dress," he said.

Suddenly Ilsa was terrified. She threw the pen at him and began to run, but he caught her arm and pulled her dress up over her head. Then he tore her slip. She kicked and screamed, but he covered her mouth. He was driven by passion; his eyes were glazed over with hunger, not only for sex, but also for power. Before she knew it, she was naked. Trying to hide her private parts with her hands, she could not look at him. Her face burned red with shame. "Please, don't." Ilsa begged him not to do it, but he forced himself inside her. Pain shot through her. He began to thrust himself inside her. She scrunched her eyes shut to block out his face.

And then it was done.

Ilsa was trembling as she sat up and hugged her dress to her naked body.

"You'd better not tell anyone what happened. If you do I'll tell everyone that you stole my mother's pen and that you made up this story to cover your own tracks. You'll get in trouble, not me."

"I don't want the pen," she said.

"But it's yours. You earned it." He'd calmed down now. The passion of the previous moment was gone, and although he was trying to seem in control, she saw the fear in his eyes.

"You shouldn't have done that," she said.

"I'm sorry, Ilsa," he said. "I didn't mean to hurt you."

She studied him for a moment. Looked him up and down. For the first time, she understood the power her sex had over men. And she let out a laugh. A long, high-pitched, wild shriek, like the laugh of a hyena.

CHAPTER 42

Ilsa went home that day with the pen in the pocket of her skirt. She'd endured his advances in exchange for something she wanted. A small smile came over her face. *I can get anything I want using sex. It was ugly, but it was easy. And it certainly is powerful.*

Ilsa didn't bother being angry at Klaus for what happened. She didn't even hate him. It was an important lesson, and she learned from it. Klaus taught her that men were easily manipulated with sex, and from now on she planned to get everything she wanted from them by using her body.

From that day on, Ilsa used her sexuality to get anything she wanted. She showed one boy her thigh, and he took her to the movies. She let him kiss her and caress her breast, and he gave her the money he earned that week working on one of the potato farms. It was easy, and she liked the fact that she had control. It excited her. She found that if she thought of sex as nothing but an exchange, she was able to turn off all her emotions when the boys touched her body. They sometimes felt guilty. She never did. Ilsa felt nothing.

The little farming village where Ilsa grew up was a close-knit community of families that had lived in the same area for decades. In the autumn of 1934, old man Echert, the owner of one of the farms, died of a sudden heart attack. He had two sons, Alexander, who lived on the farm, and the other, Peter, who lived in Nuremberg where he had gone to school and now practiced law. Peter Echert returned to the farm to attend his father's funeral. He was a tall, blond, and handsome man. His education gave him a sophisticated air that was uncommon among the farmers. He brought with him his young wife, who was plain and quiet, and their 2 three-year-old twin boys.

The day of the funeral, Adelle and Ilsa, like all the women in the community, brought food to the house of the mourners. Ilsa placed the pies she and her stepmother had baked, on the long wooden table that had been set up in the living room. Since Ilsa had slimmed down, her stepmother could no longer call her Butterball. However, now, instead of taunting Ilsa, Adelle watched her step-daughter with envy in her eyes. Ilsa had grown into a natural beauty, something that Adelle never was. Adelle's only attribute had been her slender figure, which had softened and filled out since she'd given birth to her son, Falk. The hatred between Ilsa and Adelle still burned. But Adelle found she often needed Ilsa's help with Falk as she did today at the home of the mourners. "Can you keep an eye on Falk for a minute?" Adelle asked Ilsa.

Ilsa nodded. No one knew it, but Ilsa hated her stepbrother because, unlike Ilsa, Falk was given plenty of love and attention by both of his parents. Sometimes, when no one was looking, she pinched him until he cried.

Ilsa sat down on the floor and made a half-hearted attempt to keep Falk amused. As she played with her brother, she happened to catch a glimpse of Adelle ogling Peter. The look she saw in Adelle's eyes was familiar to her. She'd seen it in the eyes of the boys who tried to kiss her or touch her. It was the look of desire, the look of longing. In a single instant, she knew that her stepmother had grown discontented with her father, who was little more than an ignorant farmer. Adelle was yearning for a different life, a better life. And she was wildly attracted to this handsome, young man in his fine suit.

A smile washed over Ilsa's face. This was what she'd been waiting for since the day Adelle first called her Butterball.

CHAPTER 43

ILSA HAD A PLAN.

She began by walking over to Peter and making casual conversation. "I'm sorry about your father," she said to him, making her big blue eyes wide.

"Thank you," he said.

At first, he seemed disinterested, and she was afraid her plan might fail, but she continued to chat with him. She asked him general questions about his children, about his law practice, but the conversation kept stalling. Then she began to talk to him about the Nazi Party.

"I'm a member," he told her proudly. "I am very excited about Adolf Hitler and what he plans to do to improve our fatherland."

"Yes, so am I. In fact, I belong to a group called the Bund Deutscher Mädels. Are you familiar with it?"

"I have heard of it, but I am not really familiar with it," he said.

Then she began to tell him all about the organization. "It's the girls division of the Hitler Youth. We spend time doing wonderful things like sports and cookouts. But we also learn about our fatherland. We study the words of our great führer and learn what it means to be a part of the superior Aryan race. Being an Aryan woman is a big responsibility. We must know what will be expected of us when we grow up and how to be good German women." She was alight with passion as she declared her love for the party and for the fatherland. And in between her patriotic declarations she made sure to cross her legs and show him just enough of her thigh to spark his interest. They spoke on and off throughout the remainder of the evening.

Peter and his wife stayed on at Peter's father's farm for a week to help his brother get settled. During that week, Ilsa found reasons to see him but so did her stepmother. They dropped by often bringing food for the grieving family.

On the night before Peter was to leave to return home, Ilsa and her mother brought over a noodle casserole. The family was about to sit down to eat when Ilsa passed by Peter and gently brushed against his arm. Then careful to make sure no one saw her, she slipped him a note.

"Meet me in the barn at nine p.m.," the note read.

He read the note and quickly tucked it back into the breast pocket of his suit jacket. He stared at her, and she could see in his eyes that a spark of desire had been ignited. Ilsa smiled.

CHAPTER 44

FROM THE MOMENT HE FIRST SAW ILSA, PETER WAS INTRIGUED BY her beauty, but he tried to fight his fascination. This was not the first time he'd found himself attracted to a girl who was too young for him. To make matters worse, after their children were born, his wife became less exciting to him. She smelled of breast milk and was always busy caring for their babies. It wasn't that he didn't love her, but the passion had gone out of their lovemaking. She didn't approach their coupling with the same passion she'd had when they were young. Now it seemed to have become a chore to her, an obligation.

When Peter looked at Ilsa, he saw a young, vibrant, and tender peach. And since they met, Peter couldn't stop thinking about her. Whenever they spoke, she either bent down to expose just enough cleavage for his imagination to run wild, or she crossed her legs and allowed her skirt to travel up her thigh sending his fantasies soaring. Even though he knew he would hurt his wife if she ever found out, Peter wanted Ilsa. He'd hoped that he would find a way to keep his desire in check, so when Ilsa gave him the note asking to him to meet her, he was both excited and terrified of his own emotions. He knew he should tear that note to shreds and not go to meet Ilsa alone in the barn that night. The right thing to do was to spend the evening packing and getting ready to return home with his family. He should put the little vixen out of his mind. But Peter Echert knew that he wasn't going to do any of those things. He was going to get dressed, make an excuse to his family, and race out of the house to meet Ilsa at the barn. It was already seven o'clock. Two more hours. And . . . he could hardly wait.

CHAPTER 45

ILSA KNEW HER FAMILY WOULD BE ASLEEP WHEN SHE SNUCK OUT OF the house to meet Peter. It had rained earlier that afternoon, and the grass was still wet. She loved the darkness of night. It was mysterious and full of danger, but sometimes it scared her too. Occasionally, she saw monsters in the shadows as she did tonight. She ran faster.

There was no light in the barn at all, and she didn't have a candle. The sounds of wild animals outside made her jump. And for an instant she thought about running back home, but then the door creaked open, and she heard his voice.

"Ilsa . . ."

"I'm here," she whispered.

The door creaked shut.

She pulled him down into a pile of soft hay and began kissing him. She let him put his hands all over her. But when he tried to take off his pants to have intercourse she refused.

"You're leaving tomorrow," she said.

"Yes, I have to."

"And you're married."

"Yes."

"So, what do you want with me?" she purred.

"You asked me to meet you here."

"And you came," she said, smiling in the dark.

"I'm mad about you."

She let out a small laugh. "Are you?"

He didn't answer her. He was breathing heavy, and his hand was caressing her breast. She removed it. "You want something from me? I want something from you."

"What is it? What do you want? Money? A pretty dress?"

She laughed again. This time it was that same high-pitched hyena shriek. "No, silly, nothing like that," she said, then she touched his cheek and continued, "I want you to seduce my stepmother."

"What?" he asked, shocked.

"You heard me."

"Why?"

"I want her to fall in love with you and leave my father, for you."

"I can't do that. What am I going to do with her once I've done that? I certainly don't want my wife to find out about this."

"She would never tell your wife. And once you've seduced her you can be done with her. She won't be able to tolerate living with my father anymore. And Adelle would be too ashamed to ever tell anyone. So she would be very discreet. Believe me, I know she wouldn't want everyone in town to find out. So she will keep her mouth shut. Besides, she's attractive for her age. Don't you think?"

He nodded. "I suppose. But not as pretty as you."

She laughed. "And you want me, yes? You are obsessed with the wanting of me. You want to feel my naked, young body under you, now, don't you?"

"Yes," he admitted.

"Then . . ."

"Ilsa? How can I do this? You ask for the impossible."

"Very well, if it's impossible, then I will leave here, and we will never meet again."

He grabbed her arm, squeezing a little too tight. She wiggled away.

"But I thought you liked me. I thought that perhaps I would come and visit you every few months . . ." he said. "I would bring you pretty dresses, ribbons for your hair. Jewelry, even."

"Don't be a fool. I know you're married. And I know that once you have had me you'll never come back. Let's face the facts, Peter. You are never going to leave your wife. I am nothing but a toy to you."

"That's not true . . ."

"I may be young, but I know what is going on. And I know you want to make love to me. You want it very much, no?"

He nodded. "Yes," he whispered, defeated. He did want her. He wanted her so badly that his manhood ached.

"You want to have your fun? I understand. And I am willing to give you what you want. But nothing comes without a cost. If you want me to spread my legs for you, then you must do as I ask."

She stood up and buttoned her dress. Shaking the hay from her clothes and legs, Ilsa sighed. Then she began to walk toward the door.

"Wait," he said. She'd conquered him. Then he added, "I'll do it."

"I thought you would." She smiled in the darkness.

"So, come back here?" He beckoned and pointed to the bed of hay beside him.

"No. Not yet. First you must do as I ask. Then you get your reward." She walked out and ran back home through the darkness.

CHAPTER 46

PETER BRUSHED OFF HIS CLOTHES AND WENT BACK TO THE HOUSE. He needed to leave the farm and return to work, but he couldn't. This wild, young girl was all he could think about. He smelled her cheap perfume when he tried to sleep. He remembered her soft white skin illuminated in the moonlight. How he wished he'd never met her.

This was not the first time Peter had found himself obsessed with a girl under sixteen. It had happened twice before. There was something sweet, forbidden, and exciting about a girl who had never given birth to a child.

One of the girls he'd become infatuated with was his law partner's niece, who came to visit on Christmas, and the other was a girl who worked in the hat shop where he bought his hats. Neither of them ever knew of his secret desire. And although his heart fluttered when he saw them, he never let things progress. Instead, he made excuses why he was unable to attend his business partner's holiday party. And to avoid the other girl, he found an alternative shop to buy his hats.

In the beginning of his marriage he was satisfied, if not completely happy, with his wife. She was obedient. And she was not an altogether bad person even if she did brag to the other women about how much money he made. And even though she did spend his hard-earned money far too readily, she took care of his home and family. But for years now, since his twins were born, he'd felt as if something inside him had died. His sexual desire for his wife had completely faded. He began to think it was just a symptom of aging. But since his tryst with Ilsa in the barn he began to feel alive again. His sexual juices had begun to stir. He tried masturbating to quench his needs. But all that served to do was make him want Ilsa even more. He yearned for her so deeply that he could not return to the city. He lied to his wife and told her that he was not ready to go home because he was still prostrate with grief over losing his father.

"You take the children and go home," he told his wife. "I want to stay on here for a while. If I am here, I can help my brother with the farm. And besides that, I need to be close to my father's grave. At least for a little while longer."

"I don't mind staying with you."

"No. I want you to go back. Take the children and go back."

"But why? And what about your job?"

"I need to be here alone. I just need you to do as I ask. As far as my job is concerned, I will speak to them. I am a partner, and I've never taken a holiday, so they will understand. You go home now. Your mother and sisters are in the city. They will help you with the twins. Besides, I think having the children around is too hard on my brother and his wife right now. I think seeing the children is a constant reminder to my brother's wife that she is barren." He was firm. And his wife, a girl who had always done as he told her to do, finally agreed to go home.

Then Peter told his brother his plans to send his family back to the city. "I'm going to stay for a short while to help you on the farm," Peter told his brother, Alexander.

His brother was surprised as Peter had never shown any interest in farming. But working the farm alone was a daunting task, so he just nodded and said, "Thank you. I could certainly use the help."

After Peter's wife and children boarded the train back to the city,

Peter left the train station and made his way to the Guhr family farm.

"Peter?" Adelle quickly smoothed her hair as she opened the door. "What brings you here?"

"I came to buy some things for my brother and his wife."

"What can I get for you?" she asked. Her hands were trembling, so she tried to hide them in her apron.

"Milk, cheese." He smiled. *This will be easy. I can see it in her eyes. She is very attracted to me. And Ilsa's right, she's no beauty, but she's not a bad-looking woman for her age. Still not nearly as exciting as her stepdaughter.*

They went out to the cooler by the barn. She bent over to retrieve a round wheel of cheese.

"Let me help you. A beautiful and delicate woman like you shouldn't be lifting something so heavy. You might hurt yourself." He smiled. Her lips quivered as she returned his smile.

"Thank you," she stammered.

"I don't want you to think me forward, but well, I don't know how to say this . . ."

She looked away.

Then he continued, "I sent my family home. But I stayed on. Do you know why?"

She shook her head.

"I stayed on because, well, because I wanted to get to know you. I realize we are both married. I realize that I have no right to speak to you this way, and you are probably going to slap my face, but I am very attracted to you. I think you are beautiful. I have wanted to say this since the first moment I saw you."

Adelle glanced up at him. "Oh!" she stammered, suddenly shocked and embarrassed. Her face turned red and hot. You should go," she said in a soft but unconvincing voice.

"Yes, I probably should."

She nodded. "Let me get you the milk."

"By the way, when do you go to the market?"

"What?"

"Do you go into town?"

"Not often. Why?"

"Have you ever been to a nice restaurant?"

"I've never been to any restaurant."

"I'd love to take you." He smiled.

"Peter, I don't think so."

"Oh, come on. I promise to behave."

Adelle quickly glanced into his eyes. He was so handsome. His clothes were tailored, and his shoes looked like fine leather. She compared him to her husband. Hans was a farmer, dirty and sweating most of the time. He had never been a very demonstrative man. And he had never been one to openly show appreciation or affection. She assumed Hans loved her, but he never told her so. In fact, in all the years they'd spent together he'd never once said she was beautiful. *It would be so exciting to go to a real restaurant. I don't have a nice enough dress though. I would have to wear my church dress. It's wrong. All this is very wrong, and I must be mad for even considering it.*

"I can't go to a restaurant with you. What if someone sees us?"

"I know a very secluded little place where no one would ever find us."

She looked at him and thought about his wife's beautiful clothes. Her fine leather shoes and handbag. Her expensive hat. She thought about her own handmade dresses and how she had to beg Hans for money to buy fabric when she needed a new one. And he'd always insisted that she fix her old clothes rather than buying anything new. In fact, it had been years since she had made a dress for herself.

"Dinner?" she said, cocking her head. "In a restaurant? What would I wear?"

"It doesn't matter. You would look beautiful in whatever you chose to wear."

She hesitated for a moment. *I will not be young forever*, she thought. Then she said, "All right. I'll go."

CHAPTER 47

ADELLE PUT ON THE ONLY DECENT DRESS SHE OWNED, THEN SHE walked into the kitchen where Ilsa was shelling peas. "Ilsa," she said, "you must watch your brother for me for a few hours. I have to go into town."

"At this time of evening?" Ilsa toyed with her.

"Yes," Adelle said. Then when Ilsa gave her a questioning look, she added, "Yes, Ilsa. I don't want to tell your father yet because I don't want to frighten him. But I am going to see a doctor. I've been having female problems."

Since Adelle almost never left the house without her son, Ilsa assumed her stepmother was going to meet Peter. She had to cover her mouth with her hand to hide her smile. *Everything is going according to my plan*, she thought.

"Of course I'll watch him, Mother. You go on," Ilsa said in her sweetest voice. "I hope everything is all right."

Ilsa heard the door open to the little farmhouse at nine o'clock in the evening. She giggled a little as she lay in her bed. *I wonder if my stupid father will believe she went to see a doctor in his office at this time of night.* Ilsa wished she could hear the conversation between her father and Adelle, but they were too quiet.

The following morning, Ilsa made her way to Peter's father's farm with a freshly baked pie. "I just wanted to drop in and see how you were all doing." She ignored Peter addressing his sister-in-law instead.

"As best we can without Dad," she said.

"I understand," Ilsa said. "Well, my stepmother asked me to bring this over." She handed the pie to the woman. "I hope you enjoy it."

"Tell her thanks so much. I am sure we will."

Ilsa smiled then she left. As she was walking back home, Peter caught up with her.

"You sure do walk fast," he said, out of breath from running. "I am glad you came by. I was hoping to see you."

She stopped and turned to look at him. "And? Did you ever do anything about what we talked about?" Ilsa wanted to be sure that Peter and Adelle had seen each other the previous night.

"In fact, yes. I did. I was going to tell you in church on Sunday. I saw Adelle last night."

"And? Did you?"

"Have intercourse?"

"Yes, did you?"

"Yes," he said.

"Good. That's perfect. When do you plan to see her again?"

"I don't know. What about us? What about you and I?"

She giggled. "One more time with Adelle. Then I'll keep my promise to you. But this time I want to know where and when you are going to meet her. I have to catch the two of you together to verify that you have really done what I asked."

"You're not serious?"

"Oh, yes I am."

"Meet me at the creek tonight at ten. I'll go and see Adelle this afternoon while your father is out working. I'll arrange a time and place. I'll give you all the details tonight."

She nodded. He touched her hand then brought it to his lips and kissed her palm. Ilsa pulled her hand away. "Not yet," she said.

. . .

That night, Ilsa arrived at the creek fifteen minutes late. Peter was waiting for her, pacing anxiously.

"So, did you arrange to meet Adelle?"

"Yes, your father is going into town on Monday. He should be gone for the entire day. Adelle is planning to send you and the baby to visit her sister, your aunt. She said she will arrange to be alone, and I can come and see her at your house."

"What time are you coming?"

"Early afternoon. About one"

"Perfect. Take her to bed, and keep her there all day if you can."

He grabbed her and pulled her into his arms. Then he kissed her. She let out that high-pitched cackle that had become her sound of triumph. "Soon enough," she promised.

CHAPTER 48

ON SUNDAY NIGHT WHEN EVERYONE WAS ASLEEP, ILSA WENT downstairs and loosened the wheel on her father's wagon. It would take a few miles of riding before it fell off entirely. That would be perfect. It would give Peter and Adelle just enough time to get into bed and get started.

In the morning, Hans hitched the wagon and grabbed the lunch Adelle had packed for him. Then he set out to go to town.

"I want you to take the baby and go to Aunt Mary's farm. She said the apples are ready for picking. Go with Falk and pick a basket. You can stay there for the day. Tomorrow we can make some pies. I know how much you enjoy picking apples," Adelle said.

"Have you asked Aunt Mary if it's all right?"

"She said she would love to have you and Falk for the day."

"Then I'll get the baby and go." Ilsa smiled sweetly.

Adelle had been treating Ilsa much nicer since she and Peter had been seeing each other. That was because she needed Ilsa to care for Falk so that she had the free time she needed. It made Ilsa smile to know she was about to expose Adelle's secret.

Ilsa walked about a half of a mile, then she sat down on the side of the road with her stepbrother and waited. She tried to amuse the child so he wouldn't cry. He giggled and tugged at her hair. Then he threw his arms around her neck and kissed her. Falk loved attention, which Ilsa found annoying. She would have preferred he weren't with her.

Once the sun was high enough in the sky to let her know it was well past noon, Ilsa began to head back to her parents' farm. She came into the house quietly, but her brother cried out. "Mama. Where is Mama?"

She would have liked to strangle him to keep him quiet. *Damn you, Falk,* she thought. Surely Adelle had heard him. Ilsa had to work quickly now. Ilsa searched the house, running through the rooms as fast as she could, but Peter and Adelle were not inside. She put her brother into his crib. He immediately began fussing and reaching for her. She didn't pick him up. She closed the door, and when she did she heard him begin to wail.

Quickly, Ilsa walked out to the barn, then she stood outside and listened. A smile washed over her face when she heard her step-mother moaning. *This is even better than finding them in the house. This is perfect. Take your time, Peter,* she thought. *If my calculations are right, my father should be home any minute.* It was a quarter of an hour before her father came riding home on the horse without the cart. She ran to meet him. "What happened, Father? Are you all right? Did you have an accident with the cart?"

"No, the wheel fell off. I had to come back home to get some tools to fix it," he said in his matter-of-fact voice.

Then, just as Ilsa had hoped he would, her father walked into the barn. Ilsa followed behind him. Peter and Adelle were naked lying on a pile of hay. Ilsa saw the look of shock and fear on Peter's face. He hadn't been expecting Hans. He thought Ilsa would come in alone, but here was Hans red faced from heat. There was shock, disbelief, and then pain in Hans's eyes. Adelle grabbed her dress to cover herself. She got up and ran to Hans. "I'm sorry," she said. "I don't know what came over me. I never meant to do this."

He shook his head. "I never thought you would do anything like this," he said. He looked at Peter and at the straw where he'd just seen his wife naked beneath another man. Then he turned his gaze back to Adelle's eyes. In a small voice Hans asked, "Have I been such a bad husband to you? Have you ever gone hungry?"

Adelle began to cry. She reached out her hands for Hans, but he turned away leaving her in the barn with her head bent. Peter glared at Ilsa. She cracked a smile. Peter stood up and got dressed quickly. Then as he was about to leave, he walked over to Ilsa and whispered in her ear, "Meet me at the creek at ten tonight?"

"Yes, you've earned it." She smiled, remembering what the boy had said to her when he gave her his mother's pen. Then she said, "I'll be there."

Peter could not look at Adelle. Once he was dressed he walked out of the barn.

Adelle began putting her dress back on. Her hands were shaking. "Your father is going to leave me," she said, "and I deserve it." She was still crying. "Where is the baby?" she asked.

Ilsa didn't answer. "You stupid bitch," she said. "You don't even know what happened, do you?"

Adelle looked at Ilsa blankly. There was pain in her eyes. She'd hurt Hans, and she felt terribly guilty. "I don't know what you mean."

"I set you up. It was me. It was all me—Butterball. I sent Peter here to seduce you, and you fell for it like an overripened apple falls to the ground. Of course my father is going to leave you. Peter is going to leave you too. He'll go back to his family. You will be all alone, and your reputation will be so soiled that no one will have anything to do with you. And by the way, I just saw you naked, and you're getting fat. Perhaps your new nickname should be Butterball." Ilsa let out her high-pitched shriek. Then she turned away from Adelle and left the barn.

Ilsa was glad that her father was in his bedroom with the door closed when she went into the house. As quickly as possible, she gathered the few things she owned and put them into a cardboard suitcase that had belonged to Adelle. Then she took all the emergency money her stepmother kept in a jar in the kitchen and tucked it into her dress pocket. Falk let out a cry, but Ilsa ignored him. The front door of the farmhouse where she'd lived her entire life snapped shut as she walked out and began trekking down the dirt road. Not even once did she look back. Everything in that house was in her past. And Ilsa Guhr was done with the past.

The dusty road was covered with the colorful leaves of fall. She marveled at their beauty. Then she thought of Peter waiting for her by the creek tonight. She thought of how shocked and hurt he would be when she never came. *He is nothing but a pig. He deserves to suffer. That stupid man was more than willing to ruin a woman's life just so he could take a young girl, who is too young for him, into his bed. I don't feel a bit sorry for any of them. They all got what they deserved.* Ilsa shook her head. Then her high-pitched laughter broke the silence of the afternoon. She laughed so hard that she had to stop walking for a few minutes and clutch her side.

Then she took the money she'd stolen, out of her dress pocket, and put it into her handbag. *My new life begins today!*

CHAPTER 49

November 1934

Ilsa got into town just before sunset and wandered into the local beer hall. She ordered a beer and smiled at an older man who was sitting across the bar. She didn't recognize him, and being that it was a small village meant he was not from the area. Within a few minutes, he was sitting beside her buying her drinks and rubbing her thigh under the table.

"I need a ride out of here," she said bluntly.

He nodded. "All right."

Ilsa grabbed her suitcase and followed the man outside.

She never knew his name, but it didn't matter to her. Ilsa gave him sex, which was what he wanted, and he drove her all the way to Berlin. Once they arrived, they checked into a cheap hotel where they had two days of wild sex. In the morning on the third day, he told her that he'd had a good time with her, but he had to get home to his wife. She wasn't upset that he didn't care about her. She'd never expected him to. But as he walked out the door, she felt a little afraid being alone in a big city. Taking her handbag, she descended the flight of stairs from her room to the main lobby of the hotel.

She walked up to the clerk and explained that she would like to pay to keep her room for a full week. But when she opened her handbag, all the money she'd taken from her stepmother's emergency fund was gone. *Damn that bastard. He stole my money.* If that man would have been standing in front of her, she would have grabbed the scissors off the hotel clerk's desk and stabbed him. Desperate, Ilsa begged the hotel clerk to let her stay for a few days until she was able to find work and pay, but the woman refused. "I'm sorry, it's not our policy. Pay in advance is the way we do it here," the clerk said.

It was early November, and a dagger of fear struck through Ilsa's heart when she thought about the upcoming winter. Having nowhere else to go, she walked to the train station and sat down on the bench. Looking around the crowded station, she felt like crying. *That bastard stole all my money. Now I have to find a job in a hurry,* she thought. *I need a place to stay. Sitting here is accomplishing nothing.* Her stomach growled with hunger too. So she got up and walked back into town. All day long she went from shop to shop looking for employment, until she saw a woman's dress shop. The sign above the store said Weinstein's Fine Apparel for Women. The large picture window was filled with lovely dresses and suits. Ilsa looked down at her worn-out, handmade dress, and she turned away. *I can't go in there looking like this,* she thought. *But what difference does it make? So what if they laugh at me? I am so hungry that I can't keep wandering around. And as it is, I am going to have to go back to the train station to spend the night.* She entered the dress shop and huddled in the corner. There was a man and his wife behind the counter and several elegantly dressed women scanning the clothing racks. The man was short and heavyset; his wife was short but slender. The wife spotted Ilsa and came out from behind the counter. She wore black, high-heeled pumps that clicked on the floor as she walked over to Ilsa.

"Can I help you, dear?" the woman asked.

Ilsa shook her head, and intimidated, she turned to walk out of the store.

"Wait," the woman said.

Ilsa turned around.

"You look hungry. Are you?"

"Yes, I am very hungry. And I need a job," Ilsa said, then she fabricated a story. She told the woman that she had come to Berlin with her new husband, and he left her there alone.

"Well, that's terrible. Why don't you follow me, and let's see if we can't get you something to eat."

Ilsa felt tears welling in her eyes. "Thank you."

"Marsha, get this girl some latkes, will you?"

A pretty, young girl with dark hair and bright blue eyes came walking out of the back of the store. "Of course, Mama," she said.

"I'm Esther Weinstein. This is my husband, Sam, and this is our daughter, Marsha." The older woman said, "You look to be close to Marsha's age. What's your name, child?"

"I'm Ilsa Guhr."

"It's nice to meet you."

Marsha set a plate of latkes in front of Ilsa. "I'm afraid they might have gotten cold. They were left from our lunch, but that was several hours ago. I hope you enjoy them anyway."

Ilsa gobbled the latkes with a dollop of applesauce. She ate so fast that she couldn't stop to speak.

"We could use some help here in the store, couldn't we, Sam?" Esther Weinstein said.

"Sure. We can always use help here."

"Let's get you a few dresses to wear when you're working. And, by the way . . . where are you staying right now?"

Ilsa looked down. "I was going to sleep in the train station."

"Nonsense. We have a room right here behind the store. You can stay here."

Ilsa began to cry. "Thank you," she said. "Why are you being so kind to me?"

"It's a mitzva. Thank you for allowing me to do a mitzva." Esther smiled. "That means a blessing. I am blessed because I am able to help you."

In the beginning, Ilsa was grateful to the Weinsteins for their generosity, but as the months passed, and she watched Marsha waltz out of the shop after work with her wealthy American boyfriend, wearing lovely dresses and delicate jewelry, jealousy began to stir in Ilsa.

That summer, Marsha took Ilsa to Munich for a few days to thank her for all her hard work. The Weinsteins adored their daughter and they indulged her. She attended university and took piano lessons. Even though Marsha was very kind to Ilsa, Ilsa resented her. Ilsa's father had never loved her like that, and she could hardly remember her real mother.

Winter came again, and this time the Weinsteins gave Ilsa a brand new wool coat for Christmas. Even though they celebrated Hanukkah, they wanted Ilsa to feel like a part of the family. They wanted her to know that they accepted and respected her religion too.

Ilsa's jealousy started small but it grew, and as it did, Ilsa began to plan revenge. Using her sexuality as a weapon again, she set about to seduce Marsha's boyfriend. He succumbed to her sexual advances rather quickly. However, when she threatened to tell Marsha what had happened between them, hoping to hurt them both, she was disappointed to find out that Marsha and the American were only childhood friends. He had come to Berlin to study art for the winter. They had no plans to marry. Marsha intended to start medical school. She had plans to become a doctor. This infuriated Ilsa even more. However, Marsha's American friend didn't trust Ilsa. He told Marsha everything that happened between himself and Ilsa, and he warned that Ilsa was not a friend to the Weinsteins, especially Marsha. Marsha told her parents what her boyfriend said, and they fired Ilsa.

"Can I just stay the night? I'm so sorry for what happened. I know you don't believe me, but it was all his fault. He seduced me. I don't know why I let it happen. I got caught up," Ilsa begged, with tears in her eyes. Now that she had to face the consequences for her actions, she regretted having done such a pointless and stupid thing. "Please, I'm begging you. It's so bitter cold outside. And it's late."

"Very well, we aren't going to turn you out in the middle of the night. But it's best that you go as soon as possible," Mrs. Weinstein said.

"I will leave early in the morning. You won't see me again."

Mrs. Weinstein didn't say another word. She turned and left the store.

Ilsa sat on the cot where she'd slept since she'd begun working for the Weinsteins. She was angry at herself for doing what she'd done. *Why do I do these things? Why can't I let myself be happy? I had a place to stay that was rent free. It was clean and warm too. The Weinsteins gave me a decent job. It didn't pay a fortune, but it was enough. Why did I ever do this? I was blinded by hate and jealousy of that girl. It wasn't my fault it was hers. Her's and her parents. If they had not had so much money and flaunted their wealth in my face, I would never have been so jealous. And now that bitch, Mrs. Weinstein, is sending me away in the middle of winter. Well, that's just fine. I'll leave. I'll go away and never come back. I have some money saved from the money I earned. I'll be fine. But first I am going to make them pay for what they did to me . . ."*

Ilsa took the scissors out of the drawer and walked from the backroom apartment, where she slept, into the main store. Rage filled her. Her hands shook. And by the time she was done, she had cut up all the dresses in the store that were not in her size. Then she packed the ones that fit her, along with her own clothes, and walked out without locking the shop door.

An icy wind bit her cheeks as she entered the train station. She boarded a train which took her to the other side of Berlin where she rented a cheap hotel room.

CHAPTER 50

ILSA FLOUNDERED. SHE COULD NOT FIND A PLACE FOR HERSELF. FIRST she found a job working in a factory. It was long hours and she hated it. One day she left her machine unattended to go outside and smoke. Her recklessness caused another worker to be hurt in an accident. She was let go.

Next she was hired as a waitress in a restaurant where she lasted for almost two years. The other waitresses were more friendly and outgoing than Ilsa. They made the customers feel comfortable, and consequently they were more well liked. They got the better shifts and were treated better in general. Ilsa blamed the owner for giving the others preferential treatment, deciding that the owner, through no fault of her own, just didn't like her. So she began stealing money. At first she only took a little. But soon she was taking more and more from the money box each night she worked. When she was caught by the owner, he threatened to press charges. But she wept and carried on so much that he, a nonconfrontational man, finally said, "I won't call the police. But get out of here, and don't come back. I don't ever want to see you again."

By 1939, Ilsa was miserable and desperate. When she left home, she hadn't thought that living on her own would be so difficult and that earning her own living would be a daily grind. And over the past few years Ilsa had developed a love for cigarettes and alcohol, both of which put a financial drain on her. The small hotel room she rented was a dingy, rat-infested place with a small kitchen and a lumpy mattress that had bedbugs. The bathroom down the hall was a breeding ground for cockroaches that were bold enough to run across the walls as soon as the light was turned on. She spent all her free time alone because she had no friends. Most nights after work she went to her room and drank. However, occasionally, when she was out of beer or schnapps, she went to the local tavern to have a drink. It was on such a night that Ilsa's life was changed forever.

She sat at the bar drinking a beer. The bartender had the radio on loud enough for all the patrons to hear. Ilsa took a sip of her beer when she heard the familiar voice of Dr. Goebbels on the radio. He was speaking about how the führer was Germany's savior. She'd heard him speak before, and there was no doubt that he was well spoken and very logical. Then Dr. Goebbels introduced the führer, Adolf Hitler. The führer's strong voice came through the radio, quiet at first, building momentum, persuasive and full of promise until it filled the entire room. Everyone in the tavern grew quiet to listen. Including Ilsa. She was mesmerized by the power in the führer's voice. And the truth she heard in his words resonated with her. Before she knew it, she and all the other people in the tavern were clapping and cheering for Adolf Hitler. They were raising their hands to salute him almost as if he were right there in person in the tavern instead of just a voice on the radio. It was exhilarating. Hitler was promising a better world for the German people. Promising to restore Germany to the greatness it deserved. And promising to take back all that the Jews had stolen from the Germans and return it to its rightful owners. Not only was he making these promises, he was making them with such conviction that Ilsa truly believed that every vow he made to the German people would be fulfilled.

A man who was sitting at the bar a few feet away from Ilsa smiled at her. He was not handsome, but he wore a uniform that gave him an air of power and superiority. She returned his smile.

"Our führer is quite marvelous, isn't he?" the man said.

"He is," Ilsa agreed.

"He will save Germany. I know it."

"I believe he will."

"I'm Oberstrumbannführer Fredrich, but you can call me Wolf-gang. And your name?"

"I'm Ilsa Guhr," she said.

"Are you hungry, Ilsa? Can I buy you dinner?"

She smiled and nodded. By the time they'd finished eating, he had offered her a job working as a guard at the first prison camp that the Nazis were building which would be only for women. It was to be opening in the spring. He made the job sound important and glamorous.

"Not only will you be helping to rid the Reich of her enemies, but you will be paid good wages and live in nice accommodations right on the grounds."

Ilsa smiled.

She was also promised beautiful, well-made uniforms to wear. Ilsa was elated. This new job proposition seemed to be everything she could have hoped for. It seemed to be a solution to all her problems. The name of the prison camp was Ravensbrück.

CHAPTER 51

Before Ilsa started working at Ravensbrück, she'd been looked down upon by the owners of the business where she worked. She became known as a drifter. And she always felt insecure because she was at the mercy of the whims of her bosses.

But once she started to work at Ravensbrück and the prisoners arrived, Ilsa found herself in a place of power. Never before had anyone shown her respect. Never before had she had so much control over others. All her life, Ilsa felt beneath the other girls she met. In school she'd been teased mercilessly. Then once she became an adult she always felt like an outsider. It was easy for her to use her sexuality to control men, but women never seemed to accept her. Ilsa hated these women, but she enjoyed dominating them. So she began to delve into the inner depths of her own depravation. Ilsa found there were very few rules as to what she was allowed to do to the prisoners. She imposed sadistic sexual torture on the prisoners: sometimes beating them, sometimes even killing them.

For the first time in her life, Ilsa felt like she was coming out of her shell, and she began exploring all sorts of new things. On occasion, she had sexual encounters with the other female guards. And then there were numerous dates and one-night stands with the male SS officers, some married, others not. Most of the time she had no emotions at all. She could go through the motions of a complete relationship and feel nothing at all.

Only one person, whom she met at Ravensbrück, touched her cold heart. His dark hair was shiny like black leather. His eyes were deep and mysterious. He was meticulously clean, handsome, and educated. A doctor. One of the prison doctors who was notorious for his sadistic experiments on the prisoners. He and Ilsa had worked together for a while. From the first time she met him, she felt connected to him as she had never felt to any other person. They had wild and experimental sex. But when he found out about her appetite for homosexual encounters, he said he could overlook anything but that. And he broke off the relationship. Then without saying goodbye to Ilsa, he moved to another prison. Ilsa was heartbroken. She was not ready to let him go, so she kept in contact with him by sending him letters or calling him. And even though he was cruel to her when he occasionally dropped in to see her, she could not resist him. Ilsa continued to sleep with him whenever he wanted her.

Then one afternoon, Ilsa was called to the office of her superior where she was given new orders. "I want you to show a new recruit around the camp," her superior officer said. "Her name is Hilde Dusel. Show her to her quarters, and tell her what is expected of her. Understand?"

"Yes," Ilsa answered in a firm voice.

She hadn't thought much of the new assignment. After all, Ilsa had introduced several new recruits to Ravensbrück. However, from the first moment she saw Hilde, something inside her was uneasy. Hilde reminded her of herself when she was young, fat and unattractive. Her feelings toward Hilde were mixed; she found the heavy girl repugnant, and at the same time, she felt a need to keep Hilde close to her. Ilsa could not put this girl out of her mind. She yearned to play with Hilde, to toy with her mind and her body, but she didn't know why.

Ilsa seduced Hilde. The sex between them was both appalling and fascinating to Ilsa. It almost felt like she was having sex with her younger self.

Hilde made it clear that she had not really liked their sexual encounter, but she made it understood that she deeply valued Ilsa's friendship. Whenever Ilsa saw Hilde, she was excited by the admiration she saw in Hilde's eyes. This was fun for Ilsa. And she wanted to see just how far she could push Hilde. So one night she arranged for Hilde to join her in one of her sessions where she sexually tortured female prisoners. Ilsa saw the fear in Hilde's eyes, and it made her laugh. But she also saw that Hilde was excited by the power. This aspect of Hilde fascinated Ilsa far more than the prisoners who had no choice but to bend to her will.

Each day, Ilsa explored her sick obsession with Hilde pushing things harder and further. She would treat Hilde like a best friend, and then in the next breath, she would humiliate her. Ilsa enjoyed the confusion she saw in Hilde's eyes.

One day, Ilsa didn't even know why she did it, Ilsa called Hilde by her old nickname "Butterball." The look of hurt on Hilde's face made Ilsa smile. *I have the power to make her happy or make her sad. I can decide if she is miserable here at Ravensbrück or if she feels welcome. I control her like she is my own fat, little marionette.*

But as time passed and Ilsa's cruelty toward Hilde increased, Hilde began to pull away from Ilsa. Ilsa did not acknowledge that she was losing her friend because she treated Hilde so poorly. Ilsa was quite sure Hilde did not want her around because Axel, Hilde's fiancé, had become attracted to Ilsa. *Well, who could blame him after all. I am beautiful, and Hilde is ugly.* Ilsa could not help herself from flirting shamelessly with Axel, especially in front of Hilde. She enjoyed the distress she saw in Hilde's eyes and the power she had over her.

Then Hilde and Axel were married. Ilsa had expected to go to the wedding. But Hilde had purposely arranged things so that Ilsa would not be able to attend. Ilsa was livid. Then to make matters worse, she discovered that Hilde had invited another girl, whom she called her best friend. This was a girl Hilde knew from her childhood in Berlin. Her name was Gretchen. Ilsa was jealous of Gretchen. Who was this girl whom Hilde had dared to choose over her? Ilsa vowed to someday make Hilde pay for the slight.

Hilde got pregnant quickly, but she had an early miscarriage, then she conceived again within a couple of months. And because of her problems with her first pregnancy, the doctor suggested that Hilde stop working and get plenty of rest. So Hilde left her job at Ravensbrück. Ilsa thought that Hilde would stay in contact with her but she didn't. In fact, months passed without any word from Hilde. The next time Ilsa heard anything about Hilde, she learned that Hilde had gone to Berlin to visit her friend Gretchen. Ilsa felt left out. She had thrived on Hilde's worship of her, and now that she'd lost that worship, she needed to get it back. Ilsa needed to feel that she was in control of Hilde. And because of this, she was sick with jealousy over the relationship between Hilde and Gretchen. Each day that passed made her more angry. She thought of Hilde and how Hilde had replaced her so easily, and Ilsa was overcome with a strong need to hurt Hilde.

Three days later, to add to her dark mood, Ilsa overheard some SS officers talking at a party. The officers didn't realize anyone was listening, so they spoke candidly. They said things were looking bleak for Germany, and it looked as if the fatherland would lose the war. If this proved to be true, Ilsa needed to secure a safe place to escape. However, to do this she would need money, plenty of money. She had saved, working for the Reich, but not enough to pay for papers and safe passage out of the country if things did go sour. She had to find a way to get her hands on valuables. If these men were right and Germany did lose the war, reichsmarks would be worthless.

Then one of the camp doctors told Ilsa that Hilde had returned from Berlin. She'd miscarried again. The doctor, thinking Ilsa was Hilde's friend, confided that Hilde was distraught and might be close to a nervous breakdown.

Ilsa hid her true feelings. She told the doctor how sorry she was to hear that Hilde was doing so poorly. But when the doctor turned his back a smile washed over Ilsa's pretty face.

It was early one morning, and Ilsa was on her way to the beauty salon in Ravensbrück where she was stationed as a guard. She walked through the camp thinking that today she would have one of the prisoners pin curl her hair. That was when she happened to look around and saw Axel, Hilde's husband. He had just entered the children's camp. She ducked to hide behind the building so she could see what he was doing there. She listened intently. Axel was talking to one of the prisoners. Ilsa peeked around the corner to see whom he was speaking to. The woman was sitting on the ground holding a beautiful, blond, little boy on her lap. Ilsa heard the woman beg Axel to take care of her child. And he promised her that he would. Ilsa ducked back behind the building again. She didn't want to be seen, but she continued to watch and listen. She heard movement, but no one spoke, so she peeked around the corner. She saw Axel take the little boy in his arms and carry him out of the camp. Ilsa followed Axel but not too closely. He took the little boy to his car then drove away with the child. Ilsa needed to know more about this child and why Axel had taken him. The boy's mother was sitting on the ground crying when Ilsa walked into the children's camp.

"Who are you?" she asked. "What is your name?"

"Felicia Bankowski," Lila Rabinowitz lied. She was trembling, hoping that the SS officer who had just taken Moishe would not hurt him.

"What business do you have with that SS officer who was just here?"

Lila shook her head. "None."

"Was that your child he just took with him?"

"No. He was just one of the children here in the children's camp."

"Liar," Ilsa said. Then she walked out. She had to know the truth.

For the next three nights, Ilsa took several women out of the block where Lila slept and tortured them by burning them with her cigarettes. She was trying to find out anything she could about this woman who called herself Felicia. No one had any answers. Then finally Ilsa had a breakthrough when one of the women could not bear the pain.

"Her real name is Lila Rabinowitz; the child is Moishe Rabinowitz, her son," the prisoner said. She was still holding her arm where Ilsa had burned her ten times.

"Is she a Jew?" Ilsa asked.

"Yes, she confessed to being Jewish when we were on the transport. She is a Jew, but she is pretending to be a Gentile."

"Good. That's what I needed to know," Ilsa said. Then she shot the prisoner point-blank in the head.

"Clean this up," Ilsa said to the other prisoners who were in the block.

"Lila Rabinowitz," she whispered aloud. *Now I have to find out what Axel is planning to do with the child.*

Ilsa knew a man who worked with Axel. She asked him for Axel's schedule. He was so impressed with the pretty female guard that he gave her what she asked for. Then she began to follow Axel.

Ilsa didn't want Axel to suspect that she knew anything about him taking a child from the children's camp, so she waited for a month, watching him. She decided it was best to give him time to let his guard down. Then knowing where he would be, she decided to bump into him, all the while making their meeting seem purely accidental. His eyes lit up, and then a shy smile came over his flushed face when he saw her.

"Axel, how are you? It's been such a long time. How is Hilde?"

"She is coming along. I'm sorry to say that she was pregnant, but she miscarried again. Only this time it was very late in the pregnancy. "

"A second time?" Ilsa pretended to be shocked.

"Yes, a second time. But she is doing much better now than she was when it first happened."

"Oh, I'm truly glad to hear it. I would love to see her."

"Why don't you come to our home for dinner on Thursday evening? I know she would be very happy to see you."

"I would love to," Ilsa said, giving Axel her prettiest smile. *Perfect,* she thought. *I'll bring a nice bottle of schnapps, and then while we are having after-dinner drinks, I will see what I can find out about the child. I wonder if he is arranging escape routes for children and being paid handsomely to do it. If he is, perhaps I could earn some valuables by doing the same thing. I don't want reichsmarks, that's for sure. But the Jews have diamonds and gold. And I've been looking for a way to get my hands on some things that I can sell just in case Germany loses the war. And this might be just what I have been looking for.*

CHAPTER 52

ALL WEEK, ILSA TRIED TO THINK OF WAYS TO APPROACH THE SUBJECT of the child with Axel. She knew she must choose her words carefully. However, when she arrived on Thursday night, she found that she needn't have worried. The answers to all her questions were right in front of her. There, playing on the living room floor of Hilde and Axel's home, was the little boy she'd seen Axel carry out of the children's camp. The Jewish child whose name was Moishe Rabinowitz. Ilsa hoped that neither Hilde nor Axel heard her let out a gasp when she saw the boy. She watched as Hilde coddled Moishe and then called him Anatole. Hilde was tickling the child. He was laughing. Ilsa smiled. This was even better than she'd originally thought it would be. Now she knew how she was going to regain control of Hilde.

The blond-haired little boy was charming indeed. He gave Ilsa a hug and kiss before bed. But she knew the truth: he was a subhuman, a Jew, a trickster, even at his young age.

Axel took the child to put him to bed leaving Hilde and Ilsa to catch up. Once they were alone, Ilsa told Hilde what she knew about the child.

"His name is not Anatole. It's Moishe. He's a Jew. Your husband stole him from the children's camp at Ravensbrück."

"That is simply not true, Ilsa. How can you say such a thing?" Hilde's face was flushed.

"No need to worry, Hilde. I'm your best friend. I wouldn't do anything to hurt you . . . unless, of course, I had to, but . . ." She let out a short hyena laugh. "I promise you that little Anatole's secret will be safe because I am going to help you. I know who his mother is. I'll find her and kill her. Then," she said, "the only people who will know that little Anatole is really Moishe Rabinowitz will be you and Axel and me . . . of course."

Hilde was unnerved. Ilsa could see how upset she was, but Ilsa pretended not to notice. And she'd kept her promise.

The following day, Ilsa found Lila Rabinowitz and accused her of stealing food, then she shot her. It had been that simple.

After work , Ilsa went back to see Hilde to tell her that Lila Rabinowitz no longer posed a threat. That . . . and to tell her that she'd found out that Hilde's friend Gretchen had been arrested for harboring Jews.

"How did you find all of this out?" Hilde said, her hands were shaking.

"I know even more," Ilsa said proudly. "I know that you were the hero who was responsible for Gretchen's arrest."

"I am not a hero. I am so sorry that I hurt my friend Gretchen. I feel guilty about it every day."

"And once again, your good friend Ilsa can help you." Ilsa smiled. "As you well know, I have plenty of friends."

Hilde nodded.

"So I can use my influence to have Gretchen brought here to Ravensbrück. As long as she is here, you will be able to help her, yes?"

"I would try my best."

"I might be able to arrange for Gretchen to work for you. She could be your housekeeper and babysit Anatole."

"Oh yes, Ilsa. That would be wonderful. I would know she was safe, then. Would you really do that for me?"

"Of course I would."

Hilde's hands were trembling. Tears were forming in her eyes. She'd felt so guilty about the mistake she'd made that had led to Gretchen's arrest. This solution that Ilsa was proposing was heaven sent. "How can I ever thank you?" Hilde asked.

"Nothing is free, little butterball. I need something from you too. You must return to work at Ravensbrück. I need you to steal all the valuable jewelry you can get your hands on and give it to me."

"Steal from the Reich?" Hilde asked. There was a note of fear in her voice.

"We've taken jewelry before, you and I."

"Yes, we have but only a few pieces," Hilde said.

"Now I want you to take as much as your pockets can hold."

"This is dangerous. Very."

"Of course, but you want me to bring Gretchen here, don't you?"

"Yes."

"Well, then?"

"I'll do it." Hilde bowed her head in defeat and agreed as Ilsa knew she would. After all, not only was Ilsa going to do Hilde a big favor, but she also had plenty of dangerous information about Anatole, which gave her the power to destroy Hilde and Axel.

Ilsa was pleased with how the evening had gone. As she walked back to her room at Ravensbrück, she thought, *Now, not only do I have control over Hilde and Axel, but Gretchen will be at Ravensbrück. And that will mean I also will have the power to destroy Gretchen.* Ilsa straightened her back and hummed softly to herself. She loved the feeling of triumph.

It was not difficult for Ilsa to have things arranged for Gretchen to be brought to Ravensbrück. And as soon as Gretchen arrived, Hilde went back to work and began stealing for Ilsa.

This was how Ilsa acquired what she needed to pay ODESSA for safe passage out of Germany just in case Germany lost the war. Now all she needed was a way to meet Adolf Eichmann and convince him to make the arrangements for her escape. She'd heard that Eichmann had connections to ODESSA, and he had the power to make the arrangements she needed to get out. It would be a risk to discuss it with him, treason of course, but a necessary risk. Still, she had to find a way to meet him. Then, an entire year later, an opportunity fell in her lap. She heard that there was to be a gala, and Adolf Eichmann was going to be attending. She assumed her old lover Dr. Mengele would be invited. And although she knew Dr. Mengele didn't have any deep feelings for her, she hoped he would do her this one favor. She went to see him. Once he agreed that she could accompany him to the gala, she began to make plans. She needed to make sure she would be able to meet and seduce Adolf Eichmann.

CHAPTER 53

1945

AFTER THE STRANGE MAN CAME TO COLLECT PAYMENT AT
Ravensbrück in 1944, Ilsa had not heard another word from
ODESSA until early April 1945. In the middle of the night, a man
knocked on the door to her room in Ravensbrück. When she
opened it, he handed her an envelope. Then, without a word, he
disappeared into the darkness. She closed the door and opened the
envelope. Inside were identification papers for a Jewish woman. The
woman's name was Atara Herskowitz. She was twenty-five years old
and born in Krakow, Poland. Along with the papers was a quickly
scribbled note.

"These are your forged papers. We will be sure to list this
woman's name as having been a prisoner in Auschwitz and in
Ravensbrück. By the time you will be using her name, she would be
considered a survivor.

"If things should go awry and you must leave Germany quickly,
someone will come to escort you. After you have left Ravensbrück,
you will assume the name of this Jew that is listed above. Tell no one
of your plans. However, be sure to keep a bag packed with warm

clothes, a coat, and boots in case the departure time should occur during the winter months. Also be sure to pack any valuables you may have. You must be ready to depart at a moment's notice."

There was nothing else inside the envelope.

Ilsa packed her small suitcase and then shoved it back under the bed. There was a growing fear among the guards that could be felt throughout the camp. They knew the Allies had invaded Europe, and soon they would be marching through Germany. It was treason to talk of Germany losing the war, but sometimes Ilsa overheard the guards discussing Germany's situation. A few years ago the possibility of Germany's defeat was a mere speculation. However, now it seemed inevitable. A few of the women guards who worked with Ilsa admitted to the others that they planned to run away as soon as they knew the Allies were near.

One night when Ilsa went to have dinner at Hilde's house, Hilde and Axel asked her what she planned to do if the Allies came through the camp. She never let on as to her plans. Instead, she just smiled and reassured them that she did not believe that the Allies would ever enter the fatherland. With confidence, she told them that it was treason to even entertain the idea that Germany could lose the war.

"I have faith in the führer, and I have no intentions of turning my back on our beloved Reich," she said.

It sounded almost like a threat to Hilde and Axel, so they backed down immediately, and although they were doubtful that Germany had a chance, they both agreed with her. The last thing they needed was for Ilsa to think they'd committed treason.

Ilsa patted their backs and told them not to worry, that their lack of loyalty to the party was safe with her. A quick look of fear passed between Axel and Hilde, but they both managed to cover it as quickly as it came. For the rest of the night, Ilsa was as sweet as maple syrup. She played with Anatole. She even held him in her arms and sang to him in German.

Gretchen had arrived a month prior to this visit, and since her arrival, Ilsa could see a difference in Hilde. Hilde had begun to relax. The child, too, had adjusted to his new home. Anatol called

Hilde, Mama, and Axel, Father. Hilde seemed happier. She'd even gained some weight. Ilsa complimented her on how healthy she looked. At the end of the evening, Ilsa kissed her friends' cheeks and asked Anatole for a big hug. Then she left the house and headed back to Ravensbrück. Once she was far enough away to be out of earshot, she began to cackle, and as she did she said, "Oh, Butterball, you are such a fool."

CHAPTER 54

IT ALL HAPPENED JUST AS ILSA THOUGHT IT WOULD. LATE IN THE night, she heard a knock on her door. She got out of bed, but no one was there, then she looked down to see a note.

"Leave the camp, and come into the town. Once you are there, go to the area behind the postal office. Be there by four a.m. this morning. Bring your bags."

This was it. Ilsa was sorry to leave the best job she'd ever had, but she knew that the days of the Reich were numbered, so she quickly got dressed, slid her suitcase out from under the bed, looked around one last time, and then headed out into the night.

CHAPTER 55

THE TRIP ON FOOT THROUGH THE SWISS ALPS WAS CHALLENGING for Ilsa. She'd never been much of an athlete. The rest of her group seemed annoyed that they had to wait for her because she had trouble keeping up. The terrain was difficult to navigate, especially at night, so three days later when she saw the small plane in the distance, she was both scared and relieved. It was before sunset, and the plane looked almost like a mirage, like something unreal, in the golden, afternoon sun. Ilsa had never flown before, and the idea of it made her heart race with fear. As she sat down in the leather seat, she imagined the plane falling out of the sky, then the engine roared, and the plane began to taxi. She felt dizzy, hardly able to catch her breath. As the aircraft rose into the sky, Ilsa felt as if her eardrums might burst. Then she vomited on the floor.

"Disgusting," the man who was leading the group said. He was a man with no name because he refused to reveal anything about his identity. "You'll clean that up," he growled at Ilsa.

Ilsa nodded. She felt alone, and suddenly she was frightened. It was unusual for her to feel so afraid, but she had no idea what lay in store. *South America. I've heard there's a barbaric jungle there. I wonder how far away from it we will be. Perhaps we will be right in the middle of it. And to make matters even worse, I don't like any of these people who are on this plane with me. They look at me as if they are repelled by me. They remind me so much of the children I knew when I was young and fat. I hope the arrangements can be made for me to get out of South America and to the United States as soon as possible. I have a feeling that I could be happy there. After all, they say everyone is rich in America. And I am going to need to find a way to replenish my savings after paying for this escape.*

The others dozed, read Nazi-approved literature, or gazed out the window into the darkness. Ilsa contemplated seeing Eichmann again. She'd heard that Josef Mengele would be there too, the only man who had ever broken her heart. *It was only my ego that he hurt,* she consoled herself. *I never really loved him or Adolf. I've never really loved anyone. Love is for fools. Well, I'll get away from them and out of that miserable place as soon as I possibly can, then I'll head straight for America.*

The small primitive-looking aircraft rocked through the turbulent air as night fell. Feeling lonely and strangely eerie, Ilsa wrapped her arms around herself. *If this thing crashes, my life will be over. What would it feel like to die in a burst of flames? Would it be horribly painful, or would it be fast?* Ilsa swallowed hard. *Could there possibly be a God? And . . . if there was, what would that mean to her?* She trembled at the thought.

CHAPTER 56

The Amazon Jungle in Bolivia

THERE WAS NO LANDING STRIP. THE PLANE CAME TO A ROCKY landing in the darkness in a section of the rainforest that had been cleared for this purpose. When Ilsa stood up, her knees trembled. She walked down the stairs out into the unbearable heat. The air was heavy and moist. The guide who awaited them led them down a narrow path that had been carved through the thick trees. Branches slapped her arms and scraped the skin on her legs.

"Be careful where you step. There are poisonous snakes," the guide said.

Ilsa trembled, but she didn't speak. *What a stupid man he is. How am I supposed to be careful if I can't see what's in front of me?* she thought.

Finally, they came to a small clearing where a large hut had been constructed out of what appeared to be some form of bamboo. There were two stories, and a good portion of the structure was not enclosed.

At the door to the hut stood a portly woman with a face as brown as a coconut. She had a big, yellow-toothed smile. "Welcome," she said in German. Then she escorted each member of the group to their individual rooms. Ilsa was led to a very small room with a dirt floor. In the center was a hard and uncomfortable cot that had been covered with mosquito netting.

The woman looked at Ilsa and then said, "This will be your room. We put breakfast on table just as sun come up in sky. Please, you will sleep inside netting at night or insects will attack you. And when you need to relieve yourself, hole is outside, a little walk behind house."

Ilsa nodded. She wanted to vomit. Somewhere in the distance, a wild animal let out a howl. Ilsa jumped. "Before you go," Ilsa said to the woman, "the animals? Can they get in here? I've heard that there is a big cat that lives here that is like a leopard."

"This is jungle. Anything can happen here. The cat you talk of is jaguar. Jaguar have powerful spirit, must respect jaguar spirit. But not worry, jaguar mostly shy away from people. That is unless somehow she gets taste of human flesh. Once this happens, jaguar must have more and more. So we must send out hunters to find her and kill her. If not, she keep coming into villages and she kill more people. Now, about snakes and spiders? Yes, they come in."

"Poisonous ones?"

"Yes, some are. Others not poison. Many spiders look very bad but are harmless; others look harmless but are very bad." She smiled, and Ilsa noticed that she was missing some of her teeth. Then she continued, "Mostly colorful spiders are poison. Now snakes are different. Some not poison but still dangerous. These snakes kill by wrapping around victim and squeezing life out."

"Oh!" Ilsa sucked in a deep breath.

"Don't be afraid. If you don't go walking in forest, you should be safe. As I tell you before, no need for worry, jaguar rarely come into village. And anaconda, the giant serpent with powerful dark spirit that can swallow a man whole . . . are most of time found on river. Stay here in house with others, and all will be well."

"As for bathing in the river? I heard there is a poisonous eel?"

"Yes, I think you speak of brown snake. Very powerful. If she touch you, you may be, could be, dead in minutes. Something in her magic stop your breathing and your heart instantly. Also, keep eye open for large, long insect with lots of legs. This one has very bad poison. She be smaller than snake, still very long. In fact, longer than most man's sex part. And she have strong dark spirit. Called centipede."

"Centipede," Ilsa said, so angry with Eichmann that she could hardly speak.

"I think maybe it be best if you not go all the way into river for taking a bath. Perhaps bathe using cloth but stay on land by river. Even so, still must be cautious for caiman. Hard to see. He hide in bushes, and then he come out fast. Big strong spirit. Big teeth."

Ilsa stared at the native woman.

But the woman continued to speak. "Also, you must never to go walk in forest. Tribes live in forest. Some very dangerous, hate white man. Hate others not in tribe. These not friendly. Some eat heart of others not in their tribe to steal their power and spirit."

"Oh, what a horrible place. This is an absolute nightmare. Well, don't you worry. I have no intentions of ever walking through the forest," Ilsa said, speaking more to herself than to the woman.

She didn't sleep at all that night. The sounds of the jungle unnerved her. There were the cries from the howler monkeys, and she was sure she heard the growls of the jaguars. *How am I ever going to stay here even for another day?*

Working at Ravensbrück, she'd become accustomed to bathing each day. However, this was not possible in the jungle. When she asked one of the servants where the bathing facilities were she was told that she would be required to bathe in the river.

"The river?" *The river is filthy, full of mud.*

"Yes, but you must be careful when you go in. Look where you are going because you must watch out for big green snake."

"You mean the anaconda? I heard about that." Ilsa shivered. *This place is what nightmares are made of.*

"Oh yes, of course, the anaconda, you must beware but also the eel. He live in river too. If eel bite you, you are finished."

"Where am I?" Ilsa said.

"I don't understand question?" he asked.

"Never mind." She dismissed him. Then she went down to

breakfast where she saw Adolf Eichmann. She looked everywhere for Josef Mengele, but she didn't see him or Eichmann's family. Ilsa wondered, *Perhaps Eichmann has made other arrangements for his family so that he and I can have some time for fun before his wife arrives, and he is under her thumb again. Perhaps he's done the same with Mengele. I can't be sure, but I dare not ask. He wouldn't want me asking about his wife, and he certainly wouldn't want me asking about Josef.*

The food, which was mostly beans and rice with some strange chewy meat, did not appeal to her. It was not at all what she was used to eating. But she was glad that at least a few of the servants spoke some, if not fluent, German.

Eichmann walked over to her after breakfast. She turned away from him. "You never came to visit me," she said, a little angry.

"I know. I'm sorry. I was unable to come. I was busy making all of the arrangements for these people to get out of Germany."

"I see. It doesn't matter anyway," she added, turning away. She was disgusted with him, but she dared not show it. She still needed him. " How long do I have to stay here?"

"You don't like it here?" he said.

"And you do?" she replied sarcastically.

"I don't mind it, really. It's peaceful. But don't worry. You won't be staying in the jungle. I'll have you moved to a city," he said, smiling.

"A city, here? In this place?"

"In South America, yes. Buenos Aires, perhaps?"

"I want to go to the USA," Ilsa insisted. The thought of spending the rest of her days in this hot, tropical hell made her feel desperate. "I've already paid you very well, Adolf, but I can't stay here. I'll give you more. Just get me to the United States."

"I know you want to go there. But it's harder to get in."

She glared at him. "How much?"

"A lot more. How much do you have?"

"I have a large ruby brooch, perhaps three carats, two thick gold wedding bands, seven thinner gold bands, a two-carat emerald necklace, a matching emerald bracelet, a thick gold Jewish star on a thick gold chain, and a diamond necklace."

"How big is the diamond?"

"Not as big as the last one I gave you, but at least two carats."

"Hmmm? That's all you have?"

"I have a diamond necklace and diamond earrings. I wanted to keep them for myself, but I'd rather get out of here."

"I need all of it," he said.

She grunted. "I'll pay, but hurry up and get this done for me. This place is unbearable."

"Believe me, I'm working on it."

CHAPTER 57

Ilsa held her urine until she could not hold it anymore. She was not looking forward to using a hole in the ground as a toilet. But she braced herself and walked outside.

"Which way to the hole?" she asked a native man who was making a fishing pole out of a stick.

He stared at her.

"The toilet," she said, frustrated.

He shrugged his shoulders. Ilsa thought she might cry, but then the large woman who spoke German walked by. "What you want?" she asked Ilsa.

"Toilet," Ilsa said.

"Toilet?"

"Hole?"

The woman nodded and pointed. Ilsa began walking. As she did, she passed a group of children playing a game with a stick. When she looked down at the ground where they were playing, she saw a giant hairy spider in the center of the group. They'd attached what looked like a huge, lime-green grasshopper to a stick which they were dangling in front of the spider. Every time the spider lunged for the insect they moved the stick. Ilsa felt her skin crawl as she let out a scream.

One of the servants came running. "What is it?" he asked.

She pointed to the massive spider. "That!"

"Oh." The servant laughed. "No need to be afraid. That's a tarantula. But that's one of the harmless kind. They are everywhere here. The children play with them. But you are right to be cautious because there are two kinds of these spiders. This one is all right. But the other one is deadly."

Ilsa shivered. She kept her distance as the spider danced on it's eight long, thick legs. She had to go so badly that she had no choice but to continue to the makeshift toilet. When she got there she found it to be a smelly, dirty place covered in large, black bugs. Quickly, she peed then she ran back to the house. The children were still playing with the spider. She continued to run until she was in her room. Bees buzzed around her head, landing on her face and eyelids, stinging. Not only did they buzz, but they made a peculiar sound that she'd never heard the bees in Germany make.

Throwing herself down on her cot, she thought it might have been better to face the Allies than to come here. Biting her lip, she forced herself not to cry. *Damn Eichmann. He had better find a way to get me to America quickly.*

Before dinner that evening, Ilsa joined the rest of the group for drinks in the main room of the house. She saw Eichmann standing at the bar and talking to some of the men. She immediately walked up to him.

"I must get out of here as soon as possible," she blurted as she marched over to him, interrupting his conversation.

"Excuse me," Eichmann said to the other men, then he turned to Ilsa. "Let's take a walk outside, shall we?"

She glared at him and nodded.

He squeezed her arm a little too tightly as he led her outside. "That was very rude," he said.

"I can't bear this place another minute," she growled. "I am covered in bee stings. These bees are horrible. They are so aggressive even though they are smaller than any I've ever seen. They sting, and I just can't stand to have them landing on me. It makes my skin crawl."

"They are attracted to your sweat, and that sound you hear is them licking the sweat from your skin. And being that it's very hot here, there is plenty of sweat. Even you, my beauty, have to be sweating furiously in this heat."

She gave him a vicious stare.

"Anyway," he continued, trying to sound casual, "they are called sweat bees, and they are exclusive to the Amazon rainforest. Now you can think of your situation of being here in another way. You can say to yourself, 'Ilsa, you have a seen an insect that most people will never encounter,'" he said mockingly.

"Oh, shut up, won't you? I am horrified by this place. You promised to get me out of here."

"I'm doing the best I can." He forced a smile more for the sake of the men who were watching him from inside than for her sake.

"It's not good enough. I can't stand it."

He shrugged. "I'll do what I can."

"That's simply not good enough, Adolf. I have to get out of this place, or I'll go out of my mind."

"You haven't forgotten, have you? My name is Ricardo. You must never use my old name. It's important that we don't forget our new identities."

"Go to hell." She was angry. "If you don't get me out of here by the end of the month, I swear I'll tell your wife what happened between us. I swear I will, Adolf. I'll find a way."

"Dinner is served," the heavyset, brown-skinned servant woman called out.

"Shall we go to the dining room?"

"I am serious about what I am saying to you. I demand that you get me out of here and soon."

The group of seven SS officers, including Eichmann and Ilsa, sat down at the table. Ilsa glared at Eichmann as a large, black ant crawled across the plate of rice that one of the servants had just placed in the middle of the table.

"This place is not a fit place to live," one of the Nazis said. "The animals alone are a good reason to move to the city."

"Oh, yes, you are correct. The animals and the insects are monstrous," another of the Nazis answered him. "It's uncivilized."

"I think it's rather lovely. This morning I saw a flock of iridescent, brightly colored butterflies," said a Nazi, with a head of thick, white hair.

"Lovely, yes, but dangerous. Just wait until you meet up with a jaguar," a servant boy, carrying a large platter of beans, chimed in. "The jaguar is a beautiful animal but deadly too."

"I'd rather not meet up with one," Eichmann said, "but I did hear a rather curious story about the anaconda the other day. Would you like to hear it?"

"Yes, do tell us."

Then Eichmann went on. "First off, the anaconda is the largest snake in the world. She can grow to twenty-five feet long. Some of the natives say they've seen even bigger ones."

"Are these the ones that are poisonous?"

"No, but they're constrictors. They wrap themselves around their prey and squeeze until they've squeezed the life out of their victim. And you know what I have heard? I've heard that after they mate, the female devours the male. She eats him and that way she will not have to eat again until her seven months of gestation is over."

"How vile," one of the Nazis said.

"I know some human women who are just like that. They devour the men in their lives just to serve their own ends." Eichmann laughed, but he set his eyes on Ilsa. She glared back at him to let him know that she would not back down. And if he didn't get her out of South America, she would find a way to destroy his marriage.

CHAPTER 58

EICHMANN DISAPPEARED FROM THE JUNGLE CAMP FOR TWO WEEKS. Ilsa began to worry that he'd abandoned her. During that time she'd stood at the edge of the river and sponged herself off with rags in order to bathe. She found she was unable to submerge herself in the water. The food upset her stomach so much that she'd run to the hole at least twice and woke in the middle of the night to vomit.

When Eichmann finally returned, Ilsa was relieved. He was standing at the bar when she came into the main room. Giving her a smile, he asked Ilsa if they could go to her room so they could speak privately. She agreed.

Once they were in her room, Eichmann locked the door. Then he turned to Ilsa and spoke in a whisper. "I have found a solution to your problem. I think I can get you into America."

"I knew you could do it if you tried hard enough." She was so relieved that she slumped down on the bed and let the tears flow down her face. "How?" she asked.

"Here is my plan. You are going to pose as the fiancée of a Jewish scientist. Of course, this man is not really a Jew. He, like you, is really one of us. But don't worry, the American government knows the truth. And they will keep your secret safe because the

Americans want this scientist in their country. They know of his reputation, and they want him to be a part of their outer-space program."

"The United States knows he is a part of the Nazi Party, and they are letting him in anyway?"

"That's right. They need him to further their progress in the space race."

"I can't wait to leave. Who is he? Will I be required to marry him?"

"He's an old man. Sickly too. He doesn't expect you to really marry him, so you needn't worry."

"When you get to America, you'll stay with him for a few months then you can break up. After that, you'll be free to go your own way."

"I can't wait. When do I leave?"

"Next week"

"Not soon enough," she said, but she let out a sigh of relief.

"So tonight? Shall we say our goodbyes, old friend?" He cupped her breast in his hand.

She looked in his eyes trying to hide her true feelings of hatred for him. He'd taken so much of the valuables she'd worked so hard to acquire. She was left with almost nothing. *As far as he is concerned, I have nothing left to start my new life. And now he expects this too! Bastard. But I'd better not refuse him. If I do, he might not fulfill his promise, and I have to get to America.*

Ilsa put her arms around Eichmann's neck and kissed him. Then she pulled him down onto the cot where she slept. A bee stung him in the back of his arm. He let out a little shriek. "Damn these bees," he said then added, "Perhaps we should get undressed and go under the netting."

She nodded. *At least this will be the last time*, she thought.

CHAPTER 59

New York, NY, United States of America 1947

WHERE THE STREETS ARE PAVED IN GOLD.

After the war ended, Benjamin Rabinowitz contacted Levi Mansky and told him that he was a good friend of Caleb Ornstein's. Without hesitation, Levi graciously agreed to sponsor Ben, and who then moved in with Levi and his family on the Lower West Side of Manhattan. Levi, who was a religious man and a part of a tight-knit religious community, had even secured a job for Ben as an apprentice to a diamond cutter. Although Ben had never been very religious, he recognized that his employers, two brothers, were Hasidics. He knew this by their clothes, their beards, and their payots. Many of the men who worked in New York's diamond district had come from Eastern Europe. And although his bosses had been born in America, many of the others he met, like Ben, had survived concentration camps. Although they had shared a harsh past, no one ever mentioned the Nazis or what had happened before they came to America.

Ben found the diamond cutters to be meticulous experts in their field. And they always treated Ben with kindness. Even so he knew he was not a part of their world, and often he felt like an outsider. Time had not erased his memories. He still found his thoughts consumed with people and places he feared he would never see again. Sometimes he wondered if Moishe were alive, and what Moishe might have been like—if he'd had the chance to watch him grow up. When he allowed his mind to travel down this dark, painful path his head would ache, and sometimes he would feel so sick to his stomach that he had to vomit. He thought of his little boy, and he chastised himself for being powerless to help his son. His own weakness sent him spiraling down into fits of self-loathing followed by prayers that, by some miracle, Lila had survived and had been able to save Moishe. He thought of Zelda, poor gentle Zelda. Had she somehow survived? Before he'd left Germany, he'd searched for them all. He'd registered at every agency he could find. He'd searched all the names of people who had survived and were now looking for their loved ones. But he did not see one familiar name on that list, and no one ever contacted him. Then once he received the letter from Levi telling him that the sponsorship had gone through, and he could now come to America, Ben went back to the Red Cross agency and made sure to leave all his forwarding information. But he was doubtful that he would ever hear from any of them again.

The day that he boarded the ship to take him to America he knew he should be grateful he was alive and on his way to the land of plenty. However, that was not how he felt. Ben felt beaten and alone. He had no idea what lay across the ocean, but he knew that no matter what he found he would never forget the friends, the family, and lovers he left behind.

Two years had passed since he'd arrived at Levi's tenement on the west side of the city. His first impression was shock. If this was the land of milk and honey, he couldn't see how. The tenement buildings were dirty and overcrowded; the people were immigrants from many different countries. On the streets one could hear a multitude of languages: Yiddish, Italian, Polish, German. The people, their food, and their customs were all different. However, all they shared was poverty and a dream, the dream of a better life, for themselves and their loved ones. It was far from perfect in the tenement where he lived. The buildings were death traps, made of wood, prone to fire. The work was hard, and the hours were long, but compared to Auschwitz, it was heaven.

Ben liked Levi, his wife, and two teenage boys as soon as he met them. He'd told them that Caleb died in the camp. They didn't want to know how it happened, and Ben was glad they didn't ask any more questions. He was relieved not to have to explain his unusual friendship with Caleb.

As soon as Ben began earning money, he paid a third of his wages toward the rent. He also bought food for the family and made every effort to contribute.

On a wickedly cold day in early January, the snow trickled down from a bright silver sky, and the wind blew in chilly gusts off the frozen lake. Ben was busy taking an order from a jeweler who wanted to have a large round diamond cut into a pear shape, when a woman, wearing a brown wool coat that matched her golden-brown hair, hair the color of dark honey, came into the jewelry store. She waited for Ben to finish with the customer, then she walked up to the counter.

"Good Morning," she said in broken English with a heavy German accent. "I am sorry, but my English is not so good. I need to sell these diamonds." She took a wrinkled, lilac handkerchief out of her purse and unwrapped it to reveal five large stones: each of them set in gold ring settings.

Ben looked up at her. "I speak Yiddish," he said. "It's a lot like German. I think I will understand you if you want to speak to me in German."

"I speak Yiddish too," she said, smiling. She'd learned Yiddish from the prisoners at Ravensbrück. She studied Ben. He was handsome. Very handsome. His dark, wavy hair was combed away from his strong but sensitive eyes.

"I'm Ben; may I ask your name?"

She glanced down at his arm where she saw the number

tattooed. "I'm Atara Herskowitz," she said. Then she placed her hand gently on his arm and whispered, "I'm a survivor too."

"Which camp?" he asked.

"Ravensbrück" she said.

"Auschwitz," he answered.

She nodded. "These were my mother's diamonds. I hid them all through the war. They are all I have. Please . . . get me the best price you can?"

"Of course," he said. "I will speak with the boss and explain everything to him. Can you wait for a few minutes?"

"Yes, of course."

Ben took the diamonds and walked over to speak to one of his bosses who was a heavyset Hasidic man. Chaim was a good businessman but also a kind and generous soul. He and Ben spoke in whispers for several minutes. Ben showed Chaim the diamonds and explained that the woman was a concentration-camp survivor. Chaim listened quietly, then he told Ben what he was willing to pay the woman for her gems. However, as Ben was heading back to tell the woman the price, Chaim called him back. "Rabinowitz," he said, "before you give the lady the price, come here."

The woman at the counter, who was really Ilsa Guhr posing as Atara Herskowitz, a Jew in America, almost fell over when she heard that the man's name was Ben Rabinowitz. *Is it possible that he is the father of the child Hilde stole from the children's camp? He is not at all the way I pictured him to be. But there could be more than one Benjamin Rabinowitz. I must know if it's him, but I can't push him. I have to wait for the right time.*

Ben walked back to Atara. "I have good news. First, my boss gave me one price, then he thought it over and decided to give you a little more. Probably because he understands that you need the money to start over. He's a kind man and a fair one too. How does five thousand dollars sound to you?"

Atara's eyes lit up. "Oh . . ." she stammered. You're right; he is very fair," she answered in Yiddish. "I would love to buy you a cup of coffee sometime to say thank you," she said, curious about Ben Rabinowitz and wanting to know more about him. She was intrigued because she knew so much of what had happened to his family. But he was unaware of who she really was, and she found that she was enjoying playing a part like an actress.

Atara Herskowitz was a pretty woman; Ben couldn't deny that. And he was lonely. It had been a long time since he'd spent time with a woman whom he might be interested in romantically. Each night he retired to his small room taking his meals alone, not wanting to become a burden to Levi and his family. And although he could hardly call a cup of coffee a date, he was excited to get to know Atara Herskowitz. "I would love to have a cup of coffee with you," he answered.

"Tomorrow after work?"

"I get off at seven in the evening. Is that too late?"

"It's perfect," she said.

"And by the way, instead of coffee, why don't you allow me to buy you dinner?" Ben offered. "I know a kosher deli just a block from here. It's called Leon's Deli. Do you know it?"

"I have never been there, but I have seen it."

"Can you meet there me at seven?"

"I'll be there."

CHAPTER 60

ILSA WALKED BACK TO HER COLD-WATER FLAT WITH A CHECK FOR five thousand dollars in her handbag. This was all the money she had left from the jewelry she and Hilde had stolen from the prisoners at Ravensbrück. When she arrived at her apartment, she removed her coat and scarf, then she ran her fingers through her hair. In the mirror she saw that she needed to touch up the color. Her natural blonde was coming through at the roots. Coloring her hair golden brown had become part of her routine since she'd arrived in America. She felt it was less conspicuous than her golden-blonde curls for a woman posing as a Jew.

Now that she had some cash, she planned to move out of this run-down apartment with its roaches, mice, and temperamental heater. In the morning, she would look for something better. Not anything extravagant because she didn't want to go through her money too quickly. After all, her English was not perfect, so she was not qualified for any type of work. Besides that, she still remembered how much trouble she'd had at the job where she'd worked at before she became a guard at Ravensbrück. But she hoped that if she was careful she could find a better place to live that was affordable.

Plopping down on the sofa, she took off her shoes and rubbed her toes. *I'm glad he's paying for dinner. Why spend any money if I don't have to? But I must say he is certainly more handsome than I ever expected him to be when I heard his name. It was one of the last words that came out of his wife's mouth before I killed her,* Ilsa thought as she remembered back to the last moments of Lila's life. Ilsa had taken Lila outside at gunpoint in the middle of the night. She had promised Hilde she would kill Lila, and she planned to keep her promise, but she did not pull the trigger until she heard the truth from Lila's lips.

"Do you want to survive?" Ilsa asked Lila as Lila lay hugging the trunk of a tree. "If you are alive you can try to find your son again."

"Yes, I want to survive."

"Then tell me the truth. Is your son a Jew? Are you a Jew?"

"He is not," Lila said.

Ilsa cracked Lila across the face with the plastic whip she carried.

"Tell me the truth, I said, or I'll have the child killed. If you want me to insure his safety, I must know the truth. Now tell me. Is he a Jew?" Ilsa could see the doubt, the fear, the confusion in Lila's eyes.

Then Lila hung her head and said, "Yes, he's a Jew."

"Good, very good. Now we are getting somewhere. Would you like a piece of candy?" Ilsa handed Lila a piece of chocolate. "I'm not such a bad sort." She smiled. "When you tell me the truth, I can help you, but I don't like liars."

Lila ate the candy.

"Now, what is the child's given name, and what are the given names of both of his parents?"

"Why do you need to know this?"

"I am going to help you. I am going to write down your name and the name of the boy's father. At the end of the war I will help him find you."

"I don't believe you."

"You stupid woman. I could kill you right now. I could kill your son too. What other reason would I have for asking you these questions?" Ilsa cracked the whip against the tree. Lila jumped. "You are trying my patience. Do you want my help or not? If not, that's fine with me."

Lila hung her head in defeat. The guard was right. She could kill Lila right now. She could probably kill Moishe too. Maybe she really was trying to help. Lila wasn't convinced, but she felt she had to trust her. "I am Lila Rabinowitz. My son's name is Moishe Rabinowitz. The boy's father is Benjamin Rabinowitz. I don't know if Ben is still alive."

"And Moishe is the little blond-haired boy that the SS officer carried out of the children's camp the other day. Is that correct?"

"Yes." Lila nodded.

Ilsa smiled and handed Lila another chocolate. "These are good, aren't they?" Ilsa said, but before Lila had a chance to answer, Ilsa shot her point-blank in the head.

Ilsa was brought back to the present moment by the sound of a man and woman laughing in the hallway of the building. *These damn walls are paper thin*, she thought as she got up and went into her room to undress. *This dinner tomorrow night with Benjamin Rabinowitz should be very interesting. Jews, they never cease to amuse me.*

CHAPTER 61

January, Berlin 1947

ANATOL, WHO WAS REALLY MOISHE RABINOWITZ, LAY WITH HIS HEAD on Gretchen Schmidt's lap while she was reading to him. She gently ran her hand over his golden hair. *He is such a treasure*, she thought. *But I feel so bad for him. It's been two years since he last saw Hilde and Axel, and he still asks when they are going to return. How could he know that they were Nazis and not his real parents? After all, they were the only parents he ever really knew. Some day I will have to tell him the truth, that he was a Jewish child stolen by Axel because Hilde had lost her baby. They planned to raise him as their son—as a Nazi. And when he asks about his real parents, I'll have to tell him that I have no idea what has become of his father, but then I'll have to explain that Hilde's friend and coworker, that horrible woman Ilsa Guhr, killed his mother . . .* Gretchen shivered at the heaviness of this responsibility.

As Gretchen stroked his head, Anatol looked up at her and asked, interrupting her thoughts, "What is going to happen to the world now that the war is over?"

"Anatole, that is a very grown-up question for a little boy."

"I want to know, Auntie Gretchen."

"Well, Anatol, just as the Nazis were taking over Germany, I overheard my father and uncle talking. I remember my father saying that Hitler was opening a small crack in the right-thinking minds of our people here in Germany."

"What does that mean?"

"It means that people started to forget what was right and what was wrong. A foundation of right thinking that had once been firmly in place was now cracked. Then my father said that if the German people allowed that small crack to go unrepaired, it would grow until it would become a dark canyon."

"A canyon?"

"A huge, dark hole. Hitler took power and started to do very bad things. So that crack went unrepaired, and it grew, and people forgot what was right and what was wrong. At first, only a few people followed Hitler. But by the time the war ended, many people had lost themselves in his empty promises.

"Where are my parents, Auntie Gretchen? Why did they leave me? And when are they coming back?"

"I don't know," she lied. How could she tell him that Hilde and Axel were arrested and would be standing trial in Nuremberg? If they were found guilty, they would face execution. How does one tell a child that the only parents he can remember might be killed? Gretchen decided he was too young to comprehend all the evil that Axel and Hilde had done. *Where do I begin to tell him about the camps? And how do I explain that the people he loved, who were kind to him, were guards—cruel and horrible guards? They were Jew haters. And then if I am going to tell him the truth, should I not tell him the whole truth? Does he not deserve to know that his birth parents were Jews? I don't know the fate of his father, so when he asks, I will have no answers. He could be dead or alive. All I know was that his name was Benjamin Rabinowitz. I know that the right thing to do would be to try and find his father, but if I do, I would have to give Moishe to Benjamin Rabinowitz. And I would hate to give the boy up. He is all I have.*

"Is it a real canyon? Where is it? I can't see it."

Gretchen was pulled back into the present moment by Anatol's question. "It's not a real canyon that you can see. It's a deep crack like a wound in the fabric of humanity."

"I don't understand what you're talking about, Auntie Gretchen."

"I know," Gretchen said. "It's very complicated."

"Can we ever fix this big hole?"

"I believe we can," she said.

"But how? Wouldn't we have to fill it up? What would we fill it with?"

"Millions of pebbles."

"It seems like it will take a very long time. I don't know how we are ever going to do it. Do you?"

"One pebble at a time, Anatol." She touched his hair.

There was a knock at the door. Anatol sat up straight. A look of fear and worry washed over his face. *He's been through so much. It is such a shame that a knock on the door can spark such terror in the eyes of a child so young,* Gretchen thought. Then she smiled at Anatole, trying to reassure him. "It's all right. I am going to see who is there," she said, walking to the door. She, too, was worried about who might be at the door. After all, once the Russians had marched into Berlin, it had become very unsafe for German women. Terrible things had happened to Gretchen at the hands of those Russian soldiers. Things she would never tell Anatol. However, she'd been fortunate. After the rest of the Allies arrived and split Berlin between them, the tiny apartment where she lived had fallen under the rule of the Americans, who were far better than the Russians.

She took a deep breath, glanced back at the child for a single moment, then she opened the door.

"Rebecca?" Gretchen said as she stood face-to-face with the pretty, blonde girl, who had been her best friend. "You're alive. Thank God, you're alive," she said, almost falling to her knees.

"Gretchen," Rebecca said, taking Gretchen into her arms. "I am so happy to see you. I've been so worried."

Both women were crying and hugging each other.

"Perhaps we should go inside," a handsome, blond man with a cane said to Rebecca.

"Yes, Jan. You're right," Rebecca said, then she turned to Gretchen, her eyes shining with tears. "This is my husband, Jan."

"I've heard so much about you," Jan said.

"Good things, I hope."

"Very good. Rebecca loves you very much. She says you are like a sister to her."

"I feel the same way. I love her too. Come, come inside. Let me introduce you to Anatole."

Anatole eyed the couple skeptically, then he looked at Gretchen.

It's all right," she said and patted Anatole's head. "This is my very dear friend, Rebecca and her husband, Jan." Then Gretchen turned to Rebecca and said, "This is Anatol, Hilde's son."

Rebecca gave Gretchen a look that said she didn't understand. But nothing more was said about Anatole until after they'd all had dinner together and the child was tucked safely into bed.

"He's a sweet boy," Rebecca said when Gretchen returned from checking on Anatole.

"It's true. He is."

"Is he asleep?"

"Yes."

"You said he is Hilde's son?"

"Oh, Rebecca. It's a long and complicated story. But I'll tell you. Hilde had a miscarriage when she returned from Berlin."

"You mean after she had you and I arrested?"

"Yes."

"She was distraught, so her husband stole this child from the children's camp at Ravensbrück where he and Hilde worked. The boy is really a Jewish child. His real name is Moishe Rabinowitz."

"Do you know anything about his parents?"

"Yes, his mother is dead. She was killed by one of the guards at Ravensbrück whose name was Ilsa Guhr, and she was friends with Hilde. His father's name is Benjamin Rabinowitz. I never looked for him. I was afraid."

"How do you know all of this?"

"Because Hilde and her friend Ilsa had me sent to Ravensbrück where I worked as the child's nanny for the rest of the war."

"That was where you went the day you disappeared? I was so distraught when I returned from work, and you were gone." Rebecca said.

"Yes, that was where I was taken."

"You lived with Hilde?"

"Yes. She later told me that she felt very guilty about what she'd done, so she asked Ilsa, who had influential friends in the party, to bring me to Ravensbrück."

"That day you disappeared from Auschwitz was the worst day of my life," Rebecca said. "When I returned to our block that night, you were gone. I didn't know what to do."

"I thought of you as I was being driven away. I thought of how you would feel when you got back to our bunk and I was not there," Gretchen said as she wiped a tear from her eye.

"I was so scared. Sick with worry. I didn't know what happened to you. As Jan and I took the train here today, I was so terrified that I would not find you. I was afraid . . . you were dead." Rebecca took Gretchen in her arms again.

"I searched for you after the war. I searched for you and for Eli. I signed up at every displaced-persons camp I could find. And until today I'd lost hope. I was afraid you were both dead."

"Have you heard anything from Eli?"

"Not a thing. Have you?"

"Nothing," Rebecca said. "I fear the worst."

"Yes, so do I, and it hurts me deeply. More deeply than I can ever say," Gretchen said.

"I know how much you loved him."

"I did, and I always will. There will never be another man for me," Gretchen said.

"You're still young. Don't say that. You don't know what God has in store for you."

"I know that my heart belongs to Eli, now and for the rest of my life."

"After the war, I was afraid to come back here to your apartment. I was so scared that I would find out that you had not survived. It took Jan two years to finally convince me to make the trip."

"I'm glad you did."

"So am I. Oh, Gretchen, so am I. You are the only family, besides Jan, that I have left."

"You have Jan's family too?"

"No, we don't. His father was a Nazi, an SS officer. High up in the party. Jan saved me from him. Not only from him, from all of them. Jan saved my life."

Gretchen looked from Rebecca to Jan. She had a million questions, but instead, she took Jan's hand in her own and in a voice just above a whisper she said, "Thank you." Then as tears ran down her cheeks, she stood up and took a bottle from the shelf. "Let's have a drink. We have a lot to celebrate," she said. "I am so happy to see you. I will never be able to express how much I missed you. How afraid I was." Her voice broke. "Everything is perfect tonight." Gretchen wiped the tears from her face with the back of her hand. Then she got a faraway look in her eyes that reflected the sadness she hid deep in her heart. The unspoken words that burned in her soul. "If only Eli were here with us . . . If only he had survived."

"It is a wonderful night, a perfect night." Rebecca took Gretchen's hand and squeezed it gently.

"Well, almost, anyway," Gretchen said and tried to smile.

"I know." Rebecca said the words that Gretchen could not say. "This day is one of the best days of my life. It would be perfect if Eli were here."

Then Gretchen whispered, "If only Eli were here."

CHAPTER 62

Rebecca and Jan had planned to spend the night in a hotel and head back to Poland the following day. However, Gretchen insisted they stay with her. "I have plenty of room, and I would love to spend a little more time with Rebecca. Would that be all right with both of you?" she asked.

Jan smiled and said, "It's fine with me. I'll do whatever Rebecca would like."

"I'd like to stay the night, Jan."

"Then it's settled. Come, both of you. Please follow me. Rebecca knows this room; she's stayed here before."

They followed Gretchen to the bedroom in the back of the house.

"Oh my, this room brings back so many memories," Rebecca said. She gently touched the quilt on the bed. "It's the same quilt that was here when I stayed here."

"Yes, I've had it for years. My mother made it before she died."

"How did you ever get your old apartment back?"

"Do you remember Mrs. Kulterman from upstairs?"

"Of course."

"Her daughter was renting this place when I returned. As soon as the daughter saw me, she insisted that I take back my apartment. She and her husband moved in upstairs with her mother. She said she couldn't afford to keep this place any longer. But I don't believe her. I think she was being kind. My father was always good to their family, and I think she remembers."

"She just gave you the place?"

"Yes, she did. I see her in the hall sometimes; we have coffee together. I remember when her father died, and her mother couldn't afford to buy food, my father would tell me to bring half of our dinner upstairs to share with them."

"I never knew your father. I always wished I had," Rebecca said.

"He was a wonderful man, my father was," Gretchen said wistfully.

"So what do you think of the room?"

"It's a lovely room and a very nice apartment," Jan said. "I am going to bed, so I can give you two ladies some time alone to catch up."

"Are you sure? I don't want you to feel unwanted," Rebecca said.

"I know how women like to talk. And let's face it, the two of you have been through a great deal. I think you deserve some time alone together. I don't feel unwanted at all."

"Good night." Rebecca got up and kissed Jan.

He nodded to both women and then disappeared into the bedroom.

Once Gretchen and Rebecca were alone, Gretchen put on a pot of water for tea.

"Do you remember how we used to sit here at the kitchen table and make tea, just like this? It feels so long ago," Gretchen said.

"Of course, I remember. How could I ever forget? You did so much for Eli and I. I could never begin to thank you."

"You don't have to. You never have to thank me. You are the sister I never had."

For several moments, there was quiet, then the teapot began to whistle. Gretchen rose quickly and poured the water. She wanted to stop the whistle before it woke anyone.

"Do you like Jan?" Rebecca asked.

"He seems very nice."

"He is very good to me."

"Yes, I can see that. I am glad you have found someone."

Rebecca nodded. She wished there was something comforting she could say about Eli, but all that remained was an awkward silence.

The two women sipped the tea for several minutes then Gretchen said, "I don't know what to do about Anatole. I know it's not fair to him to keep the truth a secret, but he is so young."

"You mean about his being Jewish?"

"Yes, that and all of the rest of it too. I feel like I owe it to him to search for his father. If his father is alive, he deserves to know him. I feel like he deserves to know that he is Jewish and to be proud of his religion. After all the suffering the Jews have endured . . ."

"Yes, I agree with you."

"But he's so young, and this will all be so hard for him to understand. Besides that, I don't want to lose him. If his father is alive, he will want his son back. And how could I ever blame him?"

"But we don't know if his father is alive. You're right though. You should at least try to find him. You could wait until Anatole is older, but then you would be running the risk that his father might pass away. And that would rob Anatole of ever knowing him."

"I never thought about that. Anything might happen. I should see what I can find out about this man called Benjamin Rabinowitz. Even though it hurts me to think about giving up Anatole, I love that little boy too much to deny him this."

CHAPTER 63

BENJAMIN RABINOWITZ STOPPED BY THE FLORIST ON HIS WAY
home from work. For the last three months, he'd had a standing
dinner date twice a week with Atara Herskowitz. They would
share a quiet dinner at an inexpensive café or deli, and then
sometimes they would go back to her apartment where they
played cards and enjoyed a cup of tea. Once in a while, they also
met for lunch when their schedules permitted. It was still too cold
outside to take walks, so they often cuddled next to the heater and
talked. Atara told him stories about her wonderful parents and
her younger twin sisters. She wept in his arms as she explained
that after the war a survivor from Auschwitz, who had known her
sisters while they were there, came to her and told her that her
sisters had died. They had both been murdered by a horrible,
sadistic Dr. Mengele who had used them in an experiment. Atara
learned that her mother had been gassed as soon as she arrived at
Auschwitz.

"I was originally with them, so I already knew about my mother
being murdered," Atara said, her eyes glassed over. "She waved to
me and smiled. 'I'll be all right,' she said. But, of course, she was
not."

"I'm sorry." Benjamin held her hand in his and rubbed it gently with his thumb. There was not much else to be said.

"I remember that terrible doctor too. When we first got off the transport, my mother, my sisters, and I were forced out of the train car at gunpoint. Everyone was running. It was utter chaos. But then we were herded into a line. That's when Dr. Mengele came. He pointed to my sisters who were holding hands. "I'll take these two," he said. I never saw them again. The following week I was sent to a special women's house, where things were done to me that left me unable to have children. These things, I still can't bear to talk about. From there I was sent to the all-women's camp called Ravensbrück."

"There is no need to talk about anything that makes you uncomfortable," Ben said in a soft and sympathetic voice. "I am here for you, and I will listen when and if you ever want to get all of this off your chest."

"You are very kind," she said, squeezing his hand.

Ben told Atara about Lila and Moishe and about Zelda too. He told her about the Lodz ghetto, Rumkowski, and Caleb too.

Ilsa perked up. She was interested.

"Were you in the Lodz ghetto?" he asked.

"No. We lived in Germany, my parents and I. Then when my father died from the flu epidemic before the war began, my mother, my sisters, and I moved to Warsaw to live with my mother's sister and her husband.

"What was Lila like? You did say your wife's name was Lila?" Until now, Ilsa had not been sure that Ben was Moishe's father and Lila's husband. She'd suspected, but this gave her the confirmation she needed. How strange it felt to be sitting beside him and hearing his story all the while she was aware that he did not know that she'd played an integral part in all of it. Ben gazed at her with gentle, caring eyes—innocent eyes. The poor man had no idea that she was the reason Lila would never return to him. Sometimes she found his naïveté charming. Other times she laughed at him inwardly for being such an idiot.

"Headstrong. She was difficult, but she was my wife, and she did the best she could for our son. God be with her wherever she may be," he answered with a sad smile as he remembered. "Lila was a good mother to our Moishe. And he was the light of my life."

"I never had any children," she said, looking down at the ground and sniffling as if she might cry at any moment. *I am such a good actress*, she thought.

He shook his head. "We all suffered so much . . ."

CHAPTER 64

Ɪʟsᴀ Gᴜʜʀ ᴡᴀs ɪɴ ʜᴇʀ ᴀᴘᴀʀᴛᴍᴇɴᴛ sɪᴛᴛɪɴɢ ᴏɴ ᴀ ᴄʜᴀɪʀ ɪɴ ғʀᴏɴᴛ ᴏғ the night table by her bed. She was removing her makeup with thick, white cold cream. In spite of herself, she found that she liked Benjamin Rabinowitz. He was different than any man she'd ever known. He treated her with kindness and respect. She had grown to like him so much that she felt guilty about lying to him. She wished she hadn't had to make up the stories about her family or lie to him about being a Jewish survivor. *What the hell is the matter with you, Ilsa? Are you getting soft? He's a Jew. You must not forget that. If he ever found out who and what you are, he would hate you. And although he seems to be a good person, the truth is that he is nothing but a tricky subhuman. A very attractive one, yes, but a subhuman nonetheless.*

CHAPTER 65

Ben enjoyed the time he spent with Atara. She filled the emptiness in his life but only to some extent. She was a nice person. When she told him that she'd turned her back completely on God and religion, he understood her. Ben believed that she was a good-hearted Jewish woman who had gone through hell, just as he had, and it had left her with deep scars. If he took the time to evaluate his feelings, which he often did, he liked her, but there was something inside him that was stopping him from falling in love again. He decided it was fear. All the loss he'd endured during the war had built a protective barrier inside him that kept him from sharing his heart the way he once had.

Ben liked Levi and his family a great deal. They were open and honest people, not as religious as Ben's bosses at work, but they did celebrate Shabbat with a special dinner each Friday night. Ben enjoyed these ritualistic moments. They brought him back to his childhood when his mother had said the prayers covering her eyes over the Shabbos candles. The first time Levi had asked him to join the family for Shabbat he wept. As he looked around the table, his heart and mind were clouded with tender memories. Tears rolled down his cheeks as he recalled his wife, Lila, and their son during

Shabbat dinners. He thought of Zelda and how she'd tried to keep the Sabbath even in the Lodz ghetto. Remembering the faces of Solomon and Sarah, her wonderfully inquisitive children, made his heart ache. No one from his past had ever contacted him. He had no choice but to assume they were all dead. The very thought of those children taken from the earth before they'd had the chance to taste the sweetness of life, sickened him. He tried to wipe the thoughts from his mind, but it was impossible. Often, during the course of his day, in his mind's eye he would see little Moishe's smile just the way it was the last time his mother had carried him out of their flat in the ghetto. What would his Moishe have done with his life if things had been different? What would Zelda's children have become? It was pointless and painful to think about, yet he could not control his thoughts.

Ben told Levi that he had been seeing a woman. "Her name is Atara. She, like me, is a survivor of a concentration camp," Ben explained.

"I'm glad you met someone. No one should live out their lives alone. Perhaps you might like to invite her for Shabbos dinner this Friday night? We would love to have her."

The next time Ben saw Atara he invited her to come to Shabbos dinner, but she declined. She said it brought back too many memories of the past for her, and the pain was too great to bear. Ben told her he understood and respected her feelings. He also said that if she ever changed her mind he was sure that Levi and his family would love to have her.

CHAPTER 66

EVERY MORNING, GRETCHEN WOULD DRESS ANATOLE AND THEN walk him to school. Then she went to work at the local hospital cleaning rooms, washing down bedpans, and scrubbing floors.

As she scrubbed the floor in the hall of the hospital she let her thoughts drift. *Once, long ago, I planned to go to university. I had such wonderful dreams of what my life would be like. Of course, that was before Hitler. What a curse that man was on Germany. Not only Germany but the entire world. How sweet and idealistic I'd been as a young girl. I fell so deeply in love with Eli. Even now I can remember how devastatingly handsome he was with his dark hair and deep somber eyes. Those wonderful eyes of his were always filled with kindness and wisdom.* She smiled when she thought of him. When she first saw him she'd been afraid of his black coat and payot, the uniform of a Hasidic man. But as she came to know him, she'd found everything about him, even his religious beliefs, wildly intriguing. *If Hitler had not come to power I know that Eli and I would have found a way to be together. It would have been difficult. His family would have probably been resistant to having a Gentile daughter-in-law. But our love was so strong that I am certain it would have prevailed.* Gretchen looked down at the floor she was washing and at her raw hands, red from scrubbing. She felt tears sting the backs of her eyelids.

There was no point in thinking about the past: it only depressed her.

For months after Rebecca's visit, Gretchen fought an internal battle. She felt it was only right that she search for Benjamin Rabinowitz and if she found him, tell him about his son. *I am holding on to this child because he is all I have. Once he is gone, there will be nothing left for me. I am so happy for Rebecca that she has found her true bashert, but I wish she and Jan lived closer. I would love to be able see her more often. We swore we would keep in touch. But she has her life now, and I don't know if or when she will return to Germany. And I don't earn enough money to travel to Poland. I am a German woman in Berlin, under Russian occupation. I am lucky to have a job and a place to live.*

One night, Gretchen had a dream. In the dream, Eli came to her. He spoke clearly in his soft voice telling her that she must search for Benjamin Rabinowitz. And if she finds him it is only right that she return Moishe to his father. She felt Eli's hand warm on her shoulder, and she knew that the time had come.

CHAPTER 67

Summer Berlin, Germany 1947

GRETCHEN HELD THE PAPER IN HER TREMBLING FINGERS. ANATOLE was playing on the floor. She faced away from him so he could not see her expression as she opened the letter.

"Benjamin Rabinowitz

Last known phone number and address:

Phone: 212-588-4268

357 Delancey Street, Apartment 415

New York, New York, United States of America"

According to this letter, Moishe's father was alive. The very thought of it made her feel dizzy.

She forced herself to pick up the telephone receiver and held it tightly for a moment. It felt cold in her hand. *If I dial this number, my life will change. And I've been through so many changes, so much loss. I could hang up this phone and hide this number, and then things would go on as before. What would happen if I never told Anatole the truth? What if he never knew anything about his past? Only Rebecca, her husband, Jan, and I know his real identity. And if I asked Rebecca to keep it all a secret she would do as I ask. She loves me that much. Even though she knows it's wrong, she will do whatever I ask. But do I love Anatole as much as I claim to? What is love? Is love keeping someone with you and forsaking their happiness for your own? Can real love ever be built on lies? If I lie to Anatole, won't there always be something between us, keeping us apart, keeping us from ever being really close?* Gretchen's fingers trembled but she dialed the number. The phone rang. It was an strange and empty sound. *Probably because I am calling America*, she thought. Three times it rang. Then an operator answered.

"What number are you calling?" she asked in perfect English.

Gretchen spoke English well enough to understand the question. She responded, "212-588-4268."

"I'm sorry, that number is not in service at this time. Please be sure you're calling the correct number."

"Not in service? What does this mean?"

"The number is not working, ma'am. I'm sorry."

"Not working?"

"That's correct."

"But why?"

"I don't have that information. I'm sorry. Please be sure you are calling the correct number," the operator repeated, sounding more like a machine than a person.

"Thank you," Gretchen said, placing the receiver back in its cradle. For a few moments she breathed a sigh of relief, then she shook her head. *I would like to let this all disappear. After all, I did try to call. So when Anatole grows up, I could say that I tried to find his father. And it would be true. I did try but not hard enough. I love that child, and the truth is I owe it to him to go to New York and find Benjamin Rabinowitz. Even though it is very expensive to go to America, I must find a way to get the money.*

Again, Gretchen picked up the telephone receiver. This time she dialed the number Rebecca had given her in Poland.

Rebecca answered on the first ring, "Hello?"

"Rebecca, it's Gretchen," she said. "I don't know if you can help me or not. But . . . I need to borrow some money. It's very impor-tant. And to make matters even worse, I don't know how I am ever going to pay it back to you."

"Don't worry. Jan and I have some money saved. It's yours."

CHAPTER 68

AT FIRST ANATOLE WAS VERY FRIGHTENED BY THE OCEAN LINER THEY
boarded to America. He hid behind Gretchen whenever anyone
tried to talk to either of them. After a couple of days at sea, he was
dizzy and vomiting. Gretchen had told him nothing more except
they were on their way to America for an adventure. That, she
decided, was enough information at this point for a ten-year-old boy.
He had not wanted to go. His first reaction was fear. It was always
that way with Anatole. It seemed he was afraid of everything. But to
soothe his nerves, she told him stories about the brave American
soldiers who had helped to defeat the Nazis. This seemed to calm
him, and he agreed to go. Gretchen knew that he was a nervous
child. He had a bad habit of pulling out tufts of his hair and biting
his nails to the quick. It broke her heart. But she understood him.
Anatole had been through so much in his young life that he was
always afraid that something bad was about to happen.

On his first day of school, he'd broken out in hives and vomited
twice on the walk there. Gretchen didn't know what she was going
to do. But he'd finally adjusted and for that she was grateful. But he
still hadn't made any friends, and sometimes she found him crying
alone in his room. "The other children at school hate me," he said.

"They are mean to me. Promise me that you'll never leave me, Auntie Gretchen." Even though they had been together for several years, he still asked her at least once a week if she was ever going to leave him. She'd never promised that she would be with him forever because she wasn't sure if he would be going to live with his father some day. But whenever he asked, she told him she loved him, rubbed his back, and read to him. And somehow that seemed to calm him. But since she was not sure what she was going to find at the end of her journey, she didn't want him to agonize over the outcome.

Even though she had an address, it was still possible that Benjamin Rabinowitz was not there anymore, or even worse that he had somehow perished. The less Anatole knew about Gretchen's plans, the better. If it turned out they were unable to find his father, then they would return to Germany without Anatole ever knowing the reason for the trip until he grew older. If they did find Benjamin, there was always the possibility that he might not want the child. He may have started a new life, have a wife, or even another child. In that case, Gretchen would take Anatole home and raise him with all the love in her heart. But then there was always the possibility that Anatole's father would want to be reunited with his son. In that case, Gretchen would have to allow him to take the boy. She would have to find the courage to say goodbye. And that was her greatest fear.

They arrived in the New York harbor on a hot and dusty Monday afternoon in the middle of August. Gretchen held Anatole's hand as they walked through the park to the train station where they would catch the train into the Jewish section of the city. Anatole followed obediently, but he was trembling.

"It's exciting, isn't it? To be here in America?" She tried to sound optimistic.

"Yes," the boy lied. She knew him well enough to know he was lying. Then in a soft voice he whispered, "I wish we could go home to our apartment in Germany. I don't want to be here."

"Anatole," she said, crouching down so that she could be at eye level with him. "You have so much to see and do in your life. You can't let your fear keep you from living."

"Auntie Gretchen . . ." he said.

"Yes?"

"If I had my choice, I would never go to school. I would never leave the house. You and I would stay at home together, safe, safe from all the bad people who hurt other people. We would never, ever leave."

"Anatole," she said, shaking her head, trying to keep the tears from forming in her eyes. "That's not living. That's existing. Living is getting out and being a part of the world."

"I hate the world. I hate the things that can happen in the world," he said.

"But good things can happen too."

"I don't believe you. Good things never happen. Only terrible things."

Have I made a mistake bringing him here? Should I have never searched for his father? Am I setting him up for another awful experience? I am so confused; what is the right thing to do? I wish I knew.

Gretchen and Anatole took the subway into a heavily populated section of Manhattan that was filled with immigrants, noise, and tenements. They checked into a cheap hotel. Gretchen needed a good night's sleep before making her way to the address on Delancey Street that could change everything in her life.

After they checked into the hotel, Gretchen helped Anatole select clean clothes to change into for dinner, then she changed as well. "After dinner, we can take a walk around the city before it gets dark. Would you like that?"

Anatole shrugged. "I don't know. It's a big city, and I don't understand the language. I'm a little afraid, Auntie Gretchen. We could just go back upstairs to our room."

"Don't be afraid," she said, smiling at him and taking his hand in both of hers.

In the small café next to the hotel, Anatole huddled in his chair, moving it as close to Gretchen as possible as they waited for their bread and soup. He kept his eyes glued to her face. For the first few minutes neither of them said anything, then Anatole asked "Auntie

Gretchen, please tell me the truth. Why are we here? Why did we come to this strange country?"

"I already told you. We came for an exciting adventure." She tried to muster a sincere smile.

The waitress, a pencil-thin woman slightly hunched over, with shoe-polish black hair, set two bowls of soup and two glasses of water, along with two hunks of heavy bread down on the table. "Do you need anything else?" she asked Gretchen.

"This should be fine," Gretchen said, "Thank you."

After the waitress left, Gretchen handed Anatole his napkin. "Please put this on your lap," she said, gently reminding him of the manners she'd taught him.

Anatole did as he was told, then he turned to Gretchen. From his expression, she couldn't tell if he was angry or just frustrated, but he blurted out, "That's what you said every time I asked you why we left Berlin when we were on the boat. You said we were on an adventure. But I don't believe you. I don't believe that we have come halfway across the world to have an adventure. I know how difficult it is for you to earn enough money for us to pay the rent. I'm not blind. I see you struggle to pay the bills each month. I am young, but I am not stupid, I know that this trip must have cost a lot of money. So there's got to be a good reason why we came all the way here. Please, Auntie Gretchen . . . tell me. I have to know the truth. Is it about my mom and dad? Are they here? Are we going to see them?"

Gretchen sucked her breath in and swallowed hard. She looked away from Anatole. *He thinks we have come here to America to meet with Hilde and Axel. He still believes they were his real parents. I know he's only ten, but he is very mature for his age. Pain and hardship will do that I suppose. And to make things even harder for the poor child, I know that soon I am going to have to tell him the truth. I've been avoiding it; it's such a horrible truth, but he must know. He must know before tomorrow because tomorrow we might actually meet with his real father. I think it's best that I tell him the truth about everything now. Eli, if only you were here to help me. You were always so wise. You would know what words to say to this child to somehow make sense of his terrible and confusing life. But you are not here.*

Hitler took you away from me. He took everything that I held dear. You and my father, and now he might even take Anatole. At least I have found Rebecca again. She is like my sister, and if I find Benjamin Rabinowitz, she will be the only family I have left. "Anatole." Gretchen swallowed hard and then said as firmly as she could, "I've changed my mind about taking a walk tonight. As soon as you've finished your dinner, we should go up to our room. I want to talk to you. I have to tell you something important."

CHAPTER 69

"Moishe Rabinowitz? My name is Moishe Rabinowitz? I don't remember anyone named Lila. You say my real mother's name is Lila?" Anatole said.

"Yes." Gretchen nodded.

"And Hilde and Axel weren't my parents; they were Nazi guards?"

Again Gretchen nodded.

"My real mother and father were Jewish?"

"I know all of this is hard for you to grasp. And . . . I don't know if I did the right thing by bringing you here, but I didn't want you to grow up and not know the truth. You deserve to meet your father if he is alive."

"I'm frightened, Auntie Gretchen. As you were telling me everything I remembered having dreams of a woman, a blonde woman, with hair the same color as mine. In the dream she and I were in a forest. I remember that she held me close to her. She sang to me. I am either imagining it, or maybe it wasn't a dream. Maybe it really happened, and she was my real mother."

"I don't know anything about your real mother except that she died in Ravensbrück. I never saw her."

He lay his head on Gretchen's shoulder. She felt his tears wet the sleeve of her blouse. "I'm so sorry that I have to be the one to tell you all of this."

"I am glad you did," he said, sounding far older than his ten years.

"Do you want to go and meet your father?"

"Yes. I'm a little afraid, but I want to meet him. I want to know everything," he said. "You'll be there with me . . ."

"Of course I will be with you. I am assuming he probably works during the day, so we will go tomorrow evening after dinner."

"What if he wants me to stay with him? Will I have to?"

"I don't know."

"What if I don't want to? What if I want to go home with you?" his voice was strained with panic.

"Then you'll tell him as much, and I'll try to arrange for a way that you can live with me but keep in contact with him. I honestly don't know what is going to happen."

Moishe's face was wet with tears, but he nodded. And when he did, his beautiful golden hair caught rays of light from the small lamp on the table.

CHAPTER 70

Every Tuesday at four in the afternoon when Ben finished work for the day, he met Atara in the city for a quick dinner. Then they went back to her apartment to play cards. Lately, they'd begun to kiss deeper and longer. They had not made love, but they cuddled. The closeness that had begun to develop between Ben and Atara gave Ben a sense of security. For the first time in a very long time, he felt a small amount of joy. It was not as if things would ever be right in his world, he had too many memories that kept him awake at night, but his deepening friendship with Atara had brightened his life if only a little.

As he did every Tuesday night, Ben stopped at the florist and picked up a small bouquet. Then he went to the café where he met Atara. She was waiting for him at their regular booth. When she saw him she smiled.

"How was work today?" she asked.

"It was work."

They both laughed.

After dinner they went back to her flat and played a few hands of cards. When they kissed, Ben took his glasses out of the breast pocket of his shirt and laid them on the coffee table. He didn't need them for everyday use. He only needed them for cutting diamonds.

They kissed, and he held her tightly. "You've filled my life," he said.

She smiled. "You've filled mine too, Ben. Would you like to come into the bedroom?" She'd prepared the previous week by etching a series of numbers into her forearm with a dark blue fountain pen.

He nodded. It had been a long time since he'd been with a woman in that way. He longed not only for the release but for the intimacy of sharing himself with another person.

Atara led him into the bedroom. She took off the pearls she wore around her neck. They were the same pearls that Hilde had coveted all those years ago and the only piece of jewelry she still owned. The rest she'd had to sacrifice for her escape. Five thousand dollars. That was all she had to her name. It was a nice sum, but it would not last forever. *Ben is the kind of man who would work hard to support a wife. Once he finishes his apprenticeship as a diamond cutter, he should make a nice living. And even though he is a Jew, he would be a good husband to me. I could count on him to support me.* There was deep sincerity in Ben's dark eyes as he stared at her. He was so serious that it made her want to laugh. She controlled the impulse.

"Are you sure you're ready for this? I don't want you to feel rushed," Ben said.

She nodded.

"I want you to know that I'll wait as long as you need me to. I like you very much, and I am hoping our friendship will develop to something even deeper than it has. I am not saying that I don't want to make love to you. What man wouldn't? You are beautiful, and it's been a very long time since I have been in the presence of a beautiful woman. But I want you to feel sure that this is what you want to do. You are very important to me, and I want you to know that there is no hurry for this."

"You sound reluctant," she said, cocking her head.

"I'm just . . . oh, I don't know . . . I'm just trying to let you know that your feelings are very important to me."

She kissed him and unbuttoned her blouse.

CHAPTER 71

NEITHER GRETCHEN NOR MOISHE HAD MUCH OF AN APPETITE that Tuesday evening as they sat at the same café and ordered the same soup as they did the night before. After a half hour, Gretchen looked across the table at Moishe. He was playing with his food.

"Are you ready?"

"I think so," he said.

He is so old for his age. Hitler made old men out of adolescent boys. It hurts my heart to look at him sitting there. He's so afraid to face the truth.

"We don't have to do this if you don't want to. I want to give you the option to leave now if you want to."

"I don't know what to do, Auntie Gretchen. If he is really my father and he is still alive, I think I should meet him. But then, I am really scared, and I would rather get on the next boat back to Germany without ever knowing him. I am not sure of what to do."

"I have thought about all of that too. But I am afraid that later, when you are older, you will wish we would have gone to see him. And then, well, who knows . . . it could be too late."

"You mean he might be dead?"

"Yes, he might. We don't know how old he is or if he is in good health. In fact, we know almost nothing about him. There is also the possibility that he might move away without leaving any forwarding address. And if that should happen, we might never find him," she said. "I realize that you are very young to be faced with all of this. However, you must make this choice. I can't make it for you, Anatole. Or would you prefer I call you Moishe?"

"Anatole is my name. It's the only name I know . . ."

"I understand, and I'll call you Anatole."

CHAPTER 72

It was not difficult to find the address on Delancey Street. For several moments, both Anatole and Gretchen stood outside staring at the brown bricks of the old tenement. It was dark, and the only light in the starless sky was a full, rounded silver moon.

"Shall we go to the door?" Gretchen took Anatole's hand.

He didn't speak, but he began to walk forward slowly like a man on death row.

They silently climbed four flights of rickety, wooden stairs then walked down a dark corridor until they saw Apartment 415.

"This is it," Gretchen said.

"He might not even be here. He might have moved away," Anatole said more to himself than to Gretchen.

"I'm going to knock. All right?"

"Yes," Anatole managed.

She knocked and they waited. A pretty, young woman, with a graying white scarf that almost completely covered her dark hair, answered the door.

"Hello, my name is Gretchen Schmidt. Is this the home of Benjamin Rabinowitz?"

"Yes." She looked at Gretchen skeptically.

"I think he will want to see me. I have come here all the way from Germany. This is his son, Moishe."

A veil of shock spread over the face of the pretty woman. Her hands were shaking as she gestured to Gretchen and Anatole. "Please, won't you come in? Ben is not at home, but I expect him to arrive any minute. He usually comes home at about eight thirty on Tuesday night, and it's already after eight."

"You are his wife?" Gretchen asked.

"No." She shook her head and managed a wry smile. "He is living here with my husband and I and our children. He is a good friend of the family."

"Oh," Gretchen said.

"Are you related to Ben?" the pretty woman asked.

"No, I am a woman who has been the guardian of his child. Ben and I have never met. The war made everything very confusing for everyone," Gretchen offered.

"Won't you sit down? Can I get you something to drink?"

Gretchen sat on the sofa with Anatole beside her.

"Who's here?" Levi came into the living room. "I heard a knock at the door."

"This is Gretchen Schmidt. The little boy is Ben's son. Gretchen has been caring for him."

"Oh!" Levi said.

Before Levi could say another word, they all heard a key turn in the lock. Then the door handle turned.

Anatole began biting his nails. He huddled into Gretchen. She could feel him trembling.

The door opened, and there stood the handsome, unassuming, soft-spoken Benjamin Rabinowitz. He glanced around the room, cocking his head with a puzzled look in his eyes. For what seemed like hours but, in fact, were only seconds, no one spoke. Then Gretchen stood up; her legs felt unsteady. "I'm Gretchen Schmidt. This is your son, Moishe. I've been taking care of him."

"Moishe?" Ben said. His voice was hoarse, his eyes shining with disbelief. "Is that really you?" Ben walked closer to the child. "My God, you look just like your mother." Ben could hardly stand up straight. He practically fell onto the sofa beside Moishe. "How are you? Where is your mother? Oh, dear God, I can't believe it's you."

Ben put his arms around Moishe who tensed up. "I'm sorry," Ben said. "You don't know me. Of course you don't remember anything, and now here I am trying to embrace you, and . . . well . . . what was I thinking?" He was crying and laughing at the same time. Moishe just looked at him wide eyed.

Then there was a knock at the door that quieted the entire room. Everything about this night had a dreamlike quality. "Who could that be?" Suddenly Ben looked around; his voice had a trace of fear. Perhaps it was seeing Moishe again that brought back the memory of the Gestapo coming to his home to arrest him and his entire family.

"I'll get it," Levi's wife said.

"Hello." A very pretty, petite woman stood in the doorway. "I am Atara Herskowitz, Benjamin's friend. He left his glasses at my apartment. I know he will need them for work tomorrow. Can you give them to him for me, please?"

Ben heard Atara's voice and said, "Come in. I have some wonderful and exciting news to share with you."

Atara walked inside.

"This is my girlfriend, Atara Herskowitz," Ben said.

Gretchen's mouth fell open. But she was not the first person to speak. The first person to say a word was Moishe. "Auntie Ilsa? Is that you?"

"Ilsa Guhr, how dare you come into this home? How dare you pose as a friend to Benjamin Rabinowitz when it was you who murdered Lila, his wife . . . Moishe's mother. I know you. I know all about you. A little hair dye isn't going to be enough of a disguise for you," Gretchen said as she was pointing directly at Ilsa. She had been so shocked to see Ilsa that she had spoken without thinking. She'd forgotten that Moishe was sitting beside her, listening. She looked over at the child whose face had turned gray as a mourning dove, and she immediately realized that this moment would change the boy forever. This was a terrible way for him to learn the truth. But it was too late. Several seconds passed and no one spoke.

"Ilsa Guhr?" Ben said in disbelief. "Who is Ilsa Guhr? Lila? You know Lila, Atara? There must be some mistake."

"There is no mistake, Ben. Atara's real name is Ilsa Guhr. She worked as a guard at Ravensbrück. She helped a married couple, who were also Nazi guards at Ravensbrück, steal Moishe. They took him because he looks so Aryan, and they were unable to have children. In order to bury this secret, Ilsa murdered Moishe's mother." Gretchen had to tell him the entire truth.

"Liar," Ilsa said.

"Am I? I have an old photograph of you with Hilde. I carry it in my wallet. Here, look . . ." Gretchen pulled out the picture of a smiling Ilsa with her arm around Hilde's shoulder. Both women wore the gray-skirted uniform of the Ravensbrück guards.

"Oh my God," Ben said. "What did I do tonight? How could I have done what I did with you," he said.

"You are a stupid, foolish Jew, Benjamin. And you, Gretchen, you were always a Jew lover. And I always laughed at your friendship with Hilde. She was nothing but a mental deficient. She should have been done away with when the party was ridding itself of such scum."

"Let me get this straight," Ben said, his eyes blazing. "You killed Moishe's mother? You murdered my wife?"

"Don't make more of this than it is, Ben. It was something that had to be done, that's all." Ilsa turned to walk out the door, but Ben ran over to her and grabbed her from behind before she could leave. He spun her around like a dreidel on Hanukkah and then began choking her. Levi's wife let out a scream. Ilsa's eyes were bulging, her throat was turning red, which became a deep bruised purple.

Gretchen ran over and tried to pull Ben off Ilsa. "Stop, you're going to kill her," he screamed, but Ben would not stop. He was raging, and he pushed Gretchen away. She ran back and shook his shoulder trying to shake sense into him. "Let's call the police," Gretchen begged. "Don't kill her. Please, Ben, it will be murder. You'll go to jail or worse. And she isn't worth it!"

Moishe started crying and rolled himself into a fetal position in the corner of the sofa. Levi, too, tried to pull Ben off Ilsa but he was unstoppable. And by the time Ben's rage was spent, Ilsa was dead.

Levi double-checked Ilsa's arm for a pulse. There was none. He shook his head. "She's dead."

Ben hung his head, his anger was gone. "Call the police," he said in a soft voice. "Tell them what happened. Tell them to come and get me."

As they waited for the police, Ben turned to Gretchen. "Take my son back home with you. Please, will you raise him? Do you love him?"

"Yes, I will raise him. And I do love him very much."

"I know what I did was wrong tonight. I lost control. I wish Moishe had not seen this."

"Yes, the poor child has seen far too much."

"Please, before you go, leave me a phone number and an address where I can reach you. I don't know what is in store for me, but maybe sometime, who knows, we will meet again," Ben said, then he gave Gretchen a sad smile.

When the police arrived, Ben did not fight. He went with them . . . willingly.

CHAPTER 73

It was almost two full weeks before Gretchen was able to secure passage back to Germany on an ocean liner. During those two weeks, Anatole hardly spoke. He'd wet his bed in the hotel twice, but he'd been too embarrassed to tell Gretchen. However, the hotel staff came to the room to complain about the bed-wetting. They insisted that Gretchen find a way to make this stop. Gretchen felt so badly for Anatole. She blamed herself for bringing him to America. She explained to the hotel manager that she could not promise that the bed-wetting would stop, but she agreed to pay extra to have the sheets double washed and the mattress cleaned. That seemed to satisfy him.

Gretchen tried to talk to Anatole; she wanted him to open up to her. Even if he yelled at her or wept, it would be better than this terrifying silence. But he refused. She was quickly running out of money. Rebecca had given her what she could, but Gretchen had never spent so much money before in her life. So because Anatole hardly ate, they began splitting a bowl of soup each night. He was awakened by terrible nightmares almost every night, but he wouldn't tell Gretchen what he'd dreamed. Instead, he just sat on the chair curled up in a ball waiting for the light of dawn. She was miserable with guilt. *I tried to do what was right for Anatole, and I ended up hurting him. I don't know if he'll ever recover.*

Gretchen called Rebecca. It was an expensive indulgence to call Poland, but she needed to talk to someone. The cost prohibited them from speaking for very long, but hearing Rebecca's voice gave her some small comfort.

Finally, the day arrived, and Gretchen and Anatole boarded the ship. Nothing changed for Anatole during the voyage. He remained withdrawn and anxious. There was another boy close to Anatole's age on board, and Gretchen tried to encourage Anatole to make friends, but he had no interest.

When they arrived back at their apartment in Berlin, Anatole went right to his room and closed the door. He'd been begging Gretchen for a dog for several months, and she was seriously considering adopting one. It would be another expense she didn't need, but the child was a mess, and she owed it to him. So she decided she would look into it.

The day after their return, Gretchen returned to work, and Anatole went back to school. Two days later, he came home with a black eye and blood crusting around his nose.

"What happened to you?" Gretchen said when she arrived home from work.

"Nothing." He shrugged.

"Yes, something did. You've been fighting."

He shook his head. "Nothing," he said again.

"Please talk to me, Anatole. I need for you to talk to me so I can help you." Gretchen was desperate, almost in tears. But Anatole just walked away and went into his room.

Gretchen sat on the sofa in the living room, an unopened novel on her lap and a cold cup of tea on the coffee table. She was thinking about the dog. It would be difficult for her to afford to feed a pet, but it might be worth it to help the child.

There was a knock on the door. Gretchen looked at the clock

and trembled. It was 9 p.m. *Who would be coming here at this time of night?*

She got up from the sofa and walked to the door. She glanced through the peephole, but one of the lights in the hallway had burned out, and it was too dark to see anything. Taking a breath, she opened the door.

Her hands flew to her throat. She could hardly speak. "Eli."

He nodded. Tears ran down his cheeks, then they ran down hers as well. He took her into his arms and held her tightly, both of them still in the doorway. "I thought you were dead," she said.

"I almost died in an uprising. I was left for dead then rescued by a band of Gypsies." He was squeezing her, taking her in, breathing in her hair, the scent of her skin.

"Oh Eli, how I've missed you." She pulled him inside the apartment and closed the door. Pulling him close to her she whispered, "I missed you so much . . ." She was weeping and laughing at the same time.

"I love you, Gretchen. My love for you was the only thing that kept me alive." He kissed her all over her face.

"Auntie Gretchen?" It was Anatole. "Who is that?"

"Anatole." Gretchen looked at the child who was staring at her. "This is Eli. You've heard me talk about him. Do you remember Rebecca spoke of him too when she came?"

Anatole nodded. "You both said you thought he was dead."

"But he isn't. We were wrong. He's right here."

Anatole looked from Gretchen to Eli. "I have to go pee," he said and ran out of the room in the direction of the bathroom.

"Who is he?" Eli asked in a gentle voice when the child was gone.

Quickly, and in whispers, Gretchen explained the situation with Anatole including that his real name was Moishe. "I don't know what I am going to do. He is traumatized by what happened with his father and rightfully so. I feel like it's all my fault . . ."

"Don't worry, my love. I am your partner in all things. I am here to share in your life if you will have me. I will help you with this boy. We will raise him together. I don't know how we will help him, but we will. You'll see; it will be all right. Together we will ask God for his help. And God will show us the way. He will give us the right words. I am here now, and you are here in my arms. This is what is most important. God brought me back to you. And I have never been so filled with joy in my life."

"I am so happy, Eli. I am so happy to feel you here close to me. It's like a dream," she said, touching his face. "You can't know how much I love you."

"I know how much I love you, and if it's even half as much, then it is a lot." He kissed her again. "I heard you mention that you have been in contact with Rebecca?"

"Yes, she is married."

"We are blessed. I give thanks to Hashem; may his name be blessed. We have all survived. In the morning we should contact Rebecca. I would like to tell her that I am alive, and that I am glad she has found her bashert and she is happy. I will ask her for a *get*, a Jewish divorce, so I can marry you. I am sure she will comply. Will you marry me?"

"Oh yes. Oh yes," she said. They kissed again, and when they opened their eyes, Anatole had returned. He was standing there in his pajamas watching them.

"Anatole," Eli said. "Hello, my name is Eli."

Anatole stared at him, cautiously backing away until he was huddled into the wall.

"You know what?" Eli said in an upbeat tone of voice. "I heard that there is something very special about you. Would you like to know what it is?"

"Special? About me?" Anatole asked with a child's curiosity. "What is it?"

"I heard your real name is Moishe."

"It's not. It's Anatole."

"Very well, Anatole. But I would like to tell you a story. Would you like to hear a story?"

"What kind of story?"

"A story about another man whose name was Moishe."

"Yes, I guess I would like to hear the story," Anatole said.

"Come, we'll both sit down here on the sofa, and I'll tell you all about this man."

Anatole nodded in agreement and sat down, but he crouched into the side of the sofa as far away from Eli as possible and watched Eli skeptically. Eli smiled at him warmly.

"This is the story of Moses. Moishe is the Yiddish name for Moses." Eli looked at Anatole, his eyes warm, inviting, and tender. "Have you ever heard this story?"

"No," Anatole said. He shrugged, trying to look as if he were not interested, but Eli could see the inquisitiveness shining from his eyes.

"This is a very important story. It comes from the Bible," Eli said, then he continued, "Moses, or Moishe, was born a Jewish boy. He lived during a time in history when Egypt had enslaved the Jewish people. And the Jewish people were being worked to death and starved. When little Moses was born, his mother wrapped him in a Hebrew blanket and then put him in a basket. Then do you know what she did?"

"No," Moishe said, "what did she do?"

"She took the basket and put it in the Nile River then allowed the basket to float down the river. She had to do this. It was the only way to save his life. You see, the Egyptians were killing all the Jewish baby boys. And if they would have found Moses they would have killed him too. Can you imagine the trust his mother had to put in God to send her son away in a basket on the river? Anything could have happened to him. He could have drowned or been eaten by crocodiles—but he wasn't. Do you know why?"

"No."

"I'll tell you. It was because God had bigger plans for Moses."

"Crocodiles? What are crocodiles?"

"They are long, dangerous lizards bigger than any man."

"And they live in that river where Moses' mother put him?"

"Yes, they do. But even though there were dangers, Moses' mother trusted that God would protect her child."

"God?" Moishe asked.

"God. Hashem, our Creator. May his name be blessed. He watches over all of us."

"Me too?"

"Yes of course you too, Anatole. And I know that you have been through terrible things. You have suffered a lot for someone so young. But you are here now. You have survived because God was with you. And like Moses, God has a plan for you."

"Are you sure of this?" Anatole asked.

"Oh yes, I am very sure," Eli said as the child moved closer to him. Eli put his arm around the boy, then he continued to tell his story. "Now it just so happened that the daughter of the pharaoh saw little Moses floating in the river. She was barren. That means she could not have children of her own. And she had always wanted a child. So she took off the Hebrew cloth that Moses had been wrapped in and hid the fact that Moses was Jewish. In fact, she raised him as her son. Because she was the pharaoh's daughter, this put Moses in line to become the next ruler of Egypt. Moses grew up as an Egyptian. He was happy in his life. But God had saved him because he had a very important task for Moses. The Jewish people had been suffering, and God heard their prayers, so he'd sent Moses to help the Jewish people break out of bondage. Soon, although the pharaoh's sister tried to hide Moses' Jewish background, the Egyptians discovered that Moses was not really one of them. They learned that he had been born a Jew," Eli said, never losing eye contact with the child, as he spoke in his deep and wise voice.

Anatole's eyes were trained on Eli with interest.

"So Moses left his comfortable life with the Egyptians and took his place as one of the Jews. He became a slave and he was tortured. But with God's help, Moses led the Jewish people out of bondage. He was a great and powerful leader. A very powerful leader indeed." Eli smiled

"And I share his name? Moishe," Anatole said.

"Moishe. Yes, you do share his name. And a great and powerful name it is. "

"Moishe?" Anatole repeated. "And he was a great leader?"

"One of the greatest leaders of the Jewish people. One of the strongest and most important men ever to live according to the Bible."

"I guess I like my real name, Moishe."

"I don't blame you. It's truly an honor," Eli said, nodding. "So would you like me to call you Moishe?"

"Yes, I think I would," Moishe said, and a single tear ran down his cheek.

Gretchen stood on the sidelines watching Eli with Moishe. Her hands were clutched in fists against her mouth. How she loved this man and his wisdom; how she loved this lonely, little boy. Her face was wet with tears of joy. She smiled, and her heart swelled. Eli was alive. He was home. And although there would be difficult times raising this troubled child whom she loved, she knew that all would be well because she and Eli would raise him together.

AUTHORS NOTE

I always enjoy hearing from my readers, and your thoughts about my work are very important to me. If you enjoyed my novel, please consider telling your friends and posting a short review on Amazon. Word of mouth is an author's best friend.

Also, it would be my honor to have you join my mailing list. As my gift to you for joining, you will receive 3 **free** short stories and my USA Today award-winning novella complimentary in your email! To sign up, just go to my website at www.RobertaKagan.com

I send blessings to each and every one of you,

Roberta

Email: roberta@robertakagan.com

Keep reading to get a sneak peek at the third book in the A Holocaust Story Series:
Sarah and Solomon

SARAH AND SOLOMON

Solomon could hardly catch his breath as he looked into his mother's eyes. "Take care of your sister," she said somberly. Solomon rubbed the sleep out of his eyes. And even though he was in the familiar small room that he shared with his sister, Sarah; his mother; and his mother's friend, Benjamin Rabinowitz, it was the middle of the night, and the stars that came through the window gave the small space an eerie glow. For a moment he felt that the entire situation was not real. His heart was pounding. Perhaps, he thought, he might be trapped in a terrible nightmare.

"Mother?" he said, sitting up in bed.

"Yes, Solomon."

"Am I dreaming?"

"No, son. I wish to God that you were. But this is not a dream. So you must wake up quickly, and get your wits about you. Now, I know I am asking a lot of you, and what I am asking is a big responsibility for a boy your age, but you have always been my little man. From the first day I held you in my arms, I knew you were special. You have an old soul, Solomon, and I love you more than you'll ever know. But, my son, my dear beloved child, I have no choice but to send you and your sister away."

So it was true. He'd heard her correctly. It was not a dream at all. His mother was sending him and Sarah away from the ghetto, and she wanted them to leave immediately.

Zelda, Solomon's mother, continued as she stroked his hair. "My son, my dear sweet boy. My Solomon. As much as I would like to keep the two of you here for as long as I can, and every moment I can share with you and your sister is precious to me, I know that we must act quickly. There is no time for sentiment. As much as it hurts me, I know in my heart that this is the only chance the two of you will have to survive the Nazis."

She wiped a tear from her cheek with the back of her hand.

Then she touched his shoulder. "My babies, my two precious babies."

"We're not babies anymore, Mama. I'm nine, and Sarah is five," Solomon said, trying to sound strong.

"Of course you're not. But to me, you will always be my babies." Then she forced herself to smile. "Now, I know how smart you are, Solomon, and I am depending on your quick wit. You'll need to be smart and alert at all times." She went on. He could see, by looking at the pain in her eyes, just how distressed she was, and it frightened him.

"I know what a strong boy you are, and I'm counting on you to use every bit of street savvy you have to protect Sarah," she said, touching his cheek softly. "Your sister is only five, and she has been protected and is not nearly as wise as you. She is going to need you, Solomon."

Solomon felt the bile rise in his throat. He wished he were still asleep, still an innocent child trying to keep his mother from finding out that he'd been sneaking out of the ghetto or palling around with a wild bunch of older boys.

"Tomorrow, Mordechai Rumkowski . . ." she said, and he turned away from her, not wanting to face the truth that she was about to share with him.

He knew who Rumkowski was. He was the head Judenrat of the Lodz ghetto.

Zelda gently took her hand and put it on his chin. Then she

turned his head back to face her, and her eyes fixed on his. "Rumkowski made a speech today. He said that tomorrow all of the children, who are under ten and living here in the Lodz ghetto, would be sent away on a transport to fulfill a quota for the Nazis. He didn't tell us where they would be sent. But everyone who has been living within these prison walls of the ghetto, knows that those who are sent away on transports, never come back."

Solomon had heard that anyone who went on a transport was murdered. "I've heard the rumors. I've heard that the people who are sent away on transports are murdered."

Zelda could not speak. She let out a gasp as she pulled Solomon close to her and buried her face in his hair.

"Mama, you're crying."

She nodded. Zelda found it hard to believe that even the Nazis could be so cruel as to murder her children. However, she dared not trust them or Rumkowski. These two precious lives must be forced to leave her and get as far from the ghetto as they could. Then maybe, if God would only watch over them, they might have a chance to live. Her mind whirled with terror. She searched for any other solution, but could not find any. Her two children would be all alone. Wandering the streets of Poland with no money and no food, they would be at the mercy of strangers. But if she went with them, they would most assuredly be caught.

The children were small, and Solomon knew how to slip in and out of the ghetto wall, but she was too big to get through. *Dear God, what am I to do? Am I making the right choice? How will they live? What will become of my babies? These two precious lives, lives that you, God, have entrusted to me.* She closed her eyes and remembered how she'd held them in her arms at night when they were sick. How she'd rocked them to sleep when they were scared and taught them as much as they could comprehend about reading. She'd shared books with them and given them her own food when the family had run short. And now, her only choice was to entrust them back to God. If they stayed here with her, they would be ripped from her arms in the morning. *Watch over them, dear God. Please keep them in the palm of your mighty hand.*

Although Solomon was very young, only nine, he was tough. His friends were less-than-savory characters, who were much older than he. They'd taught him how to maneuver his way in out of the ghetto walls. Solomon knew where every opening was and how to get through. He prided himself on how easily he'd learned all of it. He was tall and muscular, looking much older than his nine years. And he'd already had several years of experience slipping in and out of the ghetto at night to make deals with the Polish underground to buy and trade on the black market. His mother had begged him to stop. She was afraid he would be caught, but he was incorrigible, running around as if he were indestructible.

Many nights he would make his quiet escape from the bed he shared with his sister after she fell asleep and return before sunrise with necessities, like extra food for his family and a little more to sell. It was dangerous, of course, but at that time, at least he had been able to return to the apartment where his family lived. After tonight, he knew he could never come home. When his mother awakened him, she warned him that no matter what happened, he and his sister must never return to the ghetto. He'd steeled himself, trying hard to be a man. But the truth was he wanted to run into his mother's arms and cry like a baby.

"When this is all over, I will find you and your sister. But for now, you must stay far away from here," his mother warned.

"How will you find us?"

"I don't know. But I will. Now, you must trust me. And go, hurry, get as far away as you can before the sun comes up." Zelda wiped her tear-stained face on her nightgown.

Benjamin Rabinowitz awakened. He'd crawled quietly out of his bed and was now standing by Zelda's side with his arm around her shoulders.

Solomon glanced at Benjamin, who looked worn out and very sad.

"Mama, I don't want to go," Sarah said. "I want to stay here with you."

"I know. But you must go with your brother. And you must mind him. Do you understand?"

"I don't want to go," Sarah moaned again.

Solomon took both her hands in his. "Listen to me. I'll take care of you. And before you know it, Mama will come and find us."

"I don't believe you, Solomon."

"Have I ever lied to you?"

"No."

"I won't this time. I promise," he said. "Now come. We must go."

Zelda hugged her beloved children for several moments. Her mind went wild with worry, sadness, and terror. How could she be sending these two little children out into the world alone. But . . . she had no other choice, and she knew it. If she didn't send them away, Rumkowski would take them.

"Go. Please go, and hurry." Zelda had wrapped all the food she had left from her rations in a clean towel, which she gave to Solomon. Then she placed his father's gold ring into his hand. "This was your father's. It's real gold. Sell it to buy food or whatever else you need. I know you'll be careful," she said as her body was trembling.

Sarah saw her mother give Solomon the ring. "That's Papa's ring," she said angrily. "He'll want it when he comes back."

"It's all right. Papa told me to give it to Solomon," Zelda said. Her husband, Asher, who had been a volatile and abusive man, had been sent away on a transport. She didn't know if he would return. But if he did, she would worry about the ring then. Right now, she wanted Solomon to take it and use the money to provide for him and Sarah.

Solomon took the food. He plunged the ring deep into his pants pocket. Then he grabbed Sarah's hand. "Let's go. The guards in the tower are less likely to notice us while it's still dark."

"Mama? Are you sure I have to go?" Sarah said, shaking and holding her doll tightly.

Zelda nodded, then she said, "Sarala, I love you. Solomon, I love you too, my little man."

He nodded, trying hard to hold back his tears, then he forced himself to smile at his mother, hoping he was reassuring her as he gently dragged his sister out into the darkness. He felt his stomach lurch with fear. But he couldn't stop. He knew he must do as his mother asked. So, still holding tight to Sarah's hand, he pulled her, and within seconds they disappeared onto the route that he'd come to know so well. Before long, he knew they would come to the crack in the ghetto wall where he would push Sarah through and then follow behind her.

The streets were dark. Sarah gripped Solomon's hand tightly. He moved fast, but all his senses were on high alert. He'd done this a million times before but never with a five-year-old child hanging on to him. From the intensity of Sarah's grip, he could feel her terror. She needed comforting. He knew that; he could feel it. But it was not safe to stop and coddle her right now. He had to stay as vigilant as possible and get them out as quickly as he could, so even though he could hear her softly sobbing, he just squeezed her hand and pulled her along. Her short little legs made her slower. He was annoyed, but at the same time he felt sorry for her as she struggled to keep up with him clutching her doll in her arm.

"Who goes there?" It was the voice of one of the Germans. Solomon thought he could tell the Judenrat henchmen from the Nazi guards. This was a Nazi. *Damn*, he thought, breathing heavily.

When she heard the guttural German voice of the Nazi, Sarah let out a gasp. Solomon yanked her into an alley that was on the side of a building and put his hand over her mouth. She struggled to break free.

"Shh," he whispered into her ear. "If you promise not to say another word, I'll let you go."

She nodded, but when he let her go, she said, "I couldn't breathe with your hand over my mouth, Solomon! I'm telling Mama you hurt me."

"Shhh . . . I said shut up." He was harsher than he'd meant to be. He felt bad, but there was no time to explain. He had to get them out of there and fast. If they were captured, it would be bad, very bad. Sarah's body was shaking. She was crying silently now. He knew she'd been crying since they left, and he knew she was scared.

Solomon's hearing perked like the hearing of a dog as the

guard's bootheels hit the pavement. The Nazi was getting closer. Solomon knew he must act immediately. There was no time to think, only to act. He grabbed Sarah's hand roughly and pulled her along. He was pulling her so fast that she tripped and fell and skinned her knee. She let out a cry, but Solomon did not stop. He only dragged her harder and faster until they arrived at the wall. Then without stopping for a second, he pushed Sarah through the crack and followed her. Once they were on the other side, he lifted her up and ran with her until they reached an alleyway behind a general store. Then out of breath, he put her down.

"Stay quiet. We aren't safe yet," he whispered.

"I lost my dolly," Sarah said angrily. "She fell out of my hand when you pushed me. You pushed me so hard, Solomon. Mama would be angry if she knew. You hurt me. And you made me fall down and cut my knee too."

"Sarah, be quiet. You have to be very quiet. If they find us, they'll kill us. So don't make another sound." His tone of voice was harsh. She glared at him, but she didn't say a word. Instead, she put her thumb in her mouth and whimpered. Solomon glanced at her as she sat there looking small and frightened with her tear-stained face illuminated by the moonlight. He was sure she'd stopped sucking her thumb a year ago. But she'd reverted to it to comfort herself. Well, he didn't care if she did it now. He didn't care what she did so long as she kept quiet.

Solomon let out a long, low whistle like the call of a night bird.

It was several minutes, and then Solomon let out the whistle again. Just as Solomon expected, a man slipped out of the darkness. "Sol," he said. It was Wiktor, one of the men he dealt with from the Polish underground, who acquired things for him through the black market.

"It's me. I'm here," Solomon responded.

"What are you looking to buy?" Wiktor asked.

"Food. A gun, bullets."

"How much you got?"

"I got a gold ring. It's solid gold."

"Can't be worth much. Besides, how do I know it's real gold?"

"You're just gonna have to believe me. That's all. I've been working with you for over a year. I haven't tricked you yet. Why would I start now, Wiktor? This ring is worth plenty, and you know it."

"Sol, for a kid so young, you sure got a good head on your shoulders. All right. I'll get you a gun and bullets. I'll do what I can as far as the food. It's so damn scarce. But I'll try."

"And listen," Solomon said as he looked back at Sarah, who was huddled in the corner where he'd left her. "Can you get me a doll? Doesn't have to be a new doll or an expensive one. Just a doll."

"A doll? You want to waste your money on doll? Are you crazy?"

"I might be crazy. But I need a doll for my baby sister."

"That should be pretty easy, but it sure is a waste of money, don't you think?"

"Of course it is. Don't you think I know that? But . . ." Solomon looked back at Sarah, who was watching him with wide eyes. "Get it for me anyway."

"You want to pay? What do I care? I'll get you a doll. Meet me here tomorrow night. After dark, say eleven?"

"I'll be here," Solomon said.

MORE BOOKS BY ROBERTA KAGAN

AVAILABLE ON AMAZON

The Auschwitz Twins Series

The Children's Dream

Jews, The Third Reich, and a Web of Secrets

My Son's Secret

The Stolen Child

A Web of Secrets

A Jewish Family Saga

Not In America

They Never Saw It Coming

When The Dust Settled

The Syndrome That Saved Us

A Holocaust Story Series

The Smallest Crack

The Darkest Canyon

Millions Of Pebbles

Sarah and Solomon

All My Love, Detrick Series

All My Love, Detrick

You Are My Sunshine

The Promised Land

To Be An Israeli

Forever My Homeland

Made in the USA
Monee, IL
16 April 2022

94876264R00177